MW00438299

CRICKETS 2

OTHER BOOKS BY WILLIAM C. DIETZ

THE WINDS OF WAR SERIES
Red Ice
Red Flood
Red Dragon
Red Thunder
Red Tide
Red Sands
Red River
Red Dog

THE CRICKETS DUOLOGY
Crickets
Crickets 2

AMERICA RISING SERIES
Into the Guns
Seek and Destroy
Battle Hymn

MUTANT FILES SERIES
Deadeye
Redzone
Graveyard

LEGION OF THE DAMNED SERIES
Legion of the Damned
The Final Battle

CRICKETS 2

WILLIAM C. DIETZ

Wind's End Publishing
Copyright © 2023 by William C. Dietz

All rights reserved. No part of this publication may be reproduced, distributed, or transmitted in any form or by any means, including photocopying, recording, or other electronic or mechanical methods, without the prior written permission of the publisher, except in the case of brief quotations embodied in critical reviews and certain other noncommercial uses permitted by copyright law.

This is a work of fiction. Names, characters, and incidents either are the product of the author's imagination, or are used fictitiously, and any resemblance to actual persons living or dead, business establishments, events, or locales is entirely coincidental.

Cover Art by Andrzej Kuziola
The cover for Crickets 2 was created by Andrzej Kuziola, an award-winning 3D artist based in Edinburgh, United Kingdom. Please visit Kuziola.com to learn more about Andrzej and his amazing art.

This book is dedicated to the roughly 2.79 million civil servants who work for the United States government.

Though much maligned, they go to work each day to carry out the thousands of tasks that keep our country running, and mostly do so with little or no recognition.

Thank you for your service.

CONTENTS

CHAPTER ONE

In a tunnel near Julian, California

The man on the stretcher had been dead for five days. During that time his body had been producing hydrogen sulfide, methane and putrescine—all of which combined to produce a horrible stench. The man's name, according to his driver's license, was Fred Harris. He was an organ donor. And, in this case, that meant *all* of his organs.

Based on previous experience, Marine Corps Captain Lester Evans knew that the Prax could smell a dead body from a mile away. And the odor would summon some of the carnivorous aliens to the ambush site. A rotting animal carcass might work. But not always. For some reason the Prax preferred to feed on human flesh. And that's where Fred Harris came in.

Timing was important however. If the Prax arrived too quickly, before the ambush was ready, the Marines could find themselves in a disastrous shootout.

The Eagle Mine dated back to 1869, when former slave Fred Coleman saw something glimmer in a creek, and discovered gold. That triggered the third California gold rush, which led to the creation of gold rush towns, including Julian. A normally peaceful place that had been terrorized by Prax raids during the past month.

After being scouted by a tunnel drone two weeks earlier, the goldmine "hit" had been assigned to Charlie company, a component of the 2nd Battalion 1st Marines.

1

The Second was a specialized unit, recently designated the "Tunnel Rats," in honor of the Australian and American combat engineers who cleared enemy tunnels in Vietnam.

Like the original Rats, the men and women of the 2nd squad, 1st platoon, were armed with pistols. But, because cricket tunnels were consistently larger than those in Viet Nam, the soldiers carried submachine guns as well.

Moreover, Evans and his Marines were equipped with hard hats, night vision gear, very low frequency radios, hydration packs, and short handled shovels. Their objective was to suppress enemy activity until the entire battalion could go in and sterilize the nest. A mission slated for later that month.

Thanks to his night vision gear, Evans could see clear evidence of a Prax presence. That included sliding scuff marks on the floor, the usual nav symbols spray painted on the walls, and the green luminescence connected with alien habitats.

Most noticeable, however, was the throat-clogging blue cheese stench which, according to the experts, was sometimes associated with formic acid.

Evans decided to breathe through his mouth as he led the squad into the chamber where the ambush would take place. The ceiling was nine feet high, the cave was roughly thirty by fifty, and—judging from the marks on the walls—filled with water at times.

"Plant Mr. Harris in the middle of the cavern," Evans instructed. "Attach the Claymores to the south wall, and take cover behind the rocks to my right. Hurry."

Evans' greatest fear was that too many aliens would show up. If that occurred the Marines were going to die.

Each minute felt like an hour. But, because the evolution had been practiced above ground, the rats knew what to do, and did it quickly.

"All right," Evans said, "take cover." And not a moment too soon.

The Prax scout was about five and a half feet tall, had a rounded head, and a predatory beak. It was wearing body armor and carrying an assault weapon.

Skinny thighs were connected to knobby knees and back-slanted legs. The scout had very little resemblance to an actual cricket. But that's the name the press applied to the aliens early on, and it stuck.

The alien's large, light gathering eyes swiveled back and forth as it looked for danger, saw none, and fastened its gaze on the body. *It's thinking,* Evans reasoned. *That's a human body. It smells good. But how did it get here? Some meat bodies are rigged with explosives. I will check.*

The scout approached the corpse carefully, scanning for detonator wires, or anything else that might be suspicious. Then the crick produced a coil of cord, dropped a loop over a blueish foot, and backed away. Once clear of the potential blast zone, the alien made use of both claw-like hands to pull on the cord. Henry's body shifted, and shifted some more. Then it stopped. That was good enough for the Prax, who spoke into a communicator. A rapid *clicking* sound was heard. Evans didn't have to tell his soldiers what would happen next. They knew.

Less than a minute passed before five crickets entered the cavern, and made straight for the body. Then, without hesitation, they began to feed. It was a disgusting sight. "Prepare to detonate the Claymores," Evans whispered. "Detonate."

Two camo-covered, command-detonated mines were attached to the south wall. Each consisted of a layer of C-4 explosive which was secured behind a matrix of seven hundred, 1/8-inch diameter steel balls.

There were two overlapping explosions followed by a steel hailstorm that literally tore the aliens to shreds. "Good work," Evans said, as he stood. "Let's get the hell out of here."

Fred's remains were left behind.

* * *

Washington, D.C. The White House

President Vanessa Seton and senior members of her staff were meeting in the Situation Room as they had each day for months. And now, in the wake of the massive effort called "Operation Clean Sweep," they were assessing the results of a nationwide attack on the Prax.

The good news was that, according to early estimates, seventy-six percent of the known Prax habitats had been destroyed, and something on the order of one hundred thousand cricks had been killed.

The bad news was that American casualties, both military and civilian, were thirty-seven thousand killed, and twelve thousand seriously wounded. That was two percent higher than anticipated. And Seton was about to share the news, both good and bad, on a televised press conference.

After a brief session with a make-up lady, and still another cup of black coffee, Seton followed Press Secretary Milton Hughes to the James S. Brady Press Briefing Room in the West Wing of the White House. It was packed, and silence reigned as the reporters awaited the briefing, their cell phones at the ready.

"Good morning," Seton said. "Operation Clean Sweep was a success thanks to the thousands of Americans who risked their lives, or gave their lives, to make victory possible. To them, and to their loved ones, I send our nation's gratitude.

"But understand this... Even though our forces destroyed crick habitats, and killed at least a hundred thousand aliens, the Prax are in control of nations all around the world. And are battling to subdue others. Sadly, Operation Clean Sweep is the beginning, rather than the end, of our fight to survive."

Suddenly the wall mounted screens behind Seton came to life and a creature with four arms appeared. There was consternation in the briefing room along with comments like, "What the hell?" "Is this a joke?"

Seton was as shocked as the rest of them. The thing, whatever it was, had been able to hijack the most secure comm system in the world.

"No," the apparition grated, "this is *not* a joke. We are the Mechans. We serve the Xyfor."

The Mechan had a vaguely humanoid appearance, red eyes, a pugnacious jaw and wire mesh instead of skin. The creature's mouth, assuming it had one, was concealed by the mesh. And, its "clothing" consisted of a work-worn paint job.

"Twelve thousand years ago our avengers chased the Prax fleet into what you call the Oort Cloud," the Mechan told them. "And that's where the pestilence managed to evade our ships by executing a simultaneous two-second hyperspace jump.

"The filth could have emerged anywhere in your solar system but—by chance—the jump ended near Earth. Knowing that we would search for them, the Prax rushed to hide their ships beneath your oceans, and deep inside caves similar to the pus pits in which they evolved.

"The ruse succeeded. Because, when our scouts arrived here, they found no trace of the Prax. And, while on the rise back then, your ancestors were so primitive they couldn't provide useful information.

"But we are the Mechans. We never gave up. For thousands of years our avengers continued to check each planet in your system.

"Eventually, during the last hundred solar rotations, you devised the means to detect our scouts. You called them 'UFOs.'"

The reporters had been silent until then. But the UFO announcement elicited gasps of surprise and expressions of disbelief.

Seton wasn't sure what was taking place but knew it was vitally important. "Quiet! Trace this feed. Where's it coming from? And how did this creature override our systems?"

"In answer to your question," the Mechan replied, "this worldwide broadcast is originating from a warship in Earth orbit. One of many sent to help you fight the pestilence.

"Over the millennia the Prax have stripped multiple planets of protein and left them in ruins. You—however—you will have our help. Consistent with orders from the Xyfor, Mechan avengers and troops will begin to land one planetary rotation from now. Our mission is to cleanse your planet. Then we will depart.

"But be warned," the Mechan added. "This task is likely to take months ... And, during that time, there will be many battles between my kind and the Prax.

"Our mission is to not only cleanse your world of the infection, but to ensure that the pestilence can't colonize other planets, and seize control of your galaxy. So, should humans interfere, they will be sacrificed.

"Also, having observed your kind for thousands of years, we are well aware of your propensity for war. Should any group of humans stand in our way, or attack us, they will be eliminated. That is all."

The screens snapped to black, static appeared, and was immediately replaced by the presidential seal. Those in the room sat in stunned silence. Hughes turned to Seton. "My God. Prax ... Mechans ... Xyfor ... What are we going to do?"

"Use the Mechans if we can," Seton answered grimly. "And fight them if we must."

Everything had changed.

***

The Candelaria Caves, in Guatemala

The Candelaria Caves were located in the limestone mountains of northern Ala Verapaz. They were sacred to the *Q'eqchi* Mayans who believed that the subterranean caverns were passages into the underworld.

And the Mayans were correct. There *was* an underworld. Because *another* level of caverns and passageways lay deep beneath the cave system and had been, until recently, home to thousands of hibernating aliens.

Now the Prax were awake. And, like bears emerging from a long sleep, the aliens were hungry. That was the reality the new Prime had to deal with. That, and responsibility for nests and colonies worldwide.

The new Prime's gelatinous body was floating in a nutrient rich bath consisting of sugars, proteins, and fat. A concoction which, thanks to tech functionaries, was kept at a comfortable sixty-eight degrees. The temperature at which a Prime functioned best.

Like its progenitors, Prime was a bioelectronic computer. One of the many which had led the race during its long life. And thanks to the billions of tiny airborne spy eyes that swarmed the human cities, the new Prime could monitor "meat" TV broadcasts. Thus, it was watching Guatevision when the Mechan appeared.

Prime wasn't capable of feeling fear. But the computer intelligence could register strong concern in response to an existential threat, and the sudden arrival of Xyfor machines was the most serious threat possible.

The racial awakening had been going well up until then. Yes, some of the modern humans had proven themselves to be excellent warriors. But even so, they'd been dying by the thousands. That was a waste of meat, but couldn't be helped. And, in spite of what the North Americans called "Operation Clean Sweep," the Prax were winning.

Or had been winning prior to the previous Prime's deactivation. But now, with the arrival of Xyfor Navy vessels, and the race's robotic soldiers, the Prax were in danger of being annihilated.

What to do? Fight? Or flee? The answer was obvious. The Xyfor fleet was in orbit and ready to destroy any ship, or ships, that the Prax might launch. So Prime would fight. And there was no reason for delay.

Thanks to the old Prime, work was underway establishing planetary defenses. These defenses included surface-to-space plasma cannons. And, according to the data flowing into Prime's electronic brain, four Xyfor ships were well within range.

As for ammunition, the cricks had an inexhaustible supply of that in the form of geothermal energy harvested from the planet's mantle and processed into bolts.

There was a limitation however, and that was the half hour interval required for the plasma accumulators to recharge. But, assuming that each shot produced a kill, Prime would be satisfied. Orders were given, and orders were received.

Prime allowed itself to sink deeper into the nutrient bath. It was warm and soothing. Prime felt something akin to pleasure. And that was enough.

* * *

Aboard Xyfor ships in L4 and L5 orbits around the Earth.
The meeting consisted of six Xyfor Controllers, each representing a primary clan, and with which they shared the same surname.

Strict rules governed how such meetings were conducted—including how they were led—which was on a rotating basis. And it was Ecor Rinn's turn to serve as chair. He sat facing a semi-circle of holo tanks with one of his peers visible in each.

The controllers could have met in person, but had chosen to communicate remotely to ensure continuing leadership should one or more ships be lost in battle.

"The meeting is now underway," Rinn said. "And phase one has begun. The humans have been notified of our presence and warned that hostilities are about to begin.

"I think it's safe to assume that the pestilence has access to human communications nets and are prepared to resist. I hope they do ... Our Mechans will annihilate them."

Controller Mezo Zorg cleared his throat. His skull implant was a dull red, signaling negative emotions. Dark eyes peered out from under prominent supraorbital ridges, and the feeding tentacles that surrounded his mouth began to writhe as he spoke. His voice had a rasping quality. "I have a question. Rather than send the Mechans down to fight, why not place a planet buster in orbit, withdraw to a safe distance and trigger it?"

Rinn's implant turned purple. "We have discussed that possibility before," Rinn said irritably. "Many times. Did you learn nothing from the Ning tragedy? According to the revised clan code, sentients must respect sentient life, and the humans are sentient.

"In fact, as CU001 (Command Unit One) stated during the announcement, we are committed to helping the indigent population. And won't harm them unless they harm us."

"That is correct," Las Tith agreed. "And I would like to add that ... "

None of the other Controllers got to learn what Tith was going to add, because that was the moment when a plasma bolt struck her ship and destroyed it.

Her holo went dark, light strobed Rinn's viewport, and ten thousand Mechans were vaporized. The battle for Earth had begun.

* * *

The base Theatre, Camp Pendleton, California
Building 1330 Mainside served the base as both a theatre and a training facility. And on that particular morning the facility was reserved for the 2nd Battalion 1st Marines.

To enter the theatre, it was necessary to pass through a recently constructed security lock. The lock employed electromagnetic pulses meant to destroy any ubiquitous spy eyes—which would swarm the theatre if they could—and send Intel to the Prax.

The lock could handle twenty people at a time. Evans was accompanied by his executive officer First Lieutenant Glen Riley, Gunnery Sergeant Ralph Hollis, and the company's platoon leaders. Senior noncoms followed along behind.

Seats were waiting for the Marines directly behind the representatives of Bravo company, some of whom turned to say "Hi," or make disparaging comments.

But, in spite of the lighthearted insults, Evans could feel the tension in the auditorium as he sat down. By then everybody knew about the Xyfor. The new aliens hated the Prax. That's what they said. But was it true?

And, if that wasn't enough, a big operation was in the works according to the scuttlebutt. A rumor that Evans believed. Why else would the colonel hold a full-on group grope?

The hum of conversation died away as Bat XO Major Tracy Folsom appeared, made her way to the podium, and adjusted the mike. Her hair was high and tight. "Good morning. Oorah!"

The reply was a roar. "OORAH!"

Folsom smiled. "Damned straight. As you've heard there's a whole lot of weird shit going down, so without further ado, here's Colonel Brock."

Brock was tall, skinny, and famous for outrunning everyone in the battalion. He looked around. "Good morning. 'A whole lot of weird shit is going down.' I've had better introductions." The audience laughed and Folsom grinned.

"However," Brock continued, "I must admit that there *is* some weird shit going down. First, we had to deal with an invasion from within the planet. And now we're confronted with an invasion from outer space by four armed robots." Most of the audience chuckled.

"The good news," Brock said, "is that the Xyfor maintain they're here to exterminate the Prax. And, according to a rare interview with a now deceased Prax core, that's believable.

"The core claimed that the Xyfor landed on its native planet about a million years ago and captured a number of specimens— including a core—which they transported to their home world. After being placed in a Xyfor zoo, the core became a Prime, and directed its functionaries to engineer an escape. It was successful.

"That led to the founding of a nest, followed by rapid reproduction, and a series of wars that eventually rendered the Xyfor planet uninhabitable.

"By that time the cricks had mastered Xyfor technology, including space travel, which allowed them to emigrate to another planet."

"The Prax laid waste to it by eating, eating, and eating—until there wasn't enough food to sustain their population. So, they were forced to board spaceships and depart for another world. It suffered the same fate. And that's the cycle the Xyfor are trying to end. It's what they claim anyway—and hopefully it's true. If so, we'll have a powerful ally in the war against the cricks.

"But, for the moment," Brock added, "we're on our own. Which has everything to do with why we're gathered here today."

"*This*," Brock said, as a photo appeared on the screen behind him "is the entrance to the SubTropolis in Kansas City, Missouri.

"The developers call it 'the world's largest Underground Business Complex,'" Brock added. "The SubTropolis is roughly 160 feet below the surface, is accessible by more than 10 miles of well illuminated roads, and occupies more than 7 million square feet of underground space. And, for the moment, the cricks own it." That admission elicited a chorus of groans and swear words.

Brock nodded. "Yeah, it sucks…That's for sure. But I'm pleased to inform you that we're going to go in, kick some Prax ass, and take the place back."

The "Oorah!" came from someone in the back of the theatre and was echoed by the rest of the audience. "OORAH!"

Brock smiled. "Okay, here's how it's going to work."

A schematic appeared and Brock turned to look at it. A map of Kansas City took shape. "Our objective is here," Brock said, as a red dot circled an X.

"Alpha Company and Bravo Company will roll in from the south, cross the river using the 435 bridge, and exit. That will put them in close proximity to the SubTropolis.

"It seems safe to assume that they will make contact with the cricks almost immediately. And, since the bugs are well dug in, we can expect heavy resistance.

"Both companies will pause at that point, while our cannon cockers pound the bastards, and our gunships mow the lawn.

"Meanwhile Chinook helicopters will ferry Charlie company in, and land *here*."

Evans found himself looking at a large bald spot in the middle of a stunted forest. It was home to a small concrete building protected by a cyclone fence.

"The LZ is tight," Brock observed. "So, it will be imperative to land, and deass the aircraft quickly. The concrete structure houses a fire exit, which may, or may not, be defended.

"The first Marines to arrive will open the door by whatever means necessary."

"Then," Brock continued, "Charlie company will fight its way down to the bottom of the stairway, attack the defenders from behind, and take control of the main entrance.

"At that point the rest of the battalion will pour in. Our ACVs (Amphibious Combat Vehicles) will lead the way, followed by JLTVs (Joint Light Tactical Vehicles), and infantry.

"It will be a tough job," Brock allowed. "But well worth it. Taking control of the SubTropolis will be the first step toward liberating the rest of Kansas City. Because, as things stand now, the SubTrop is a base from which raiding parties depart every night.

"Brock eyed the audience. If you have questions, this is your opportunity to ask them."

There were questions. Lots of them. But the *big* question, the one on each person's mind, was: "*Will I survive?*" Evans was no exception.

CHAPTER TWO

FEMA TRC 1106 (Temporary Relocation Camp) adjacent to Whites City, New Mexico

FEMA Community Response Team Leader Cassie Lang's day began the way it always did, with a cold shower in the curtained cubicle next to her ancient motorhome, followed by a brisk towel-down inside.

Electricity was provided by a jury-rigged solar system that some of Lang's residents had cobbled together. And, while it couldn't provide juice 24/7, the system came on at 6 a.m. So that was when Lang heated water, took a single packet of Starbucks instant out of her hoard, and made a mug of coffee. That was followed by a Chocolate Chip Toaster Pastry from a Menu 4 MRE which she washed down with a few gulps of water.

Then it was time to put on what Lang thought of as her uniform. It consisted of a fleece lined Levi jacket, a long-sleeved top, jeans, boots and a pink ball cap.

The final piece of apparel was a western style gun belt, with loops for .45 rounds, and a holster for her single-action Colt revolver. The weapon wasn't something Lang wanted to carry, but something she *had* to carry, because some of the residents in Camp 1106 were mean as hell. Not to mention the drifters who stopped in each day looking for handouts, and were usually armed to the teeth.

That was the good thing about the United States, and the bad thing as well. When the crickets appeared, the fact that there were 120 firearms per 100 residents in the U.S. meant American citizens had the wherewithal to battle the aliens. Unfortunately, the humans could prey on each other as well, and that was all too common.

After locking her motorhome Lang went for her usual hike. Camp 1106 was located adjacent to a privately owned, seven-person hamlet named Whites City.

It had been founded by a man named Charlie White back in the '20s, and survived by providing goods and services to the steady stream of tourists who made the pilgrimage to the Carlsbad Caverns.

And there, on the ridge behind the Whites City tourist center, were two communications towers. The perfect place for a lookout station. And that was Lang's destination.

The climb was steep enough to keep Lang in shape without wearing her out, and a way to show the volunteer lookouts that she cared. It took fifteen minutes to reach the top of the ridge. An awning had been set up to provide shade and shelter the lookouts from rainstorms.

On that particular day, the team consisted of Ray Owens and John Becker, both of whom were typical Camp 1106 residents. They were in their sixties, had been driven from their homes by crick raids, and happened upon the camp by chance.

Most young adults were in the military. So it was the elderly who found their way to FEMA camps, often with grandchildren in tow. A situation that forced FEMA staff to try and provide elder services and schooling at the same time.

A mutt named Riley barked and came bouncing forward to greet Lang. She bent to pet him, and offered the usual treat, which was a piece of her breakfast cookie.

"Good morning," Owens said. "I'm happy to report that we have nothing to report."

"What about the contrails?" Becker interjected.

Becker pointed and Lang looked up. Sure enough, a wild tangle of white contrails was visible—as if a child had been scribbling on the sky. The Air Force perhaps?

No, Lang decided. There were far too many of them. That suggested that the Mechans were entering the atmosphere in force and searching for the Prax.

Lang sighed. Even if the latest aliens weren't hostile to humans, which was far from certain, their activities were sure to fuel more chaos. And that would create more refugees.

"You're right John, something's going on up there. That's for sure. Can I use your binoculars?"

Owens nodded. "Anytime. You know that."

Lang smiled. "'Never assume.' That's what my mother taught me."

A large pair of binoculars sat atop a homemade tripod. Lang aimed them at the camp. Lang used them every morning. Tendrils of gray smoke twisted up into the sky, light glinted off some of the vehicles in the parking lot, and tiny people were moving about.

The camp was shaped like a pie with the so-called "arena" in the middle. It served as a place for residents to meet, or gather if attacked.

The arena was bordered by three "slices," the oldest of which was called "Uptown." The name stemmed from the fact that the bright-white FEMA trailers were the most luxurious accommodations available.

Once all the trailers were occupied, Lang's predecessor requested more housing, and eventually received a shipment of military tents. The Deployable Rapid Assembly Shelters weren't as fancy as trailers, but they were weather proof, and durable. They were set up on the second slice of the pie.

The rest of the camp consisted of a wild hodgepodge of civilian tents, camper trucks, and makeshift shacks. That was where latecomers had been forced to live—because the government no longer had the means to supply anything more than MREs. And those were increasingly hard to come by. The housing inequities were a continual source of friction, and something Lang was powerless to fix, but generally blamed for.

Lang stepped back from the binoculars, and was just about to thank the lookouts, when a *roar* was heard. "Look at that!" Owens shouted as he pointed to the south. "What is it?"

Lang turned to see a flying barge. The construct looked worn, alien hieroglyphics were visible on its side, and guns were mounted fore and aft.

Lang's first concern was that the barge-like thing would wreak havoc on the camp. Then, when it became clear that the thundering machine would pass to the east, she heaved a sigh of relief. What was the leviathan up to anyway? Searching for cricks? Hopefully.

Lang turned to the lookouts. "Just one more thing to watch for gentlemen. Thanks for volunteering. You're awesome."

As always, the downhill trip was a lot easier than the uphill climb, and took half as long. Lang arrived in camp to find that some of her residents were all stirred up.

A man named Getz was pissed off as usual. He was waiting next her motorhome along with six other residents. "Why didn't you tell us that thing was coming?" Getz demanded. "My wife was terrified."

"I didn't tell you because I didn't know," Lang replied.

"That's the fucking government for you," Getz said angrily. "President Seton doesn't have a clue! We need someone competent in the White House."

"It was an alien machine," Lang told him. "A Mechan machine. The president had nothing to do with it."

"I'll shoot at the next one that comes along," Getz promised. "That'll show the bastards."

"Please don't do that," Lang replied. "If you shoot at the Mechans, they might decide to slaughter us.

"What you can do, is take the water tanker over to the caverns, and fill it up. You're one of the few people who know how to operate it."

Any appeal to Getz's ego was a surefire winner, and a smile appeared on his florid face. "I was a professional trucker. Did you know that?"

"Yes," Lang answered. "Fortunately for us."

The truth was that *she* could have driven the 2006 International Durastar. But Getz didn't know that, and didn't need to. The ex-trucker hurried away.

Luckily, the other people who were waiting to speak with Lang were more pleasant. One of them needed to see a doctor in El Paso, Texas, 145 miles away. A request that called for a vehicle, a volunteer driver, fuel, and at least one armed guard.

Another resident was angry with a neighbor who insisted on listening to loud music well into the night. And she wasn't the only one. Other people were upset with the noise pollution too.

Then there was the retired teacher in the wheelchair. She wanted to volunteer. Lang sent her over to the DRASH tents that housed the camp's school.

Lang was in a good mood as she crossed the compound to the dispensary. It, like everything else in TRC 1106, was an improvised affair

The clinic occupied a rusty 40-foot cargo container and was staffed by a physician's assistant named Miguel Ortiz, a retired nurse, and a disabled Navy medic.

There was a line as usual. And Lang took the time required to greet each person, and sympathize with them prior to spending a few minutes with Ortiz.

"I found a volunteer," she told him. "A resident with a Harley. He's going to make a high-speed run to El Paso tonight, pick up your meds, and return. He'll be able to travel fast, take back roads, and outrun anyone who chases him."

Ortiz made a face. "Please tell him that I'm grateful. And wish him Godspeed."

Lang was about to reply when a teenage boy barged into the container. "Come quick, Miss Lang! Some bad men are here."

Lang felt a stab of fear. "Bad men." That could mean anything. Drifters, gang bangers, or cult members. "Where are they?"

"They forced their way into the warehouse," the boy replied. "And they're stealing stuff."

"The warehouse," was an adobe structure which had been converted into storage space for rations, equipment, and ammunition. All of which were worth stealing. "Take my scooter," Ortiz offered. "And be careful."

Lang left, hopped onto the sun-faded Vespa, and turned the key. It started up.

A crowd had gathered by the time Lang arrived, including three elderly "Minutemen" who were the only defense force that the camp had. They stood facing the seven intruders, but were clearly outmatched by the thieves, who were young and heavily armed.

Deserters? Quite possibly. Or draft dodgers. They were standing in front of the warehouse next to a pile of the loot they planned to steal.

Wally, the man in charge of the storage facility, was lying on the ground with blood leaking out of his scalp. "Look!" a man with long scraggly hair said. "Mommy's here! And she's a looker. I'm calling first dibs."

"I don't know," the man wearing goggles said. "She's packing heat."

"Forget the six shooter," the first bandit said. "I'll take my chances."

Lang made her way over to stand next to the Minutemen. A single glove was tucked into her gun belt. She tugged it loose and slid her left hand into the smooth leather.

"I'm going to give one, and only one, chance," Lang said. "Go to your vehicles and leave."

Goggle face laughed. "Or *what?* Or the grandpas will gun us down?"

"No," Lang replied. "Or *I* will gun you down."

The Colt had been heavily modified by Lang's father, a fast draw champion, to accomplish one thing… And that was to fire six bullets in rapid succession. The pistol had an unfluted cylinder, a custom action, and a reinforced frame.

The Colt cleared the holster smoothly. And, as it came up, Lang's left hand was already starting to fan the extended hammer. The shots came so quickly the reports seemed to overlap each other, and a cloud of smoke obscured the targets.

Once it cleared there was only one bandit standing. A man wearing a headband and imitation war paint. His buddies were dead. Their bodies were sprawled next to him.

Lang could see the fear in the man's eyes, as well as what might have been a glimmer of cunning, as the cretin managed to produce a thought. "You had your six," the thief croaked. "And now it's … "

No one ever got to hear what paint-face planned to do, because that was the moment when a seventy-two-year-old man named George Walker fired his twelve-gauge shotgun.

The load of double-aught buck struck the bandit's midsection and nearly cut him in half. A puff of dust rose as the body hit the ground. Lang nodded. "Thanks, George."

"Any time, Cassie. Sorry about the mess."

* * *

Whiteman Air Force Base, Missouri

Evans was peering out a window as the Boeing 777-300 circled Whiteman Air Force Base and prepared to land. The base was big, flat, and completely unremarkable except for the twenty-foot-high berm that had been thrown up to keep the Prax out.

Of course, some of the aliens were equipped with bioelectronic wings, and could fly over the berm. A capability Evans had witnessed firsthand during the battle for the Air Force base, in El Segundo, California.

But the radar-guided, 20mm, minigun turrets spaced along the top of the earthen barrier had proven to be quite effective at preventing cricks, attack drones, and Turkey Vultures from over-flying the base. And, according to Charlie company's preflight briefing, subsurface defenses were in place as well. The exact nature of which were classified.

Did that make Evans feel warm and cozy? Nope. Evans hadn't been there at the time. But he'd seen news footage of how Ellsworth Air Force Base had been overrun. Nothing was safe.

The tires hit with a thump, and the pilot activated the plane's thrust reversers, forcing the passengers to brace themselves. "This is the copilot speaking," a cheerful voice announced. "Thanks for flying with us, and we hope you enjoy your stay."

"Oh yeah," a voice said. "This will be lots of fun."

"Cut the crap," a stern voice ordered. "See me later."

Evans smiled thinly. Some poor bastard had soared to the top of the Gunny's shit list. Not because he was wrong, but because he'd been stupid enough to make a comment that might impact morale.

The next couple of hours were a blur. Wait to deplane. Collect gear. Board buses. Get off the buses. Enter the transient barracks.

Choose a rack. Take a pee. And follow a guide to the chow hall, where it was necessary to pass through a microdrone-killing EMP "toaster" before getting in line.

Evans ate with his executive officer and platoon leaders. "Tell 'em what you're going to tell 'em, tell 'em, and tell 'em what you told them." That was the old axiom.

"So, let's go over the plan one last time," Evans said, as he surveyed the faces around him. First Lieutenant Lester Russo was the company's XO, Second Lieutenant Andy Yamada was in command of the 1st Platoon, Second Lieutenant Maya Christou was in charge of the 2nd and Dwight Dawkins had the 3rd. The company's fourth platoon leader, Lieutenant Abbey Wilson, had been called away to meet with Bat supply.

"Alpha and Bravo companies will attack at first light," Evans told them. "And that's when the shit will hit the fan. Meanwhile a Chinook will take the 1st platoon in for a landing on LZ Baldy. As soon as they deass the helo, Rusty's EOD team will blow the door.

"The first Chinook will be gone by then, freeing space for the second to land.

"After that the 1st platoon will engage the cricks, or if there aren't any, start down the stairs. The 2nd and 3rd platoons will follow. From that point forward, we'll play it by ear.

"The objective hasn't changed. Our job is to reach the front entrance and pry it open. Any questions?"

"Yes," Dawkins put in. "Can I have the rest of your fries?"

Most of the officers were picking at their food. But the 220-pound Dawkins was always hungry and determined to eat his fill.

"Yes," Evans said, as he pushed the plate across. "And Dwight…"

"Sir?"

"You'll be in charge of our six. Keep your eyes peeled."

"Will do," Dawkins replied. "Please pass the ketchup."

* * *

Evans hit the rack early, but found it difficult to sleep, and eventually gave up. It was O-dark-thirty when he went out for a run. The air was cold, and Evans could see his breath, as a series of sonic *booms* rolled across the land. Air Force jets? Or Mechan fighters? The second option seemed the more likely of the two.

Evans heard the *slap* of footsteps approaching from behind and turned to find Russo running beside him. "You too?"

"Yeah," the XO said. "Do me a favor ... Don't get killed. I'm not ready to be company commander."

Evans grinned. "That's bullshit. But I'll do my best."

They ran in silence after that, and were on their way back, when they heard the distant *thump* of artillery shells exploding. The canon cockers were prepping the area in front of the objective. The battle had begun.

Reveille was at 0400 for Charlie company's Marines, who were herded through the chow hall, and returned to the transient barracks at 0515. Then it was time to gun up, board buses, and ride to Heliport 3. A fully caffeinated Evans was waiting for them. "Good morning, Marines. Your helo awaits. Please don't spit, pee, or throw up in it. To do so would be to soil our reputation."

Those close enough to hear the joke laughed. The rest of the company would get the message by word of mouth. Evans could be tough, but he had a sense of humor, and that was more than most Marine corps officers could say.

The Chinook's rotor blades were already turning as the 1st platoon boarded, found seats, and strapped in. The liftoff was smooth. Evans was grateful for the short flight. That meant less time for his Marines to worry.

Were the cricks using their micro drones to track the Chinook? *I hope not,* Evans thought. *Because the bastards might have SLMs (surface launched missiles).*

But if the Prax were aware of the Chinook, they let it pass. And the trip ended twenty-eight minutes later. The announcement was made over the PA system.

"We're five from dirt," the copilot informed them. "Be advised that the LZ is clear." That was excellent news, since landing under fire would suck.

Evans made his way back to the aft end of the Chinook as the crew chief lowered the ramp. First off, last on. That was part of his job.

The Gunny felt the same way, and was there to offer a fist bump. Hollis had to yell in order to be heard. "It can't be no worse than California, sir."

Evans smiled. "That's right, Gunny… Let's kick some cricket ass!"

Rather than land, the pilot chose to hover. Evans made the two-foot jump with Hollis right behind him. The crew chief offered a thumbs up once the Chinook was empty and spoke into her mike. "All clear right and left." The engine noise increased as the helo started to climb.

Lieutenant Yamada ordered the 1st platoon to establish a defensive perimeter around the concrete shelter and they hurried to obey.

Then, while Evans was still getting his bearings, dirt covered lids were thrown aside, and Prax fighters came pouring up out of the ground. "Shoot the bastards!" Yamada bellowed, as the alien soldiers deployed their bioelectronic wings and took to the air.

That was the moment when Evans realized that Hollis was wrong. LZ Baldy *was* worse than California.

CHAPTER THREE

Near Gatesville, Texas

The Mack truck roared out of the alley, hit the prison bus, and flipped it over. Canned meat. That's what the crickets were after. And they preferred to hunt at night.

Eighteen-year-old Addy Rogers was seated toward the back, behind the single guard, and the teen knew an opportunity when she saw one.

The guard was trying to reorient his chunky body, when Rogers passed her hands over his head. Her handcuffs were connected by a short length of chain. It cut into the guard's throat. He made gargling noises as he attempted to free himself.

That was a mistake. Had he acted quickly, the guard might have been able to pull his pistol, and fire it back toward his assailant. Even a near miss might have been sufficient to save him. But the guard failed to think of that. Slowly, but surely, Rogers pulled the garotte toward her. The noises stopped. Cowboy boots kicked futilely. A loud fart was heard.

* * *

Meanwhile, oblivious of what was taking place in the back of the bus, the driver was fighting the crickets. And doing a good job of it too.

The bus was resting on its left side, and the aliens were determined to enter through the shattered windshield. The driver shot one, then another, creating a barrier that the surviving cricks had to remove in order to get at him. And, by the time the obstruction was cleared, the corrections officer had a shotgun. He fired, and continued to fire, killing crick after crick. The smell of formic acid caused him to gag.

***

The guard was dead. Rogers raised her hands, managed to pull herself over the upended seat in front of her, and went for the key chain that dangled from the dead man's duty belt. It came free. A few seconds were enough to unlock the cuffs.

The battle up front was still underway. But the driver was out of ammo and struggling to fight a crick off with his bare hands. Rogers knew which one of them would win, and hurried to grab what she could. She went for the guard's nine mil first, took his backup magazine, and came across a phone. A bonus if it worked.

The bus driver was screaming by that time. And no wonder, a ravenous alien was feasting on his right leg. Rogers knew she was going to be next, and wanted to run, but forced herself to point the phone at the dead guard's face. Boom! She was in! Rogers made a note to change the access code ASAP. A cricket was coming her way over the sideways seats and Rogers shot it twice.

"This way!" a voice said, and Rogers turned to find that the only other prisoner on the bus had been able to kick the rear window out. Her name was Marsha something.

Rogers said, "Thanks! I owe you," as she made her way to the back of the bus. "Here, take these."

Marsha Haley flashed a smile as she accepted the keys. "You lead, I'll follow."

"No," Rogers replied. "You'd be safer with the crickets. Run, find a cop, and turn yourself in. Shoplifting, right? You'll be back on the street in a month. Trust me, I know."

And with that Rogers squirmed out into the night. She heard the rattle of automatic fire in the distance, a helicopter clattered overhead, and new stars populated the sky. Mechan ships? Yes. But that didn't matter. She was on a mission.

***

Dallas, Texas

The sky was clear, the sun was up, and the metroplex glowed. Clayton could pick out the Bank of America Plaza, now ranked as the city's second highest building, having been overtopped by the new Pinnacle Building.

He could see the Renaissance Tower as well, along with the Comerica Bank Tower, and the eye grabbing Fountain Place. All of which were at least partially occupied by the alien menace. Especially underground, where the Prax had been able to seize control of seldom used tunnels, and were gradually working their way up floor by floor.

That, in spite of desperate efforts to seal off elevators and stairways. The result was a thicket of skyscrapers which were only accessible via skybridges and helicopters. So corporate executives fled, taking their subordinates with them, and set up shop in burbs.

But nature abhors a vacuum, and Clayton had seen the TV news reports. New businesses had taken root in the high rises, including a wild variety of nightspots, after hours poker "clubs," and strip joints. Operations that were thinly patrolled by a city police force stretched to the breaking point by the crick menace.

Shouts were heard as guardsmen pointed west, where a flotilla of dark shapes could be seen, all coming Clayton's way.

The Ranger heard a steady *thrumming* sound as the Mechan battle platforms passed between two skyscrapers, and wondered if the Xyfor would turn out to be a blessing, or another curse. Clayton watched as robots equipped with jet packs rose from the platforms, and hovered for a moment, prior to descending into the concrete canyons below.

And that, Clayton thought, *is where I need to go. Because, according to the signal from the phone Rogers stole, that's where she is. Does she realize that we can track the phone? Probably. But she doesn't want to give it up.*

More than 24 hours had passed since the prison bus had been ambushed, allowing Rogers to escape, and leaving another dead man in her wake.

The fifth, according to what the prosecutor said. The other four were beefy middle-aged men who Rogers lured into motel rooms where they were murdered.

Why? Because the victims looked like her foster father, that's why. A sick bastard who, according to Rogers, had raped her dozens of times as a child. And Clayton believed it. As did the other people working the case.

But there wasn't enough proof. Just the teen's word against Ralph Waring's. And Rogers had a rap sheet a mile long. Since aging out of the foster home system she'd been a stripper, a prostitute, and a thief. So, the murder verdict was guilty. And Rogers had been on her way to the Hilltop prison for women in Gatesville, when the crickets attacked the bus.

Clayton's thoughts were interrupted by a sergeant. "You've been cleared to enter the city, sir. I realize you're a Texas Ranger and all, but seriously, it's crazy to enter the city alone. Especially at ground level."

Clayton nodded. "I hear you, Sergeant. But we're short of personnel at the moment. Thanks for your service."

* * *

The national guardsman watched the Ranger drive away. *The cricks will have him for dinner,* the noncom predicted. *Maybe they'll find the white hat.*

* * *

Rogers was being tracked. That's what she assumed. But the phone gave her a way to access information about the Dallas pedways, the city's sky bridges, and her escape. So, it was a keeper. For the moment anyway.

Rogers' goal was to access the Pinnacle building, reach the top floor, and enter the Sky-High nightclub. That's where Ralph Waring worked. But *how?*

Getting into the downtown area was easy to accomplish. All Rogers had to do was circle around a checkpoint, sprint across an overpass, and keep to the shadows.

Other human skulkers were out and about, but not many, and they were easy to spot. It was the crickets Rogers worried about.

Her next goal was to find a way into the underground pedway which, though dangerous, was better than being on the streets. Or so Rogers assumed.

After trying two points of entry, both of which were locked, Rogers arrived at a third. Bingo! The door had been blown off its hinges. By whom? Humans or cricks? She didn't care.

The light projected from the cell phone played across some incomprehensible graffiti as Rogers followed a flight of stairs down into the underground. Then the phone played "Dixie."

Rogers eyed it. The incoming number meant nothing to her. And there was no reason for her to answer. But curiosity got the better of her. She thumbed the phone. "Yeah?"

"Hello Addy," a male voice said. "This is Ranger Pete Clayton. How's it going?"

"Better than yesterday," Rogers answered.

"I get that," Clayton replied. "And I understand why you're headed for the Pinnacle building. Ralph Waring is a piece of shit."

"You got that right," Rogers said, as she heard a scraping sound. "Hold one."

Rogers killed the light before peeking around a corner. A crick was up ahead gnawing on an arm. She took aim.

* * *

Clayton heard two shots followed by the sound of Rogers' voice. "The crick was a loner thank God … Where were we?"

"We agree that Waring is a piece of shit," Clayton told her. "But it would be a mistake to kill him. The jury found you guilty. Who knows? Maybe you'll get life instead of the death penalty."

* * *

"Don't bullshit a bullshitter, Clayton," Rogers replied. "They're going to find me guilty of multiple murders and sentence me to death. This is Texas.

"I suggest that you take a break, and let justice prevail. That's what you're all about, right? Justice."

* * *

The line went dead. Clayton swore. Rogers was right in a way. He was sixty-six years old and still on active duty. The crick crisis was one reason for that. The other was a deep-seated belief in the law and, more than that, in justice. So, there was something to be said for the girl's proposal. At least some of the perverts had it coming. Rogers was underage when some of the homicides took place. And that, most likely, was why the "Johns" were attracted to her.

Plus, Clayton was tired of hunting, tired of the long hours, and tired of the governmental crap. So why not hang it up? And let Rogers kill the man who started it all.

The answer was straight out of the book: *"Recognizing that I volunteered as a Ranger, fully knowing the hazards of my chosen profession, I will always endeavor to uphold the prestige, honor, and high esprit de corps of the Rangers."* And, Clayton decided, nothing had changed.

The Ranger got out of the car, put the headlamp on, followed by his radio headset. The knapsack contained food, water, and ammo. The hat came last.

Skyscrapers loomed ahead of him. The lower floors were dark. *Well,* Clayton thought, *this will be fun.*

* * *

Rogers paused to check the phone. She still had reception, but for how long? It made sense to map a route.

But it soon became apparent that the online pedway maps were woefully out of date. Doors that should open didn't. Some of the elevators were boarded up. After an hour of futile effort Rogers felt defeated.

Then, as if to make a bad situation worse, the Mechans arrived. They were strange looking creatures with vaguely humanoid features, mesh-like skin, cheek sensors, and pugnacious jaws. Though bipedal, each robot had four arms. Two long and two short.

Rogers attempted to hide from the robots initially, but soon discovered that was impossible, and unnecessary as well. Because each time a Mechan saw her it turned away.

They're searching for crickets, Rogers reasoned. *And they don't see me as a threat. Good.* When a column marched by, she followed it.

Shortly thereafter Rogers discovered that the androids were strong enough to kick steel doors open. A process that led to brief gunfights with crickets who were determined to defend their underground turf. The pistol was ready, but there was no need to fire it.

The follow-the-Mechs strategy worked for a while, but Rogers had to turn away when the robots left her line of travel.

Considerable progress had been made though. And, according to an online pedway map, the Pinnacle building was directly ahead.

* * *

The lobby had been created so that tourists could sit and look at the view, which included the Pinnacle building on the far side of the street.

In order to reach the lobby, Clayton had been forced to climb twenty-three flights of stairs and kill three cricks, not to mention a man with a machete.

The Ranger was tired. Bone tired. So, he welcomed the opportunity to sit down on one of the vinyl seats, open the knapsack, and grab a Hershey bar. The chocolate, plus some swigs of water, helped.

The Ranger's backup, to the extent he had any, was an operator named Mindy. Clayton had never met her, but was grateful for the support. She answered right away. "This is Mindy. Go."

"Please notify Ralph Waring that Addy Rogers is in Dallas and looking for him. She's armed and she's dangerous. I recommend that he leave the downtown area as quickly as possible."

"Will do," Mindy replied. "Standby."

Clayton finished the candy bar while he was waiting, folded the wrapper into a tiny square, and put it in a pocket.

The view through the floor to ceiling glass was amazing. The Pinnacle building was worth looking at, but so were the passing combat platforms, which seemed to float on air. What held them up? Some sort of anti-gravity technology? His phone chirped. "This is Clayton."

"I spoke with Waring. He was shocked to hear about her escape."

"And?"

"And he hung up."

"Okay, then," Clayton said. "We did what we could. I'll be in touch."

The Ranger stood, shouldered his knapsack, and made his way over to the turnstile that fronted the so called "Air tunnel."

The tourist attraction consisted of a four-person-wide, clear plastic tube which ran across to the Pinnacle building. "It will feel as if you're walking on air!" the sign over the entrance promised. And that was the last thing that an acrophobic like Clayton wanted to experience.

The Texas Ranger had no choice however. Not if he wanted to reach the Pinnacle building. The air tunnel was made of high-tech plastic and completely clear. *Don't look down*, Clayton cautioned himself, as he passed through the turnstile.

That strategy worked at first. Clayton's heart was beating like a triphammer, and his chest felt tight, but he managed to put one foot in front of the other.

Then, after twenty feet or so, a Mechan battle platform passed under him. The movement drew Clayton's eyes downward with predictable results.

A wave of dizziness forced Clayton to his knees. He closed his eyes. *Crawl*, Clayton told himself, *and keep crawling.* A gust of wind struck the tube and Clayton felt it vibrate. He was crawling on air.

***

In the Sky-High nightclub on the 79th floor of the Pinnacle building in Dallas, Texas
Ralph Waring was in charge of security for the dayshift. He was a *big* man, with a shaved head, and lots of tattoos. Plus, he was carrying two pistols. One on his hip and a second at the small of his back. Yet, in spite of that, Waring was frightened.

Of course, I'm scared, Waring told himself. *The bitch is a serial killer.*

But deep-down Waring knew there was more to his fear than Addy's status as a killer. Was Addy's miraculous escape from the bus a matter of happenstance? Or a divine punishment aimed at him? Waring hoped it was former, and feared it was the latter. So, he was determined to run.

In order to fund his escape Waring took all the cash out of the nightclub's safe, removed two additional weapons from the gun room, and placed a call for an air taxi. Waring eyed his watch. Thirty minutes. Then he'd be safe.

***

Finally, after threading her way through the underground pedways, Rogers emerged two blocks away from the soaring Pinnacle building. She could see it, but how to get inside?

The answer was waiting half a block away. An armored car was parked in front of a bank. The lobby was on fire and two bags of money had been left on the sidewalk.

Was Rogers looking at a last-ditch attempt to rescue some cash? That's the way it appeared. Currency spilled out of a bag and fluttered as a breeze blew it away.

Rogers approached with her pistol at the ready. Two dozen empty shell casings suggested a gunfight. Then she spotted the blood trails, both of which led to an open manhole. Crickets then... On the hunt. Who else would leave the money, and take the bodies?

The driver's side door was open. Rogers peered inside. Was that what she thought it was? *A fucking key in the fucking ignition?* Yes! It was. Her prayers had been answered, assuming God was on her side, which seemed unlikely.

Rogers put the pistol away, climbed up into the cab, and slipped behind the wheel.

The behemoth started right away. She had never driven anything so large, but the controls weren't that much different from a pickup, and her destination was nearby.

Every building had a loading dock. The only question was which side of the building back entrance was on. Rogers braked for a stray dog, circled the building, and sure enough... A trash strewn driveway led down a ramp to a steel gate. Rogers aimed the truck at the obstacle, fastened her seat belt, and put her foot down.

The armored car lurched forward, gathered speed, and crashed into the gate. It was no contest. The barrier collapsed, the truck roared into the area beyond, and collided with a green dumpster. Metal screeched as the bin was shoved up against a wall.

Rogers released the seatbelt, turned the engine off, and got out.

* * *

Clayton's eyes were closed, and he was crawling, when his fingers found carpet. *I made it,* Clayton decided, as he opened his eyes.

The lobby was very similar to the one he'd left. An empty counter, lots of seats, and architectural photography on the walls. He got to his feet. The cavernous room was empty. *Thank God for that*, Clayton thought. *Imagine a photo of me crawling through the tunnel in the Dallas Morning News. I'd never live it down.*

A bank of elevators was waiting on the other side of the lobby. Clayton hurried over, pushed both buttons, and swore when neither one of them lit up.

Clayton was standing in front of the opposite bank of elevators, poking the "Up" button over and over, when he heard a door open behind him.

The Ranger whirled, saw Rogers, and recognized her. The fugitive flipped him the bird and jabbed a button. The doors started to close. Clayton took a running dive but fell short as the doors met. Clayton swore, scrambled to his feet, and made the call. "Mindy ... I'm in the Pinnacle building, and so is Rogers. She's on an elevator headed for the top floor! Warn Waring."

"Got it," Mindy replied and broke the connection.

Clayton pushed the "Up" button and eyed his watch. If Rogers was aboard the only elevator that worked, how long would it take for the car to return? Assuming she didn't poke the emergency "Stop" control. Would Rogers think of that? All Clayton could do was hope that she wouldn't.

* * *

Waring heard a *ding*, and thumbed his phone. The helo was late, ten minutes late, and he was going to chew the pilot out.

"Hello, Mr. Waring ... This is Mindy with the Texas Rangers. This is to inform you that Miss Rogers is in the building, and headed for the top floor."

Waring swore, put the phone away, and hurried over to the roof access door. Then, with the submachine gun at the ready, he waited for the barrier to open.

Minutes felt like hours. Waring could imagine Rogers entering the nightclub and asking for him. One of his staff would tell her to fuck off. Would she shoot him? Probably.

The rest of the employees would flee. Then Rogers would look for, and eventually find, the stairs that led to the roof.

Finally, after an eternity of waiting, Waring saw the stainless-steel handle turn, then the door partially open. He was positioned *behind* it, so that Rogers wouldn't see him as it opened.

Rogers paused as she scanned the roof from the doorway. She then stepped forward which exposed her back to Waring. He fired. Empty casings arced through the air, Rogers staggered as the bullets hit her, and collapsed. There was a *thump* as her body hit the roof.

Waring was about to take a step when a *second* person passed through the doorway. Rather than attempt to reload, Waring pulled his nine, and fired.

It was only then that he saw the hat, realized that he was firing at a Texas Ranger, and took his finger off the trigger. But it was too late. The officer landed with an arm across Rogers' body. As if to protect her. Waring's phone dinged. He was expecting to hear Mindy's voice. He didn't. "This is your pilot," a male voice said. "Sorry about the delay. I'm ten out. See you soon." *Click.*

Waring heard a *thrumming* noise and looked up. A Mechan battle platform was overhead and starting to descend. Shit! If that mother fucker landed on the roof there wouldn't be enough room for the helo! Should he stay? And try to explain? Or vanish into the war-torn craziness that was America? Waring chose option two.

The Milkor MGL grenade launcher was slung across Waring's back. He brought the weapon around and aimed upwards. The sonofabitch was so big he couldn't miss.

Waring fired all six 40mm grenades in quick succession. The orange-red explosions weren't enough to destroy the Mechan machine. But the right side of the platform tilted upwards, and robots spilled into the street below, just before the flying barge slammed into a building.

The blast wave generated by the explosion knocked Waring down. His ears were ringing as he struggled to his feet, and stood there mouth agape, as a missile fell out of the clear blue sky. It landed four feet away from Waring, and destroyed every structure within a four-block radius. A finger of black smoke pointed at the sky. The Xyfor were pissed.

CHAPTER FOUR

The SubTropolis in Kansas City, Missouri

Aslug hit Lance Corporal Davis between the eyes, someone yelled "Sniper!" and bullets kicked up geysers of dirt all around the cinderblock shelter as crickets opened fire.

The fuckers knew we were coming, Evans thought, as RTO Jimmy Metz placed the mike in his hand. *At least one of their micro drones made it past our EMP generators.*

"Ugly-One, this is Charlie-Six actual," Evans said. "We're taking heavy fire from all around. Over."

"Ugly" was the standard callsign used for heavy attack helicopters like the AH-64 Apache. The response was nearly instantaneous. "Roger that, Charlie Six... This is Cowboy. Mark your perimeter. I'll call the color. Over."

Evans thumbed his tactical radio. "This is Six. Pop red smoke all around the shelter. And dig deep. Air support is on the way. Over."

"Charlie-Six, this is Cowboy. I see red smoke. We are inbound from the south with rockets and guns. Over."

"Welcome to the party," Evans replied as the helo appeared. "You're a sight for sore eyes. Over."

The volume of incoming fire dropped dramatically at that point. And no wonder. The Prax had learned a great deal and knew that smoke was the prelude to an attack by planes or helicopters. So, as the Ugly sped their way, the aliens took cover.

"Put some 40 mike-mike on those freak holes!" Platoon leader Andy Yamada shouted. "Light 'em up!"

Grenades arced through the air and started to explode as the Apache's gunner fired his chain gun and Hydra 70 unguided rockets.

Because the Apache could turn a tighter circle than a jet fighter could, Cowboy's co-pilot/gunner was able to plow the ground all around the cinderblock shelter.

"Cowboy, this is Charlie-Six," Evans announced. "Nice work! Take a break while we tidy up." That was Yamada's cue to send teams out to fire into the crick fighting positions, often followed by a grenade for good measure.

Evans thumbed his radio. "Get the WIAs and KIA's to the LZ. We'll load them onto the next Chinook. And blow that door!"

Then it was time to check in with BAT HQ. "Hawk-Six, this is Charlie-Six. We ran into stiff resistance on landing and are fifteen late."

Evans heard a muffled explosion and knew that one of the company's combat engineers had blown the door. "We're about to enter the complex Hawk-Six, and might lose radio contact underground," Evans added. "Over."

"Roger that," a female voice replied. "Good hunting. Over."

Either Tracy Folsom, the battalion's executive officer was handling radio traffic, or Colonel Brock had been hit. Evans wondered which.

But there was no time to consider that, because Evans could hear the familiar *whup, whup, whup* of rotor blades as the second platoon's Chinook prepared to land. It was tempting to provide Christou with a sitrep. But Evans decided it was even more important to keep the company moving forward, or in this case downward, lest the cricks use the additional time to set an ambush.

"Cowboy, this is Charlie-Six actual. Thanks for the assist. Please remain on station while our Chinook unloads. Over."

"Copy that," Cowboy replied. "Over."

Evans clicked the mike twice and gave it to Metz.

Yamada and a squad had entered the stairwell by then. Smoke hung in the air as Evans arrived. *No IEDs*, Evans thought, as he followed the metal stairs downward. *Good. But that doesn't mean there won't be any further down.*

Their destination was the facility's 55,000,000-square-foot main floor, which was laid out grid style, and accessible by vehicles of every size. The roof was supported by heavy-duty limestone supports, carved out of rock using the room and pillar technique.

The lights were on in the stairwell. Was that true throughout? If so, that would make the job easier, although the Marines had night vision goggles if the need arose.

The switchbacking stairs landed inside a room with concrete walls. Rather than charge into the unknown with a single squad of Marines, Yamada had the good sense to wait for backup.

There was no need for an explosive charge this time. All Yamada had to do was turn the door handle, push the barrier open, and toss a flashbang grenade out onto the main floor. A smoke grenade followed. Evans was among the phalanx of men and women who surged through the opening. He expected to be shot at. But encountered no resistance.

The roar of engines was heard as two dump trucks appeared, beds raised. The trucks produced a *beep, beep, beep* noise as they backed toward the Marines.

Yamada ordered his platoon to fire and they did. Bullets *clanged* as they hit steel and failed to penetrate. It was a striking display of the extent to which the Prax had learned to improvise over the last few months.

Even as those realizations flashed through Evans' mind, he was issuing orders. "Flank the trucks! Kill the infantry behind them!"

Evans couldn't see the crick fighters, but assumed they'd be there, and he was correct. Clever though the dump truck strategy was, it called for the alien fighters to bunch up, making them easy targets. Not just for the 1st platoon, but the 2nd as well, which surged into the open.

Evans brought his M27 Infantry Automatic Rifle (IAR) to bear on the cricks and opened fire. Some of the aliens spread their bioelectronic wings and attempted to lift off.

But the auto fire reduced the attacking force to bits and pieces that fell into puddles of watery ichor. The 3rd platoon had arrived by then. With the 1st platoon on point, the 2nd following, and the 3rd on drag Evans led the company forward.

Their goal was to reach the main entrance quickly, eliminate the cricks stationed there, and summon the rest of the battalion. But in spite of the urgency that Evans felt, he knew how important it was to proceed with caution, lest the company walk into an ambush. Scouts were leading the way. But what if they missed something? "This is Six," Evans said. "Keep your heads on a swivel. If you see something, say something. And don't bunch up. Isn't that right, Five? Over."

Gunnery Sergeant Hollis knew a cue when he heard one. "One grenade'll get you all," the noncom replied. "So, watch those intervals. Over."

All manner of things were stored left and right. That included new trucks, like the ones used to attack the Marines, and forty-foot-long CONEX containers. Most of which had been pried open and looted. A huge glassy-eyed Santa Claus stared at the Marines as they passed by. And that was when the shit hit the fan.

Suddenly the lights went out, fire sprinklers came on, and a cacophony of screams were heard. *Real* screams it seemed ... As if recordings had been made while humans were slaughtered. *The freaks planned this*, Evans reasoned. *They continue to up their game.*

"Use your night vision goggles," Evans ordered, "and ignore the screams. The cricks are trying to get into your heads. As for the water, certain Marines could use a shower. Over."

"We're looking at you, Simmons," someone said. People laughed.

"Cut the crap," Hollis said. "You're in the Marine Corps, not the third grade. Over."

Evans smiled. It was the sort of one-two that Hollis and he had used before.

Then the drones attacked. They were green blobs, as viewed through night vision goggles, and a new threat insofar as Evans knew. And they were deadly.

What looked like bolts of lightning struck Marines and knocked them down.

"Pop gunners will fire on the drones!" Evans ordered. "As will the rest of the company."

"Popguns" were recently distributed EMP rifles which were equipped with scopes, as well as piezoelectric generators, powered by blank cartridges.

Each "hit" had the effect of creating an electromagnetic field capable of short-circuiting the drones. The name "popgun" stemmed from the *pop-pop-pop* sound that the EMP weapons produced. But the firecracker-like sounds were overwhelmed by the racket the IARs generated.

Evans felt the need to intervene. "This is Six. Aimed fire only! Conserve your ammo! Over."

Unfortunately, the cold water pouring down onto the drones from above acted to cool the machines, making them more difficult to see with infrared night vision goggles. That forced Evans to reverse himself. "This is Six. Belay the last order. Spray 'em! Over."

Massed fire had the desired effect. Drones exploded, crashed, or were neutralized by the popguns. Though muffled by the over-ear headsets the Marines wore, the screams were still audible, and Evans was worried about the potential effect on morale. "This is Six ... Destroy the PA speakers. Charlie-Three, have your corpsmen treat the wounded, and identify those killed in action. The first and second platoons will advance. Over."

Evers heard a flurry of double clicks indicating that his platoon leaders understood. That was good. But the decision to split his command into two groups entailed a significant amount of risk. What if the 3rd platoon was attacked, and cutoff?

But that possibility had to be weighed against whatever casualties the battalion was suffering outside the SubTropolis. Evans turned to Metz. "Can you reach battalion?"

The Marine shook his head.

"Okay, keep trying," Evans instructed. "And let me know when you get through."

Evans could feel the external battle through the soles of his boots as artillery shells and gravity bombs landed on, or near, the crick positions in front of the SubTropolis.

Platoons 1 and 2 were closing in on the main gate when a scout materialized out of the downpour. Evans ordered the unit to halt and assume a defensive posture. "What have you got for me, Corporal?"

"The enemy is massed up ahead on the right, sir. They're using stacked crates for cover."

"Good work. The crates ... One layer? Or two?"

"Two, sir. Stacked like bricks. So, they interlock."

As it happened Evans knew something about crates and stacking them, having spent two summers working in a warehouse during high school.

And, assuming the crates had been chosen for their weight and density, machinery had been required to stack them. "Did you see any forklifts, son?"

"Sir, yes, sir. There's a row of forklifts up ahead on the left."

Evans eyed the Marine. "Fritz, correct?"

"Yes, sir."

Evans nodded. "I won't forget."

The scout vanished as Evans thumbed his radio. "This is Six. All forklift operators to me. They don't have to be experts. On the double."

"Bat is on horn, sir," Metz said. "The colonel wants to know what the hell is taking so long. His words sir, not mine."

So, Brock was alive. That was a good thing. And Brock had no way to know what Charlie company was going through.

Even so, Evans didn't like the tone. He struggled to keep his voice level as he accepted the mike. "This is Charlie-Six actual."

"Give me a sitrep," Brock demanded brusquely. "Over."

"We're close," Evans replied. "And about to make contact with the force guarding the gate. Over."

"Well, get on with it," Brock said. "We don't have all day."
Click.

Evans winced, and returned the mike. Four Marines appeared out of the murk. "Some forklifts are parked ahead on the left," Evans told them. "Try to start them and report back. On the double. Go!"

Evans glanced at his watch. Time was passing... He suspected that if Brock were present, he'd order Charlie company to charge the enemy fortification, guns blazing.

And that might work. But if it did—and that was a big *if*—the butcher's bill would be high. *Too* high in Evans' estimation.

Especially since the relatively low ceiling would prevent his Marines from using launchers to lob grenades over the wall of crates.

Yes, they could hit them straight on, in hopes of blasting a way through, and maybe they'd be forced to do so. But Evans was hoping for something better.

"Charlie-Six," a voice said. "This is Charlie-Two-Eight. Three out of four forks are up and running. Over."

Evans felt a surge of hope. "Good! Find a large pallet for each, and load something that will provide your passengers with cover. And *hurry*. Over."

"Charlie-One, send snipers and grenadiers to join the forklifts. I'll meet them there. Over."

Evans took off and Metz followed. The forklifts were lit with all manner of lights, including rotating roof beacons! Precious minutes were spent using rifle butts to shatter plexiglass. After a briefing from Evans, it was time for the gunners to mount their platforms, and take up positions behind whatever objects the drivers had chosen.

Then the makeshift attack vehicles took off with plenty of space between them. "Charlie company!" Evans shouted. "Prepare to attack… Attack!"

And with that Evans began to jog. What he thought of as forklift three was leading the way. Columns of Marines, each led by an officer, followed each forklift, ready to close with the cricks the moment that became possible.

Meanwhile, the forklift drivers raised their loads high above the floor making it possible for their gunners to see *down* into the enemy fort. Steel gates were visible beyond, as was roiling smoke, and diffused sunlight.

The snipers had orders to pick their shots, killing any crick which appeared to be directing others, to deny the mob of leadership.

The grenadiers couldn't fire *over* obstacles, but they could hit them straight on. Successive orange-red explosions tore insectoid bodies apart, sent extremities cartwheeling through the air, and triggered secondary explosions.

Then as Evans arrived on the scene, he heard the *crack* of hand thrown grenades, and the steady *bang, bang, bang* of M27 rifles. As crates were destroyed cricks were forced out into the open. Gunfire lashed back and forth. Fighters from both sides fell. But the Marines had the advantage, and took advantage of it.

In the meantime, consistent with their orders, combat engineers swept out and around what remained of the Prax fortification to place charges on the gates. The cry of "Fire in the hole," went mostly unheard, soon followed by two explosions.

Evans forced himself to take aim as a cricket charged him, and pulled the trigger. The IAR thumped his shoulder and the alien fell. Then, as the crick attempted to get up, he shot it again. Evans could see sunlight beyond the gates, along with an Amphibious Combat vehicle, and some oncoming Marines. Mission accomplished. Part of it anyway.

But there was more to do, starting with the need to assess the company's strength, and reintegrate his command.

"Charlie-Three," Evans said. "This is Charlie-Six actual. We're at the gate. Reinforcements are arriving. What's your situation? Over."

"This is Charlie Three," Lieutenant Dawkins replied. "We have six walking wounded. Four stretcher cases are headed your way on trucks, along with five bodies. We couldn't leave them behind."

Evans winced. Five KIAs. And Dawkins was correct. If the bodies were left behind they'd be eaten.

"And that's not all," Dawkins added. "One of our fireteams is MIA. Over."

Evans swore. "Roger that. The Gunny will remain here to ensure that our stretcher cases are taken care of."

Evans thumbed his radio. "This is Six. The first and second platoons will form on me. Four Marines are missing. We will find them. Over."

Evans took off at a jog, with two columns of Marines following along behind. Suddenly the lights came on and the downpour stopped.

Our guys are in the control room next to the gate, Evans reasoned. *That will help. But, assuming they're alive, that fireteam is in some deep shit.*

* * *

Corporal Anne Kirby was frightened, ashamed of herself, and in command. Frightened because a steady stream of cricks was passing the fireteam's position, ashamed because she'd led the team astray. And in command because she was an E4.

Her team consisted of Lance Corporal Corey Hill, Private Lon Wu, and Private Luis Esteban, all of whom were lying prone on top of a construction platform. A refuge Kirby spotted shortly after she realized that she was lost.

The assignment was simple: Kirby's fireteam had orders to protect the 3rd platoon's left flank and provide intelligence. No prob.

Then the lights went out, the sprinkler system came on, and the screaming started. That was the moment when Kirby became disoriented, turned away from the platoon, and lost radio contact. Not entirely, but partially.

Kirby could hear snatches of conversation from time-to-time but had been unable to get through. Now she was trying again. Her voice was a whisper. "Charlie-Two, this is Charlie Eight-Five. Can you read me?"

Kirby's heart leapt as a female voice answered. "This is Two actual... I read you! What's your twenty? And what's your situation? Are any members of your team wounded? Over."

Kirby felt an overwhelming sense of embarrassment as she turned the volume down. "No wounds. As for our twenty, I'm not sure. Somewhere left of the line of march.

"And, because we're on top of a construction platform, I can't see any grid markers. What I *can* see is a steady flow of cricks headed your way. Over."

Kirby's report was followed by a moment of silence so long she feared that it hadn't been received. Then Lieutenant Christou spoke again.

"Roger that. Hold your position. What's your estimate of the enemy's strength? Over."

"Twenty or twenty-five so far," Kirby replied. "Over."

"Keep counting and let us know if the flow stops," Christou replied. "Over."

Kirby clicked her transmit button twice.

The flow stopped after twelve additional aliens passed the raised platform. Kirby radioed the information in. The response was nearly instantaneous. "Roger that, Eight-Five. We're waiting for your friends. If they retreat in your direction, kill them. Over."

"Copy," Kirby replied. "Over."

Then it was time for a whispered conference with the rest of the team. "Hill, I want you and Esteban to join me here. Wu, watch our six. Got it?"

"Got it," Wu replied. The others nodded.

"And one more thing," Kirby said. "I let you down, and I'm sorry."

Esteban grinned. "Ain't nothing to it Corp, no worries."

Kirby was looking forward to combat. Maybe, just maybe, she could redeem herself. The opportunity came quickly. The sound of rifle fire was heard from what Kirby thought was the west, soon followed by the *boom* of grenades. "Here they come," Wu said. "Let's grease 'em."

"Hold your fire," Kirby instructed, as she peered through her scope. "Let's make every shot count … All right, *now!* Let 'em have it!"

Unlike humans, the Prax couldn't run. All they could do was shuffle, or if the situation permitted, fly. And the ceiling was too low for that.

That meant the Marines could take their time, pick targets, and in some cases kill two aliens with a single shot. As the bodies continued to accumulate, cricks took cover behind the pile and began to return fire. "Grenades," Kirby instructed. "Kill them! Kill them all!"

Being up high gave the Marines the advantage when it came to tossing grenades. The resulting explosions sent geysers of alien pulp up into the air. Some of the goo splattered the ceiling. The rest fell in globs.

Kirby fired, and fired, and was about to fire some more when Wu touched her arm. "They're dead, Corp. All of them are dead."

Kirby wanted to cry, but managed to restrain herself. "Charlie-Two, this is Eight-Five. Mission accomplished. Over."

"Well done, Eight-Five. Follow the bodies to our twenty. We'll be waiting."

CHAPTER FIVE

Washington D.C. The White House

The Situation Room was located on the ground floor in the West Wing of the White House. And contrary to what many believed, was not underground.

Over the years the Situation Room had been used to deal with some of history's most critical moments. Now the facility was being utilized to combat the crick menace, and to manage the presence of a *second* alien race, which was waging war on the first.

A long table filled most of the narrow conference room. Everyone stood as President Vanessa Seton entered the room. She was the youngest president since Bill Clinton, a graduate of West Point, and a Rhodes Scholar. More than that, Seton had been New York's lieutenant governor and a one term senator prior to winning the presidency.

Some said Seton's success was due to her experience. Others suggested that her rise was due to good timing and a pretty face. Whatever the reason, she was generally well thought of, in spite of the emergence. "Please take your seats," Seton said, as she took a seat located halfway down the table.

As the participants sat down Seton made note of the officials who were present that day. They included Secretary of Defense Morton Jones, Marine Corps General Roy Dempsey, Deputy Secretary of Defense for Intelligence and Security Dan Eason,

Secretary of State Larry Bowes, Secretary for the Department of Homeland Security Martha Rigg, Seton's Chief of Staff Roy Jenkins, and Press Secretary Milton Hughes.

Seton smiled and nodded. "Good morning, everyone. Let's get to it. General? What kind of condition is our condition in?"

Dempsey wore his hair high and tight, had penetrating eyes, and a lantern jaw. "I'll begin with the good news," Dempsey said. "As you know, our NATO partners were caught flat footed when the crickets emerged, and were initially focused on their individual plights.

"But now, after reorganizing to meet the threat, NATO's beginning to respond in a concerted fashion. That includes the use of multinational military operations where they make sense.

"The second piece of good news is that the Mechans are acting as a force multiplier," Dempsey added. "Whatever the robots may lack in terms of imagination, is made up for in numbers and firepower. And that makes sense. The Xyfor have been preparing for a long time. Thousands of years, according to their narrative.

"But, for the moment there is no strategic or tactical coordination between the Mechans and human forces, and that lessens the impact the Mechs could have."

Dempsey paused to survey the faces around him. "Now for the bad news. While NATO is starting to make a difference, as are some standalone nations like Israel, Turkey, and South Korea—other countries have been overrun. The most notable being China. It had a strong military on paper, but hadn't fought a war since 1949, so all of the generals have been learning on the job.

"On top of that the CIA believes that President Shou was either assassinated, or killed by the cricks, which led to cascading leadership failures—followed by conflicts between factions of the military. So, for the moment, China is a patchwork quilt of poorly defined states ruled by warlords.

"That's bad," Dempsey continued, "but the situation in Russia is even worse. The footage you're about to see was captured by long range drones in and around what remains of Moscow." Heads turned as video rolled on multiple screens. No narration was necessary.

The city Russians sometimes referred to as the "First Throne"—because of its place at the center of a unified Russia—was a bleak hellscape. The sky was dark, damaged buildings faced each other across debris strewn streets, and a column of cricks could be seen winding its way through a maze of wrecked vehicles.

Seton had read the Daily Brief while eating breakfast. So, she was prepared for what Dempsey had to say, but the video was shocking nevertheless.

Though no fan of Russia's dictator, Seton felt sorry for those who'd been killed, and wondered if some towns and villages still survived.

That's what Seton was thinking when an Air Force officer entered the room, and made his way over to where Secretary of Defense Jones and General Dempsey were seated. A whispered conversation ensued. Jones nodded.

"I apologize for the interruption," Jones said. "But there's some breaking news that all of you need to be aware of. The Mechans, operating on orders from the Xyfor, dropped a missile on downtown Dallas. Not only that … They released video of the event."

"A narrated video," the officer added. "Would you like to see it?"

"No," Seton replied. "But we have to. Roll it."

There was a pause. The video appeared on all the monitors at once. It began with an aerial shot of downtown Dallas captured by a Mechan drone. The narration had the stiff quality typical of Xyfor communications.

"This is the city you call Dallas. You can see Mechan battle platforms over Dallas. And if you look closely, you'll notice a human standing on the roof of what you call "the Pinnacle Building.""

At that point the top of the tallest building was magnified in a series of jerky motions, as if a camera was changing focal lengths, to what seemed like a vantage point only fifty feet from the roof. The man in question was bald, large, and heavily armed.

Seton and her team watched as the man crossed over to the point where a stairway exited onto the roof and stood next to it. Then, the door opened and a young woman appeared. She took three steps forward and the man shot in her in the back.

No sooner had the woman gone down than a man wearing a white cowboy hat stepped out onto the roof. He was moving toward the body, when the murderer shot him as well!

At that point a new camera shot appeared. It was wide enough to show the Mechan battle platform which was preparing to land. That was the moment when the bald man brought a 40mm grenade launcher around from its position on his back, took aim, and fired six shots at the Mechan platform.

Seton watched aghast as explosions marched across the bottom of the hull to a circular construct which took a direct hit. The result was a secondary explosion, followed by a slow-motion disaster as the barge-like battle platform tilted to one side, and crashed.

"As you can see," the alien narrator continued, "our vehicle was attacked and destroyed. Actions of that sort are forbidden and won't be tolerated. Watch and learn. That will be all."

The wide shot was replaced by an even wider shot of the Pinnacle Building and the high-rise buildings around it. Then there was a flash of light, roiling smoke, and a blast wave that expanded outwards to level dozens of structures.

"Holy shit," Hughes said. "That's what I call a great press release."

All eyes swiveled to stare at Hughes. He seemed to shrink under the scrutiny. "Sorry, but it's true! The Xyfor have been studying us for years. They know what they're doing."

Seton turned to her chief of staff. "Get on the horn... Talk to the authorities in Dallas. Who were those people? And what the hell was going on?

"Also, let's put some expertise on this. Should we apologize to the Xyfor? Kill some robots? Or what? We need to know."

* * *

Carlsbad Caverns National Park, New Mexico
The Carlsbad Caverns National Park was closed, and had been ever since the early days of "the emergence," when a party of thirty-two tourists had been slaughtered in the "Big Room."

And the Big Room was where Seismologist Crew Chief Gina Jansky and her crew were supposed to set up. But large though the cavern was, they couldn't bring the hulking "birdwagen" thumper truck inside it, and would have to rely on what the crew called the "mini." It was about the size of a standard hand truck and damned heavy. The rig consisted of a frame, a spring-loaded hammer, and a car battery.

The mini's purpose was to send shock waves through the ground. Then, by measuring the amount of time it took for the reflected wave to arrive at a receiver, the crew could assess what lay below. Normally such devices were used to locate ground water, landfills, and oil reserves.

And that's how Jansky made her living prior to the emergence. Then the government hired her to search for cricket nests like the colony on the Hopi reservation in northeast Arizona. A large habitat which had attacked her crew and nearly had them for dinner.

It was during that incident that Jansky met a number of neighboring Navajos and hired three of them. "All right," Jansky said. "It's getting late. Let's get the gear inside before the sun sets. Then we'll set up camp. This place was cleared. But nature abhors a vacuum, so keep your heads on a swivel, and holler if you see anything weird."

The seven-person crew was equipped with military style tactical radios and were heavily armed. Jansky had promoted a seismic field tech named Roger Gulin to the two-slot making him the "two-boss." "You heard the chief," Gulin said. "Let's move the mini first."

As the crew went to work Jansky followed the Natural Entrance Trail inside. Directional signs pointed the way to the Visitor Center, which according to Jansky's map, was the gateway to an area called "The Giant Dome." That led to the "Temple of the Sun," and the "Big Room,"—her ultimate destination. The lights were on, and were supposed to remain so for the next two days, although the crew was prepared for an outage should one occur.

Thanks to a BS in geology, and a masters in geophysics, Jansky was well prepared to appreciate the beauty and grandeur all around her.

As the crew chief followed the trail toward the Big Room, she saw jaw-dropping rock columns, soda straws, stalagmites, stalactites, helictites, cave bacon, popcorn drapes, curtains, spires, flowstone and more.

And the Big Room was BIG. According to the information Jansky had been given, the floor of the cave was more than eight acres in size, the largest accessible cave chamber in North America. That had everything to do with the seismologist's mission, which was to take readings and make sure that the cricks didn't have a nest hidden under the floor. Because, if they did, more than a thousand refugees would be at risk.

It was all part of a FEMA plan to move the residents of TRC 1106 (Temporary Relocation Camp 1106) from Whites City to a more secure location. And after speaking to Cassie Lang, the woman in charge, Jansky understood how urgent the situation was.

TRC 1106 was just sitting there, a huge sprawl of trailers, tents and shacks with no defensive perimeter—and nothing more than small arms for protection.

Jansky paused to light a cigarillo. A bad habit to be sure, and one that prevented her from holding an office job, since smoking was a corporate no-no.

Her thoughts wandered. Would the ongoing presence of a thousand humans cause harm to the cavern? Yes, of course it would.

But, Jansky thought, *more than a thousand lives are at stake. Hell, the whole fucking planet is at stake. We gotta do what we gotta do.*

Jansky heard a scritching sound, pulled the Ruger Single Seven .327 magnum, and scanned the area. The nymph was behind her. So Jansky didn't see it shuffle forward.

But, when the little bastard bit her leg, the seismologist sure as hell *felt* it.

Don't blow your foot off, Jansky thought, as she turned to take aim. The sound of the shot was magnified by the walls of the cavern and the bullet blew the alien apart.

Jansky expected more crickets to attack, and stood with her pistol at the ready, as Gulin and two crew members arrived.

Gulin knelt next to what remained of the cricket's immature body. "A youngster," he said. "This is the first one I've seen."

Jansky returned the pistol to its holster. "If there's one, there's more. We'll keep the campsite tight—and set a watch."

Gulin stood. "So, we're staying?"

Jansky dropped the cigarillo butt and stepped on it. "Of course, we're staying. Maybe there's what they call a creche nearby. Or, maybe we're standing on top of a nest. It's our job to find out. I need a bandage."

* * *

Washington D.C. The White House

President Vanessa Seton faced a difficult decision. A day had passed since Ralph Waring fired a grenade launcher at a Mechan battle platform and caused it to crash.

An act for which all humans were punished by a devastating missile strike. The citizens of Dallas were pissed. The citizens of Texas were pissed. And the citizens of the United States were pissed. That meant both houses of Congress were in an uproar, the press was demanding answers, and something had to be done. But *what*?

Most of Seton's brain trust were in the Roosevelt Room, not far from the Oval Office, debating that very question.

There were two schools of thought. Secretary of State Larry Bowes favored an apology. "It makes sense," he argued. "Even though Waring wasn't acting on behalf of our government, he fired on the Mechans, and destroyed a battle platform. All we need to do is tell the Xyfor that we're sorry, and offer our condolences. End of story."

But would it be? Secretary of Defense Morton Jones didn't think so. "Who knows?" Morton demanded. "Perhaps the Xyfor will accept a mea culpa. But it's my opinion that the citizens of the United States won't. They want strong action."

"Strong action could get thousands, or even millions of Americans killed," DHS Secretary Martha Rigg responded. "You saw what happened to downtown Dallas. For all we know, the Mechans would respond to a counter attack by destroying D.C."

A military aide entered the room. "Excuse me, Madam President. Professor Dwight Carmody has arrived."

Seton stood. "Please send him in." Carmody was one of only a few academics who specialized in xenoanthropology, a field considered to be the province of eccentrics, until the Prax emerged. Then they were in demand. And that was even more true now that a *second* race of aliens had arrived. The door opened to admit a handsome man of middle age. He was seated in a wheelchair propelled by a young man wearing glasses and a man bun.

Carmody had shoulder length black hair, and his suit was tight across the shoulders, suggesting a powerful torso. "Hello Professor, it's a pleasure to meet you," Seton said, as she went forward to shake hands.

"And you," Carmody replied. "Excuse me if I don't get up."

It was an icebreaker that Carmody used frequently and produced the usual smile.

"Thanks for coming on such short notice," Seton said. "Before we tackle the matter at hand, I'd like to introduce my staff."

Once the introductions were complete Carmody joined the rest of them at the long table. Portraits of Theodore Roosevelt and Franklin D. Roosevelt hung on the walls. And, because the room lacked windows, a false skylight lit the scene.

Seton opened the meeting. "I trust you received the briefing document?"

Carmody nodded. "I did. Thank you."

"So, you understand our dilemma," Seton said. "The people in this room have strong opinions. Roughly half of my advisors favor some sort of apology, and the rest think we should launch a counter strike."

"First some background," Carmody replied. "Until very recently xenoanthropology was purely theoretical social science, with no basis in fact. Now we're beginning to collect some data. But most of it is based on observations rather than interactions. That's because the crickets think of us the way we think about cattle. We don't talk to cows, and for the most part, the captured cricks won't talk to us."

Carmody's analogy provoked some chuckles. Carmody smiled. "There was one notable exception however, and that was the conversation that took place between Doctor Anne Blake and a core." All of the officials in the room knew Blake personally, and were very well aware of her contributions to the resistance effort.

"With your permission I would like to play a recording of that conversation," Carmody said. "Not the entire interchange, but a portion of it."

Seton remembered the gist of the interaction, but was willing to go along. "Of course."

Carmody's assistant stepped forward to place a recorder on the table. Carmody pressed "Play." A female voice was heard. "What are you?"

"I am a Core."

"What is a Core?"

"A Core is a potential Prime."

"What is a Prime?"

"Prime is the bioelectronic computer that governs the Prax race through the Nexus."

"I see," Blake said. "Under what circumstances would you become the Prime?"

"I would become the new Prime if the existing Prime suffered a catastrophic systems failure, and my peers chose me as a replacement."

"How many Cores are there?"

"One thousand, two hundred and forty-six."

"Why are you willing to tell me these things?"

"It makes no difference what a meat knows. Your species is the most violent race we have encountered. But we will harvest you nevertheless."

"Tell me about the other species you mentioned. Did they contact you? Or vice versa?"

A burst of click speech was heard, followed by the translation. "What does 'vice versa' mean?"

"I will rephrase my question. How did the Prax race come into contact with another species for the first time?"

"The Xyfor landed on our native planet about a million Prax years ago, and captured a number of specimens—including a Core—which they took to their home world.

"After being placed in a Xyfor zoo, the Core became a Prime, and directed its functionaries to carry out an escape.

"That led to the founding of a nest, followed by rapid reproduction, and a series of wars which rendered the world uninhabitable.

"By that time my forebearers had mastered Xyfor technology, which allowed them to emigrate to another planet."

Carmody pressed "Stop." His eyes roamed the faces around him. "The information about how Prax society works is fascinating, but that isn't why I played the recording.

"There, at the end of the recording, is the reason why the Xyfor are here. The Prax laid waste to one of what we assume to be numerous Xyfor planets. And then they escaped into space. The Xyfor could have written the whole thing off to experience and continued with business as usual," Carmody added. "But they didn't. Instead, they searched for thousands of years, found the Prax hiding here—and are determined to eradicate them.

"The question," Carmody continued, "is *why*? Are the Xyfor a race of benevolent sentients who, having suffered themselves, are out to protect life in other solar systems? That's how they describe themselves. Or, are the Xyfor intent on revenge? And we're of no importance.

"Before you answer consider this: According to the Core that Blake spoke with, the Prax escaped from a Xyfor zoo. Sentients in a zoo. Think about it."

Seton frowned. "So? What should we do?"

Carmody smiled. "'The only thing power respects is power.' Malcom X said that. And he was correct."

"Okay," Bowes responded. "But if we attack, they will attack."

"It's a conundrum," Carmody admitted.

Seton sighed. "I'm stumped. Any ideas?"

A long silence followed. Then, much to everyone's surprise, Press Secretary Milton Hughes spoke. "I have the answer."

CHAPTER SIX

Joint Base Andrews, Maryland

Nearly twenty-four hours had passed since the meeting at the White House, and President Seton was standing in front of a combat ready F-15 Strike Eagle, with a runway visible in the background. The sky was gray, and threatening to rain.

In concert with Milton Hughes' instructions, Seton was wearing a leather jacket over a flight suit, minus insignia. A westerly breeze ruffled her hair.

Could Seton fly the jet? Hell, no. But she had served in the Army, which made the "combat ready" imagery more believable.

Three tripod-mounted TV cameras were focused on her. One shot was wide, one was medium, and the third was tight. A director was on hand to call the shots, along with a technical director, who would push the necessary buttons. Their job was to handle the live feed that was about to go out over the recently reconfigured Emergency Alert System (EAS) to the broadcast networks, streaming services, and mobile phones nationwide.

The so-called "Hughes Thesis" held that the Dallas attack was the result of a communications problem and should be handled with that in mind.

The Xyfor weren't trying to destroy Dallas, Hughes argued. "They were trying to communicate the extent of their power. And now, if we want respect, we have to demonstrate the strength of *our* power. And we need to do so in a dramatic way. The way the Xyfor did in Dallas."

A crew member hollered, "Ready on the set! Ten seconds to air! Nine, eight, seven, six, five, four, three, and two." Then he pointed to Seton.

Commercial networks snapped to black all across the United States. The EAS logo appeared and was immediately replaced by a wide shot of Seton with the jet behind her. Her name and title appeared below the shot as the camera zoomed in.

"My fellow Americans, two days ago an American fired on a Mechan battle platform, causing it to crash in downtown Dallas. That was a serious mistake, and we in no way condone it.

"Then, in an effort to demonstrate the extent of their power, Xyfor dropped a missile on the Pinnacle building. The purpose of that barbarous act was to intimidate our government and our citizens. Well, guess what? It didn't work."

A jet roared down the runway, momentarily drowning Seton's voice out, but serving to punctuate the president's words. The shot of Seton dissolved to a satellite image of a vaguely defined airport. "This is a shot of the old Desert Center Airport in Riverside County, California," Seton said. "As seen from orbit. It's just one of what we estimate to be more than a thousand Mechan military bases around the planet."

The camera began to zoom in. "As you can see," Seton said, "there are about two dozen Mechan spaceships of various types on the ground. The one we're going to destroy is parked in the middle of the field. It's roughly a thousand feet long, and shaped like an enormous boxcar, rather than a conventional aircraft. That's made possible by powerful engines which can lift the ship into space using brute force.

"We can't be absolutely certain, of course," Seton said conversationally, "but we believe that the vessel in question is a supply ship. That makes it valuable. And if you look closely, you can see robots hurrying to board, as dust shoots sideways all around.

"That's because the Xyfor are monitoring this broadcast and, based on what I said moments ago, they hope to save their ship from destruction.

"But that's impossible. As I speak a submarine launched Tomahawk missile, armed with a conventional warhead, is already in the air—and traveling at 550 miles per hour.

"According to our calculations the missile will score a direct hit on the Mechan ship, causing only minor damage to the vessels parked around it.

"Our intent is to send the Xyfor a message rather than inflict maximum destruction. Thanks to our world-spanning fleet of submarines, we can attack each and every Xyfor base should it be necessary. That said, we'd rather enter an alliance, dedicated to fighting the Prax, than fight the Xyfor."

The timing was perfect. The sub launched missile struck the Xyfor ship as it lifted off the ground and blew up. Secondary explosions tore the supply vessel apart.

But, contrary to Seton's prediction, a number of lesser ships were destroyed as well. "Okay," Seton said as she watched a monitor. "My bad! Some additional vessels went boom! But that's the sort of thing that can happen when potential allies fight each other instead of a common enemy.

"Thank you for watching, and may God bless our citizens, our soldiers, and survivors all around the world."

The EAS cut to black, and Milton Hughes led the applause. "And *that*," Hughes said, "is what I call a *back atcha*."

***

Carlsbad Caverns National Park, New Mexico
While her crew prepared to "thump" the Big Room's floor, Gina Jansky was outside smoking a cigarillo, and waiting for a Department of Homeland Security (DHS) helicopter to arrive.

After half a dozen Nymph encounters the previous afternoon, Jansky felt compelled to report the presence of cricks to the government lest authorities move a thousand unsuspecting refugees into the caverns. "What we need," Jansky told her boss via her sat phone, "is for a platoon of bad asses to drop in and exterminate the little bastards."

But no, that was too fucking simple for the suits in D.C. According to Jansky's supervisor a "scientific assessment" had to be completed prior to military action. So, she should expect an extraterrestrial fast response team (EFRT) to arrive at 0800 the following morning.

It was 0826 by the time Jansky heard the drone of engines and saw a speck coming her way. The speck morphed into an unmarked Black Hawk helicopter, complete with door mounted miniguns, and visored crew members.

Rotor blades clattered as the helo circled, lost altitude, and landed. A skinny dude was the first person to deass the Hawk. He made his way over with hand extended. He had to shout in order to be heard over the engine noise. "I'm Brit Sanders. And you are?"

"Gina Jansky."

"Right," Sanders replied, as the engines shut down. "You're the seismologist they told me about. What makes you believe that nymphs are present in the caverns?"

"The little bastards attacked us," Jansky replied simply. "Take a look over there." She pointed.

Sanders went over to stare at six badly mangled bodies. "They stink."

"They certainly do," Jansky agreed. "They're dead."

Sanders frowned. "There's no need for sarcasm, Jansky. Do you know where they're coming from?"

"Yes," Jansky answered. "The interior of the cave is lit. Not well lit, mind you, but lit. The nymphs are crawling up and out of what the park department calls 'The Bottomless Pit.' Except it isn't bottomless ... It's one hundred and forty feet deep according to their literature."

"I see," Sanders said thoughtfully. "That's consistent with the creches we've inspected. The cricks take up residence and install a giver. Then, if they decide to move on, they generally leave the creche behind. And once the giver finishes giving birth, it dies. So, we're likely to find a dead giver at the bottom of the pit."

"You're going down?" Jansky inquired. "What for?"

"Science," Sanders replied. "I'll take tissue samples, which will be compared to those acquired elsewhere, in order to answer some important questions. Does each giver have unique DNA? Or do they share the same DNA? Like twins do. We need to understand that sort of thing if we're going to defeat the Prax."

Jansky had to admit that the research made sense. Maybe the government wasn't so stupid after all. But one aspect of Sanders' response gave her pause.

"Okay, but there's something you need to know. It's my opinion that this giver is still alive."

Sanders looked surprised. "What makes you think so?"

"We heard movement down there, not to mention loud farting sounds, and grunting noises."

Sanders shook his head. "That isn't consistent with what we've encountered at other sites. Chances are that the nymphs produced those noises."

Jansky remained unconvinced. But she could tell that whatever she said would fall on deaf ears. "What can we do to help?"

"We have lots of gear," Sanders replied. "You could give us a hand."

"Lots of gear," turned out to be an understatement, as Jansky and her crew helped the fast response team move pieces of a crane, a reel of wire rope, a winch, two batteries and Sanders' sampling gear through the Big Room and into the area where the Bottomless Pit was located.

A number of nymph attacks took place during the back-and-forth trips, all of which ended the same way. The "specimens" were shot, loaded into ice chests, and left next to the trail. "You were right," Sanders told Jansky after the most recent attack. "This is a hot spot."

No shit, Jansky thought. *Good luck down in the pit.*

Even though the DHS personnel knew what they were doing, it still took three hours to assemble the swing arm crane, rig it, and attach a specially designed chair. Sanders was fastening his harness when Jansky took one last shot at him. "Seriously, Brit, I think the giver is alive."

"I know you do," Sanders replied. "And that's why we lowered a camera down to take a look. That's SOP by the way. The bottom of the pit is ass deep in nymphs, all trying to climb the walls, but the giver is dead as a doornail."

Sanders was so certain that Jansky felt her fears melt away. He was the expert after all, and truth be told, she was a bit paranoid. Or, so some people claimed.

Nonetheless, Jansky was armed, as were seismo crew members Roger Gulin and Billy Yazzie.

Curiosity drew Jansky to the edge of the precipice as Sanders was lowered into the pit. The lights attached to the chair were bright enough to illuminate the surrounding walls and the nymphs that were attempting to scale them.

However, the spot light attached to the seat's bottom couldn't yet penetrate the blackness below. Sanders sat with a device that looked like a pole trimmer resting across the arms of his chair. But rather than cut tree branches, this tool was designed to take tissue samples.

After bringing the tip into contact with a giver, and pulling a trigger, Sanders could take a circular core sample. Each of which was about the size of a quarter and half an inch thick.

Then, as additional "plugs" were acquired, they would push the previous samples up into the tool's hollow handle where they were stored until such time as the device was "cleared."

The winch whirred, and the chair appeared to dwindle in size as it descended to fifty feet, a hundred feet, and a hundred and twenty-five feet from the surface.

All the observers could make out was a ring of light at that point. But they could hear Sanders over two pole-mounted speakers. And, if his tone was any indication, the team leader was having a good time.

***

"The walls are covered with slime, but that's typical," Sanders observed. "As is the stench. The nymphs can see me, and they're fighting for position, ready to attack when I touch down. That won't happen however. I can see the giver now, and if past experience is any guide, it's roughly the size of a killer whale.

"Okay, prepare to stop the winch, stop. That's good! I can reach the giver with my pole now. The nymphs are going crazy! There ... I'm in contact. Now, all I have to do is pull the ... "

***

The giver jerked convulsively as Sanders pulled the trigger. A plate-sized eye popped open as the giver used part of its body to reach up and grab the chair. Sanders screamed, and the lights gyrated wildly as the giver jerked the seat loose. It fell into the seething mass of nymphs below.

Sanders was firing his pistol by then, but it was pointless. A nymph was feeding on Sanders' face as he died.

* * *

Members of the extraterrestrial fast response team were shouting, and firing weapons into the pit, as Jansky and her companions backed away.

Her voice activated radio was on. "Cly! We have a situation here … Bring the team and every weapon we have."

Fran Cly was the seismo crew's "three-boss." "Roger that, we'll be there shortly."

That was the moment when a snake-like tentacle shot up out of the hole, and began to whip back and forth. Two members of Sanders' team died instantly. A third was swept into the pit. Meanwhile the tentacle was feeling about in the same way that a blind man might. And, when the giver found a sturdy stalagmite, it secured a grip, and began to pull itself upwards.

The alien grew steadily larger as the snakelike extension was reabsorbed into its flabby body, and the creature was fully restored by the time it shot out of the hole, and landed with a ground shaking thump. Jansky and her crew were firing at the monstrosity by then. The crew chief was armed with a Daewoo USAS-12 automatic shotgun with a twenty-round drum magazine. Gulin was packing a six shot 40mm grenade launcher, and Yazzie had a light machine gun. They continued to fire as Cly and the rest of the crew arrived.

The giver made a horrible screeching noise as the massed fire tore into it. The shotgun clicked empty, and Jansky was firing her pistol, as the giver backed away and fell into the pit.

The crew chief unloaded the empty casings from her revolver and began to reload. "Gulin! Fetch some dynamite! Three sticks should do the job."

Though not appropriate for use inside the caverns, dynamite was commonly used to generate seismic waves in other situations, and the crew had plenty of it.

It took fifteen long minutes for Gulin to reach camp and return with the dynamite.

Each stick was armed with a blasting cap that could be triggered with a remote. "Throw them into the hole," Jansky instructed. "Wait for sixty seconds, and set them off! That should kill the giver and the nymphs too."

Gulin dropped each stick separately, counted to sixty, and pressed the button. The resulting *BOOM* was amplified by the enclosed space, the floor shook, and a stalactite fell from the ceiling, barely missing Joe Bitsilly.

You're a geophysicist, for God's sake, Jansky thought, as chunks of rock continued to rain down. *What an idiot.* Jansky was still berating herself as she made her way through the Big Room and out into bright sunshine, where she lit a cigarillo. Her hand trembled as she flicked the lighter. Then, after a deep drag, Jansky phoned her boss. Or tried to. The call dropped twice before she managed to get through. There was a ten-minute wait before she could speak with him. "Yeah," Howie Amin said. "Sorry about the wait. This place is crazy. What's up? Did the XT team arrive?"

"Yes, they did," Jansky answered. "But all of them were killed."

There was a long pause. "You're shitting me."

"No, I'm not."

"What happened?"

Jansky told him and Amin listened. "And the bodies?"

"There aren't any bodies."

"Shit. How 'bout your crew?"

"No wounds. And no fatalities."

"Thank God for that," Amin replied. "So, what's next?"

"We'll thump the place today, file our report, and get the hell out," Jansky told him.

"I think we killed most of the nymphs," she added. "But there's bound to be some strays lurking about. I suggest you send a military dog team in to sniff them out."

"Will do. Can you head up to Montana tomorrow?"

"Montana? What for?"

"To look for cricks—what else?" Amin said lightly. "I'll send the details via email. Check your phone. And Gina..."

"Yeah?"

"You done good." *Click.*

The hot sun felt good on Jansky's skin. A vulture circled high overhead. But, for one brief moment, death was on hold.

***

Camp Pendleton, California

A week had passed since President Seton's historic gamble. And in line with Professor Carmody's thesis that "the only thing power respects is power," the Xyfor agreed to talks.

The first round resulted in a pact to find out whether humans and Mechans could fight side-by-side. And, as a "reward" for his success in the Kansas City SubTropolis battle, Evans was seconded to a combined arms platoon made up of Marines and Mechans.

If this a reward, what would a punishment look like? Evans wondered, as he left for California. But what was, was. And upon reporting to Camp Pendleton, Evans learned that the platoon had nine days in which to train for an actual mission.

His temporary CO was a lieutenant colonel named Borski. "Think about it this way," Borski said. "The Mechans are trained, your Marines are trained, so all they need to do is figure out how to work together."

That was true to a certain degree, except it turned out that the leathernecks were straight out of a holding company, and the robots had been reconditioned. To some extent anyway. It didn't take a roboticist to see that some of the machines had lingering issues. Like "Tripod," who was one arm short of a full load.

A level three Mechan was in charge of the robots. And when Evans suggested that they flip a coin to determine who would be in command, the Mechan officer nearly had the electronic equivalent of a nervous breakdown. The concept of leaving anything to chance was completely foreign to the machine. So, it had to consult a command AI, which had to check with a Xyfor controller, before granting permission. Not a good start.

And the situation deteriorated from there, starting with interpersonal communications. Rather than a name, each Mechan had an individual identifier that consisted of a six-digit batch number, a three-digit maintenance code, a five-digit specialization sequencer, and a two-digit rank—all adding up to sixteen digits in all.

That worked well for machines that communicated via high-speed bursts of data. But it wasn't going to fly with human beings. So, after checking with his counterpart to ensure that all of the Mechans could process English, and weren't prohibited from using nicknames, Evans put his Marines to work.

They called the Mechan officer, "C-3PO," even though the dark gray Mechan bore no resemblance to the gold robot of STAR WARS fame. A unit that seemed to a bit slow compared to the rest was named, "Goofy." The heavy weapons Mechan was known as, "Yeti." And so forth.

The nicknames were stenciled on the robots front and back, and much to the delight of Evans' Marines, he ordered the machines to use their nicknames as call signs. As in, "X-Ray-Six, this is Goofy. Over." A format that always produced gales of laughter.

Once the naming issue was solved, Team X-Ray went into the field, and began an arduous series of trials. For the robots, yes. But for the leathernecks too.

The exercises included a mock assault on a steep hill, a surprise attack by an Apache gunship, a water crossing under simulated fire—and a rescue mission in a maze of subterranean tunnels. After five days of observation, Evans had the beginnings of the report he would have to submit when the training operations were over.

On the plus side, the robots were equipped with electronic sensors that enabled them to see and hear things that humans couldn't. And, thanks to hydraulics, the machines were stronger than the Marines, and were capable of greater endurance. As far as Evans could tell, the robots didn't feel fear, love, or hate. Emotions that could cloud judgement.

'Furthermore, damaged Mechans had interchangeable parts, and could be cannibalized in the field. That made them more reliable than their flesh and blood counterparts.

As for skills, everything the mechanical soldiers needed to know was programmed into them. They never broke the skyline. They never bunched up. And their heads were literally on a swivel that allowed them to conduct a 360-degree sweep every ten seconds. Never mind the fact that each mech had four arms, and could fire two, or even three, weapons at a time!

There were some negatives of course. First and foremost was their reliance on detailed orders from higher up. Before a Mechan could attack a machine-gun nest it was supposed to receive a route from a flying drone, along with instructions regarding which weapons to employ, and its role vis-a-vis that of the other units.

Then, if the situation changed, as was often the case in battle, a Mechan had to request instructions. And, no matter how fast that interaction was, it couldn't compare with a Marine who could make his or her own decisions.

Still, once the field exercises were over, Evans knew he'd prefer to fight a company of Prax rather than the same number of Mechans.

After it returned from the field Evans gave the team the rest of the day off. The Marines yelled, "Oorah!" The machines were silent.

CHAPTER SEVEN

Camp Pendleton, California

The Mechan air-land transport was roughly the size of a CONEX container and just as pretty. There was no visible cockpit. *And why would there be?* Evans mused. *It's safe to assume that the pilot is a black box, sitting next to another black box, which serves as a backup.*

C-3PO had a gravelly voice. "Humans will board and sit in the back of the assault ship."

Evans thumbed his radio. "This is Six. Follow me. Over."

The transport stood on four articulated "legs," each of which was fitted with skids. Thanks to the flexible supports the transport could land on uneven ground.

A ramp led from the ground up to the vehicle's deck. The cargo area smelled like chlorine bleach, an odor that Evans had come to associate with ozone. A pedestal mounted weapon was visible in the bow.

There were two rows of inward facing seats, an arrangement that was common on human transports as well. When Evans sat down, he discovered that the seat was not only too large for him, but too high, causing his boots to dangle like a five-year-old on a school bus.

The Marines were bitching about the seats when metal safety arms slid out to hug them in a loose embrace. Loose, because the restraints were designed to protect Mechans. *Note to self,* Evans thought. *Transport interoperability is questionable. Put that in the report.*

If the transport's AI delivered a preflight announcement, the robots were the only ones who could "hear" it. Fortunately, the Marines knew where they were going and why.

Back in the early '60s, underground silos were built to house Titan 1 ICBM missiles in northern California. Later, as Titan IIs came on line, the earlier models were scrapped. Some silos sat vacant for decades, and eventually became tourist attractions, or were purchased by private citizens. Such was the case with the silo designed to serve as a survival retreat for a multimillionaire and his family.

According to the pre-mission briefing Evans and C-3PO had received, the silo was equipped with an air filtration system and stocked with enough supplies to last the owner ten years. Sadly, the threat came from below, rather than above. And the entire family was slaughtered shortly after the emergence.

Thanks to reports from the locals, the government had been aware of the infestation for some time, but been forced to focus its attention on other more important targets.

However now, with the Mechans as allies, it was time to enter the subterranean habitat and destroy the nest. The trip to Chico took a little under three hours. The Marines passed the time napping, playing cards, and shooting the shit.

C-3PO broke the silence. "We have arrived and are about to land. All passengers will remain in their seats while the vehicle fires on the pestilence."

There weren't any windows. But Evans had seen the weapon mounted in the bow and could hear the staccato *ka-chew* sound it made.

The ship landed with a thump, and began to walk. Evans knew that because of the ship's side-to-side, back-and-forth motion. *This thing reminds me of a transformer*, Evans thought.

It was an aircraft. Now it's a tank. Replace the Mechan seats, and bingo! The Marine Corps would have a new toy.

The assault craft shuddered as something hit the hull, paused, and fired in return. Then combat ceased, the safety cages opened, and the ramp *whirred* down. "This is Six," Evans said over the radio. "The platoon will leave by the numbers, starting with one. Execute."

Each member of the team had an alternating number. Evans was one, C-3PO was two, Sergeant Colby was three—and so forth. This approach prevented both the robot and humans from forming homogeneous clumps. And that was important because part of the team's theoretical strength was going to flow from well-integrated fireteams.

Evans wasn't sure what to expect as he *clumped* down the ramp. His stomach muscles were clenched, as if waiting to receive a blow, and he was hyperalert.

Dead cricks were scattered about. The terrain was flat and mostly arid, except for the green trees located to the north. A cyclone fence topped with razor wire barred the way.

Thanks to drone footage, and his briefing, Evans knew that the entrance to the hab was inside the cluster of citrus trees. Were the Prax preparing a warm reception for the platoon? Hell yes, they were. "This is Six," Evans said. "Follow me. Stay off the paths. Keep your eyes peeled for IEDS, spider holes, and cricks that aren't as dead as they should be. Over."

A sun-bleached sign was wired to the fence. "PRIVATE PROPERTY. NO TRESPASSERS." A cricket sized hole offered a way through. A Marine examined the ground looking for mines. There weren't any.

By bending over Evans could pass through. The Mechans had greater difficulty.

Cricket trails crisscrossed the ground. And there, next one of them, was a desiccated cow carcass. Whether the animal wandered onto the property, or had been led there, wasn't clear. But one thing was for sure, most of it had been eaten. Flies buzzed as Evans walked past.

The trees were immediately ahead. "This is Six. Mind your spacing. Heads on a swivel. Over."

Evans heard a flurry of clicks, and was passing the remains of an outbuilding, when a crick opened fire on him. He took a dive as bullets stitched a line across his path. A Marine fired and the alien went down.

Evans stood. All the footpaths converged on the same spot. The silo's entrance was protected by a chest high pile of rubble.

A concrete arch was visible behind that, along with the blackened remains of a steel door. Judging from the way the metal was bent, the blast had originated from *within* the hab. As if the crickets had tunneled in and used explosives to clear the obstruction.

Evans was expecting a spirited defense, but the volume of fire that lashed out from the entrance came as a surprise, and forced the team to seek cover.

Yeti was the exception. The Mechan was holding a shield with one pair of hands, while it fired an automatic weapon with the other two, and took hits that dimpled its armor. Then a second "heavy" stepped up to join Yeti and opened fire.

"This is Six!' Evans shouted. "Put some 40 mike mike on that position! But stay off the Mechs! Over."

It was hard to say what made the biggest difference, the head-on attack by the Mechans, or the skillful use of grenade launchers by the Marines, but the volume of fire fell off. Then it stopped. *Combined arms can work*, Evans concluded. *Mention that in the report.*

"Kill the wounded!" Evans ordered, as he shot a downed cricket. "Single shots only!"

Evans could smell the blue cheese stench of formic acid as he stepped over a body and approached the entrance. Gunsmoke swirled as Yeti ploughed through the drift of bodies. The Mechan paused occasionally to administer a coup de grace before forging ahead.

Most of the light inside the hab was provided by splotches of what Evans knew to be luminescent fungi. Something he'd seen before.

A corporal marked their path with international orange spray paint so it would be easy to find their way out. In spite of the damage done by the crickets, signs of human habitation were still visible. A hand painted sign read: "Home Sweet Silo."

The half-eaten remains of a goat lay on top of the pool table in the game room. The stench forced Evans to breathe through his mouth. But that was nothing compared to what they discovered next. As Evans passed through a door, he found himself in a room filled with modern furniture, and rows of neatly hung carcasses. Each of them was sealed in a semi-transparent bag.

Cuts of beef dangled next to the bodies of deer, hogs, and a dog. Humans were visible too. Most were naked, their heads hanging, and their eyes closed.

But one was different. The man's features were hard to discern through the cloudy plastic, but his eyes were open! And he was trying to speak!

"One of them is alive!" Evans exclaimed. "Set security. Check every body. Sergeant Colby, give me a hand here."

The Marines worked together to unhook the bag, lower the prisoner to the floor, and cut the sack away. Clear fluid gushed onto the tiles, and the man coughed to clear his throat. "Thank God! I prayed you would come!"

And there were three more. As they were being freed, Evans went looking for C-3PO. The robot was standing guard in the main corridor. "We found four live humans," Evans announced. "We need to evacuate them."

"No," C-3PO replied flatly. "Our orders are to plant charges and destroy the nest. Nothing else."

"True," Evans responded. "But, as circumstances change, it's necessary to adjust accordingly. And I'm in command."

C-3PO ignored Evans, turned, and led the Mechans deeper into the complex. *C-3PO is communicating with them on a data link I can't access,*" Evans realized. *Another item for the report.*

"Don't leave," Evans said over the radio. "That's an order. Both teams will be vulnerable if you do." There was no reply. And, since all of his Marines could hear the back and forth, they knew what was taking place. A morale problem for sure.

None of the freed "meats" could walk without assistance. As a result, two Marines were required to assist each survivor. That reduced the number of combat ready leathernecks by eight.

Evans ordered Colby to lead the team out, while he assigned himself to the rearguard, the element of the column most likely to be attacked.

It took fifteen minutes to exit the hab and enter bright sunshine. Evans used his radio to contact local authorities as Colby led the team back to the LZ.

The assault craft's ramp was up. And no amount of yelling produced a response. *There's no human-machine interface,* Evans concluded. *Another fuckup.*

"C-3PO … This is Six. Do you read me? Over."

There was no answer. That didn't mean much however, since it was often difficult, if not impossible, to speak with someone underground.

Hopefully C-3PO and his Mechans were finished underground, or close to being finished, and would emerge soon. But what if they were in trouble?

Evans detailed a hospital corpsman and two Marines to remain with the survivors. Even though Evans had no way to communicate with the assault craft, he assumed the ship would protect itself if attacked, and thereby defend the humans as well.

Evans felt an uncomfortable emptiness in the pit of his stomach as he led the rest of the Marines back to the silo's entrance. Something was wrong. He could feel it.

Orange arrows led the Marines deeper into the complex, past the meat locker, and into the area beyond. And that's where they found Goofy and Oddball.

It appeared that the two Mechans had been on point. And, after triggering a Prax sensor, the robots had been killed by plasma projectors concealed in the walls. A new tactic insofar as Evans knew. And worthy of mention in his report.

Judging from appearances the Mechan third in line had slagged the projectors. Both were marked by black impact craters. Evans was about to lead the team forward, when he heard automatic fire coming from the rear, and the sound of Lance Corporal Kinney's voice. "This is One-Two ... The cricks are trying to cut us off! Two men down. Over."

Shit, shit, shit! "This is Six. We will exfil, and take our wounded with us. Follow One-Two. Over."

Evans had been on point. Now he was the tail end Charlie, and had to back his way out, laying down fire as he did so. Due to the width of the passageway, only two Prax could advance shoulder-to-shoulder, and that slowed them down.

The thirty round magazines were critical. And Evans was halfway through the last one, by the time he backed out of the entrance, and a private stepped in to lob grenades into the hab.

The overlapping explosions stopped the aliens cold, and provided the Marines with enough time to withdraw.

It wasn't until they reached the LZ that Evans learned the truth. The casualties weren't wounded. They were dead. That was when Evans understood the full extent of the disaster. Depression pulled him down. *Note to self: I failed.*

***

Las Vegas, Nevada

Jimmy Tully stared at the man in the mirror. He was African American, twenty-one years old, and well-muscled. The wary look in his eyes had been there for a long time.

Soon after Tully's father died of cancer, and the twelve-year-old was handed over to a pair of quarrelsome foster parents, he became increasingly detached—and went looking for an alternative family on the streets. And gang life had left its marks.

The top third of Tully's left ear was sliced off during a gang fight when he was fifteen. And the puckered wound on Tully's chest was the result of a stab wound suffered in Ely State Prison, just three days before the cricks broke in.

Tully would never forget that day. Pandemonium reigned as the guards fired their weapons and screamed as crickets took them down, while prisoners rattled the doors to their cells.

The warden got on the PA and ordered the inmates to be calm. "There's no reason for concern," Warden Packton assured them. "Our guards are well armed, and reinforcements are on the way." That was followed by a blood curdling scream, as ravenous crickets broke into Packton's office, and began to eat him.

Tully was one of the lucky ones. Rather than being in his cell, he was in the prison's hospital wing, recovering from the stab wound. And Tully knew an opportunity when he saw one.

So, when Tully heard Packton scream, he was up, and on his way to the doors. An attendant attempted to block the way, received a stiff arm to his face, and landed on his ass.

Tully pushed through the swinging doors, ran down a hall, and spotted a crick up ahead. The alien was armed with a short sword. And, as the alien took a swing at a guard, the corrections officer raised her shotgun to block the blow.

That was when Tully arrived, fire extinguisher raised high, and brought the tank down on the bug's head. "Good work," the guard said, as the crick went down. "Now let's get you back to ... "

Tully jerked the shotgun out of her hands. His eyes locked with hers. "Run." The guard ran, and did a good job of it too, in spite of her big butt.

With the shotgun at the ready Tully continued to advance. Through an open gate, past the prisoners who called his name, and into the middle of a fight.

A cricket aimed a weapon at a guard and fired. The officer fell.

Tully blew the alien's head off, heard a shot, and realized that a second correctional officer was shooting at *him!*

Tully yelled, "Fuck you!" and fired the twelve gauge. The load of double aught buck tore into the man's midsection and threw his body up against some bars.

A prisoner managed to grab the guard's corpse, and hold it in place, while his cellmate fumbled for the officer's keys. Tully shot an oncoming alien. The blast tore the creature apart.

Keys, Tully thought. *That's a good idea.*

So, he hurried to take the first guard's key ring, plus a pistol, which went into his waistband. *Barton, don't forget Barton*, Tully thought. *It's the least I can do.*

Frank Barton was in his thirties, and shared a cell with Tully. More than that, Barton had taken the time to school Tully in prison slang, etiquette, and lore. All of which had been enough to keep the newbie out of trouble until the fight three days earlier.

So as prisoners hurled epithets at Tully, he raced past their cells, ran down a flight of stairs, and turned a corner. Cricks were up ahead, struggling to pry a cell open, while inmates cowered inside. Tully shot the aliens in quick succession, and paused to open the steel door, before continuing on. *His* cell, which was to say Barton's cell, was immediately ahead.

As Tully skidded to a stop, he saw that Barton was just standing there, arms crossed as he awaited his fate. Keys *rattled* as Tully opened the door. "I won't forget," Barton said, as Tully gave him the pistol.

They escaped the prison together, acquiring weapons when they could, and shooting anything that got in the way. Eventually, after exiting through an unmanned side gate, the convicts wound up in the employee parking lot. The officer's keys included a remote with a Toyota logo on it. Tully thumbed it and lights flashed—they had a ride.

After that it was a simple matter to enter the pickup and take off. Tully was doing thirty when he hit a crick and sent it flying. "Good work, Kid," Barton said. "But slow down once we're on the highway. What we don't need is a ticket."

* * *

Weeks had passed since then. Tully wiped a smear of shaving cream off his face. The idiot who ran the carwash didn't care how he looked. But Tully wanted to look good for his ex. And was willing to do anything to win her back.

Samantha was living with her mother to save money. So, like it or not, that's where Tully had to go. Were the police watching the house? Maybe. But the police were focused on protecting the public from cricks, not low-level prison escapees, or so Tully hoped.

Tully had a car by then. It wasn't much to look at, but the brake lights worked, as did the turn signals. And the plates were from out of state.

Samantha's mother lived in a duplex on the west side of Las Vegas, not far from the strip.

He circled the block twice, looking for any signs of a stakeout, and didn't spot anything other than a kid sitting on a bike. A lookout for a local gang. Tully knew. He'd been one.

Tully parked the car out front, made his way to the dilapidated porch, and knocked on the door. Samantha answered and smiled when Tully offered a fistful of flowers. "You never give up! I'll say that for you."

"Never," Tully replied. "How's Lea?"

Samantha's smile disappeared. "She's in the hospital, Jimmy. We need to talk."

After saying "hello" to his ex-wife's mother, who studiously ignored him, Tully followed Samantha to her bedroom. The walls were lavender and decorated with posters. A crib occupied one corner with a box of brightly colored toys next to it. They sat on the bed. The bed where they'd had sex for the first time.

Tully felt an emptiness at the pit of his stomach. Lea had been perfectly healthy during the first months of her life. Crying, crawling, eating and pooping. All the things that babies do.

However, at nine months, Lea's progress stopped. Suddenly she could no longer lift her head, sit unsupported, or clap her hands. Tully was in prison by then.

So Samantha took Lea to a doctor, who referred the baby to another doctor, who made the diagnosis: Lea was suffering from spinal muscular atrophy, a genetic disease found in one out of 10,000 children worldwide.

"Lea's getting worse," Samantha told him, as tears began to flow. "And if we don't do something right away, she's going to die."

Tully used his thumbs to wipe the tears away. "What is it? What can we do?"

"There's a one-time treatment," Samantha replied. "It's called Zolgensma gene therapy."

"Wonderful!" Tully replied. "Let's get it."

"We can't," Samantha told him. "It costs $2.1 million dollars per dose."

Tully frowned. "You're joking."

"I would never joke about something like that," Samantha replied. "Our baby is going to die."

"No," Tully insisted. "She isn't. I'll find the money."

Sam stared at him. "Don't do something bad, Jimmy. Don't hurt people. Promise me."

"I promise," Tully replied.

Samantha nodded. "Good. And Jimmy..."

"Yeah?"

"Please hurry."

CHAPTER EIGHT

Aboard a C-17A over New Mexico

Evans sat slumped in his seat with eyes closed as the plane thumped down. That was the only sure-fire way to prevent people from talking to him. Even though the silo mission had been a failure, no one blamed him, because all radio transmissions had been recorded—and it was clear that the Mechans disobeyed orders. A lesson had been learned and steps were being taken to ensure that the same thing wouldn't happen again. But two Marines were dead. And Evans couldn't get them out of his mind. He opened his eyes. Holloman was going to be little more than a pit stop for the Marines. The second half of Charlie company was due to arrive in an hour.

Then, after staying the night in transient quarters, the unit would board helos for the trip to Whites City, which was where FEMA's TRC 1106 (Temporary Relocation Camp) was located.

"Your job," LT. Colonel Brock told Evans prior to departure, "is to provide security before, during, and after the march from TRC 1106 to the caverns. That's where the refugees will take shelter until something better is available for them."

The process of deplaning went smoothly. But that was just the beginning. The next evolution involved transporting the first load of Marines to their temporary quarters, getting them fed, and holding sick call. Then the second half of Charlie company's Marines arrived, and the process started over again.

Immediately after dinner the company's officers and noncoms received a briefing from a no-nonsense Air Force captain. Her name was Natalie Cooper. "Welcome to New Mexico. Okay, here's the situation … There are lots of cricks in this area. They steer clear of Holloman for obvious reasons. But the town of Hope was over-run recently, and none of its one hundred citizens survived.

"You're headed *here*," Cooper said, as her laser pointer wobbled on a wall map. "Don't be deceived by the name. Whites City isn't a city. Before the emergence it was a place for tourists to grab a meal and buy some postcards. It's closed now.

"But over here, right next to it, is FEMA Temporary Relocation Camp 1106. According to the last census I saw, 1,245 people are staying in the camp."

Cooper's eyes swept the room. "And make no mistake about it, these people are on the enemy's menu, and the only thing standing between them and the dinner plate is a FEMA manager named Cassie Lang—and her army of senior citizens.

"The fact that the camp hasn't been hit is nothing short of a miracle. That's why you're boarding Chinooks at 0700 and going in. You'll be supplied by air because, although we could push convoys through, some would come under attack. And we would take casualties.

"Soon, with help from the Mechans, we will secure the area. But that's thirty days out. Do you have any questions?"

Evans, his officers, and senior noncoms *did* have questions. What about water? Medical care? And air support? The briefing continued.

***

FEMA TRC 1106

It was getting dark at Temporary Relocation Camp 1106. So, headlights were used to light a rickety stage. And that's where

Cassie Lang stood, squinting into the glare as more residents arrived for what was likely to be a contentious meeting.

The problem, according to resident John Becker, was that, "People don't like change. Even if that change is for the better. That means you'll have to sell them on the value of traipsing from here to the caverns."

Be patient, Lang told herself. *Let them vent.* She raised her megaphone. "Welcome to the party! Many thanks to the grill masters who prepared dinner for us. That was, as they say, 'some mighty fine road kill.'" The comment drew laughter and scattered applause.

"Now it's time to get down to business," Lang said. "As most, if not all of you know, a company of Marines is going to arrive in the morning. And I don't know about you, but I for one, will sleep better tomorrow night."

"Damned straight!" a man hollered.

Lang nodded. "That's right … Things are getting better. And another example of that is the upcoming move to the Carlsbad Caverns. Think about it … We'll have a roof over our heads! Plus running water and electricity. Not a lot, but some."

Lang took note of the tepid applause, and felt the undercurrent of dissatisfaction. Hands went up. And the doubts started to surface. Could the caves collapse? What about cricks? Did snakes live in the caverns? And how about bats?

The questions went on and on. Lang didn't know all of the answers, and was forced to acknowledge that, which was enough to satisfy most members of the audience.

Most but not all. A perennial troublemaker named Casper Wilkins stepped forward to glare at her. "What I hear is a whole lot of guesswork, dodgy statements, and bullshit. And I'm not the only one. You can lead the herd to the caverns, but the rest of us are going to stay here, and wait for credible answers. What do you think of that?"

"I think you and your friends are making a serious mistake," Lang replied. "It's my opinion that the only reason the cricks haven't attacked the camp is that we have more than 1,300 armed residents. Enough to put up a fight. Whereas you and your group will make a tempting target. But this is a free country. And, if you want to duke it out with the Prax, then go for it."

"We will," Wilkins snapped.

Then he turned to face the crowd. He had to yell for the audience to hear him. "Do you want to be part of the herd? Do you believe Lang's bullshit? If so, do what she says. The rest of you are welcome to follow me." And with that Wilkins marched away. Fifteen people followed him. The moon was up by then. And somewhere, out in the surrounding darkness, a wolf howled.

* * *

Las Vegas, Nevada

Because the 1,149-foot-tall High Ball hotel and casino was an unmistakable presence on the Las Vegas skyline it was easy to find. But, like most street kids, Tully had never been up to the revolving restaurant and lounges.

Now however, in response to an invitation from ex-cellmate Frank Barton, Tully was on his way. He was wearing a wig, shades, and a jacket with a Las Vegas Raiders logo on the back. The bouncer outside the Strata Lounge was polite but firm. "Can I help you?"

"I'm here to have lunch with Frank Cisco."

The bouncer had a clipboard. "Your name?"

"Harkin. Jimmy Harkin."

"You're expected. Have a good time."

The interior of the Strata Lounge was sleekly modern, the lighting was subdued, and the sound track was all Sinatra, all the time.

Tully paused to look around, spotted Barton in a side nook, and made his way over. Tully's ex-cellmate looked entirely different. And that was no accident.

Barton's head was shaved, he was wearing a suit and tie, and sporting a diamond pinkie ring. "Hey, Frank," Jimmy said. "You're looking good."

"You too, Jimmy. Have a seat."

A waiter arrived, took their orders, and disappeared. The first five minutes were spent reliving the escape and the likelihood of getting caught.

Barton figured it was just a matter of time. "Get yourself a good lawyer, Jimmy. And put your affairs in order. They'll find us eventually. In the meantime, you need some scratch. That's what your message said."

"Yeah," Tully replied. "But more than walking around money. I need a big score."

Barton listened as Tully told him about Lea's disease, and the amount of money required for a treatment. "Damn, Jimmy... That's a tall mountain to climb. But I might be able to help with a portion of it. Assuming you're willing to run an errand for me."

The waiter arrived at that point, served their lunches, and disappeared. "What can I do for you?" Jimmy inquired. "And how much would it pay?"

Barton took a bite of his BLT, chewed, and swallowed. "Damn... That sure as hell beats a bologna sandwich. I need you to access the subway system, enter what used to be my night club, and retrieve a box. I was out of town when the cricks showed up and it's still there. Or, so I assume."

Tully frowned. "The cricks own the subway right now, so a trip down there would be dangerous as hell. How much are you willing to pay?"

"A hundred thousand dollars."

Tully produced a low whistle. "Damn... That's a lot."

Barton nodded. "True. But it will be worth it to me if you can pull it off.

"That said, you'll notice I'm not willing to do it myself, and two contractors failed."

Tully frowned. "'Failed'—as in—were killed?"

"Exactly," Barton replied. "I forgot to tell the second guy about the first attempt. But I'm telling you, because you did me a solid at Ely. And you're too young to die."

Tully smiled. "Thanks, man … You've got a big heart. What if I get there, and the box is gone?"

Barton patted his lips with a napkin. "I'll tell you what, if that happens, pry the lucky horseshoe off the wall behind the cash register and bring it back. Then I'll pay you. For Lea."

"Cash, right?"

Barton nodded. "Yes. Cash on delivery. Now, eat your lunch. That cheeseburger is going to cost me twenty-six bucks."

* * *

Even though a hundred-thou was a lot of money, it was only a fraction of what Tully needed, so time was of the essence. His goal was to execute Barton's mission quickly, identify another opportunity, and keep going until he could give Samantha the full amount.

The first step was to make a plan. The second step was to acquire the items needed to execute the plan, and the third step was to put the plan in motion.

After spending some time online, Tully discovered that the subway wasn't a subway of the sort found in New York. It was more of a transit system, operating on underground roads.

And true to the city's persona there were shops, fast food joints, and mini-casinos at each stop. All of which had been closed after the emergence.

One of those businesses was a club called the Mole Hole, which Frank Barton owned. It was located near Stop 23. So that was where Tully had to go.

Tully's equipment included a Ryobi electric screwdriver, a TASER 7, a long icepick with a protective cover, a vial of formic acid, a headlamp, a tiny LED flashlight, and a suppressed nine mil for emergencies. All funded by an advance from Barton, and purchased at various locations, including the trunk of a gun dealer's car.

As for clothing, Tully planned to wear a reflective maintenance worker vest, over an empty knapsack, and an all-black outfit.

After returning to his rented room, Tully spent an hour fashioning a combat harness before taking a nap. It didn't work. Tully was too keyed up to sleep, and spent the whole time thinking about his family, and dreaming of a better future.

Finally, after darkness fell, Tully consumed two candy bars followed by a half bottle of Gatorade. Then it was time to venture out into the garishly lit city. It was amazing. A thousand Prax were living under Vegas, sneaking out to snatch people every day, yet the casinos were open! It seemed as if the people with money would risk death in order to lose it.

Traffic was a good deal lighter than it had been prior to the emergence. And Tully was able to reach his entry point in fifteen minutes.

Thanks to an earlier visit Tully knew where to pull over and park. Then it was a simple matter to turn the car's emergency flashers on, get out, and raise the hood.

Would the cops ticket the beater? And tow it? Probably. But Tully didn't give a shit. They could have it.

The car's purpose was to shield Tully from police cruisers, and the reflective vest was supposed to make him appear legit, while he pried the lid up and off.

People were walking past only fifteen feet away. None of them paused to look.

Good. With satchel in hand, Tully lowered himself into the manhole, and paused to pull the lid toward him. The steel cover produced a *scaping* noise as he pulled it, followed by a solid *clunk*, as it dropped into place. *These things should be bolted down,* Tully decided. *But I'm glad they aren't.*

Tully's feet were resting on an iron rung. The first of many. Tully followed them down. He was grateful for the luminescent splotches of green stuff on the walls, but fearful as well, because the cricks might see him. Fortunately, there were none in the immediate area. He took the opportunity to fasten his home-made harness.

Tully's heart was beathing like a trip hammer as he squirted small amounts of formic acid onto his clothing, while being careful to avoid his skin.

The cricks oozed formic acid. Everyone knew that. And the aliens had the ability to smell things from a distance. So, if Tully could blend in, it would pay to do so.

Then it was time to get moving. Barton's nightclub was a block away, and would have been concealed by the curving wall, even if the overhead lights had been on.

Tully could see other things however, gruesome things, like a decapitated head, a scattering of bones, and a single word written in what might have been blood. "HELP!"

The fact that the plea was hopeless made the word all the more poignant.

Don't feel—think, Tully told himself. *Hug the wall, eyes ahead, and don't shit your pants.* There were no sidewalks except those located around shuttle stops.

Tully's right foot hit an empty pop can and sent it skittering away. The response was nearly instantaneous. He heard a *whirring* sound and a small drone appeared. It was a threat Tully hadn't considered, and one which forced him to pull the nine and take aim. A red dot appeared on the device and wobbled slightly.

Tully fired three times and, thanks to the suppressor, the *clack, clack, clack* sound was barely audible. The drone crashed and threw sparks. *Shit, shit, shit! They know I'm here. Run!*

Tully's high tops provided good traction and running was his thing. Running away from problems mostly, but at them too, as was the case when he played high school football.

Tully could see the sign up ahead: "The Mole Hole." The M was loose and dangling. His destination was in sight! He ran towards it.

Then, as Tully drew closer, a crick shuffled out of the night-club's entrance and turned his way. That was Tully's cue to pull the consumer grade Taser, pause, and fire.

Two prongs, each towing a wire, shot forward to penetrate the cricket's chitin. The alien jerked spastically as 50,000 volts shocked its nervous system.

Tully removed the electric screwdriver from its belt hook as he rushed forward. And the six-inch-long spade bit was whirring by the time he arrived.

Tully didn't know jack shit about crick anatomy, but figured the alien's head was an ideal target, and applied the drill. Chitin, goo, and bits of brain tissue flew... A medical degree wasn't required to pronounce the cricket dead. The whole thing was both quiet and in keeping with Tully's plan. *Hurry,* Tully told himself. *Tow the body inside.*

Tully took hold of an arm, and pulled the body through the shattered door, and into the club where it wouldn't be visible from the sidewalk. Then he went out to retrieve the alien's weapon, which had been left behind. It consisted of a barrel over a tube which Tully took to be a magazine. The handle-trigger assembly felt awkward, and the shoulder stock consisted of a rod, with a

T style butt. *You never know*, Tully decided. *This might come in handy.*

Tully paused to survey the room. The nightclub had been trashed. Chairs had been broken, tables lay on their sides, and the floor was covered with debris.

None of that mattered. What mattered was the raised stage in front of him. "My box is under the stage." That's what Barton said. "Step up on it. And there, halfway between two stripper poles, you'll find a trap door. It provides access to the sound system's black boxes and cabling. Open it, enter the crawlspace, and elbow your way to the back. The box is in the lefthand corner."

Glass crunched underfoot as Tully hurried to the stage, eyed the low pile carpet, and saw a recessed ring pull. That was the moment when he heard movement, followed by a burst of click speech. Crickets! Summoned by the drone.

What Tully did next was the result of instinct rather than planning. He pulled the trapdoor open, dropped into the hole, and knelt. The lid produced a soft *thump* as it fell into place.

I'll take at least one of the bastards with me, Tully thought, as he fumbled for the pistol. The click speech was louder by then. Tully heard a *thump* as one of the aliens hopped up onto the stage. Would it spot the pull? And open the lid?

Tully's blood pounded in his ears as plywood *creaked*, and shuffling noises were heard, followed by a burst of static. From a radio? Probably.

Then the noises started to recede, as if the cricket on the stage had left. Tully allowed himself to relax slightly. *The box. I need to find the box.*

Tully used his elbows to drag his body through the dust. The beam from the LED headlamp revealed the cables that snaked every which way, a ring with three keys on it, and a desiccated rat cadaver. Tully pushed the corpse aside, spotted the box, and felt a rising sense of excitement. A hundred thou! For Lea.

He pushed with his toes and suddenly he had it. The box was made of metal, with handles on both ends, and was locked. No surprise there.

The container wasn't especially heavy. So, no gold coins. Tully gave the box a shake. Nothing. Maybe the object was padded. *It doesn't matter*, Tully concluded. *My job is to get it to Frank.*

With the box resting on his forearms, Tully squirmed his way back to where the alien assault weapon was waiting, and paused to listen. The crickets had left. Or, so it seemed.

Slowly, an inch at a time, Tully opened the trap door. The coast was clear. He climbed out.

Tully removed the safety vest in order to access the knapsack beneath it. The box fit perfectly. Then, with the pack on his back, and the crick-weapon in his hands, Tully returned to the subway. Look both ways. That's what he'd been taught as a kid. All clear.

Tully turned to the left, with plans to exit the tube via the same manhole used earlier. He was half way there when he heard a loud *roar*, and saw something the size of a city bus appear in the distance.

Red lights circled an open maw similar to that of a jet engine. And the machine was coming straight at Tully! Not on wheels, but on quickly thrashing legs! Like an enormous centipede.

Fight or flight? The answer was obvious. Tully threw the crick weapon away, turned, and ran. There was no need to look back. As the *roar* grew louder he knew the machine was gaining on him. What Tully needed was a ladder. Like the one he'd used earlier. And he could see a ladder in the distance. Legs pumping, and breath rasping, Tully ran even faster.

Then he tripped and fell—the impact sent the electric screw driver flying. Precious seconds were lost as Tully struggled to regain his feet.

The pack slapped Tully's back as he ran. He heard the staccato *thump, thump, thump* of alien footfalls and knew the monster was going to overtake him! Was a crick at the controls? Trying to run him over? Or was a computer controlling the creature?

A desperate rush took Tully to the bottom of the ladder which he hurried to climb. Not all the way, but high enough to escape the monster.

Hot air laced with the odor of ozone washed over Tully, as the thing thundered by, and continued on its way. That was when Tully realized that the departing machine was a Prax plasma drill, of the sort used to create underground tunnels. He'd seen one on TV. The near-death experience was something he'd never forget.

Tully felt a surge of joy as he climbed the ladder. A hundred thou! Samantha would be impressed. Then Tully remembered the rest of it. He had to come up with two million dollars or his baby was going to die. *I'll find it,* Tully promised himself as he pushed a manhole cover out of the way … *I'll find the money or die trying.*

CHAPTER NINE

FEMA TRC 1106 adjacent to Whites City, New Mexico

Cassie Lang squinted into the rising sun as the Chinook helicopter appeared and began to lose altitude. Then, as a vapor trail rose to intercept the helo, Cassie saw the Chinook fire flares, and held her breath.

There was a red-orange explosion as the Prax weapon chased a flare and destroyed it. Lang heard a muted *boom*, and watched metal confetti fall, as the helicopter's gunners fired on a target she couldn't see. Then Lang began to breathe again. *Welcome to TRC 1106*, she thought. *And just in time too ... There are more bug sightings with each passing day.*

The Chinook's rotor blades produced a swirling dust storm as the enormous helicopter landed. Marines rushed down the rear ramp to take up defensive positions. The leathernecks were followed by two Utility Task Vehicles (UTVs) pulling trailers piled high with supplies.

Then Lang saw a solitary figure appear with a radio operator trailing along behind him. The unit's CO? Yes, she thought so, and went forward to meet him.

The Marine was tall. His hair was short, his features were even, and his eyes were blue. Creases appeared when he smiled. "Are you Cassie Lang? I'm Lester Evans."

Lang felt something jump between them as they shook hands. Something she hadn't felt since Ken. The sensation took her by surprise. "Yes, that's me. I'm sorry about the nasty reception. The cricks are closing in on us."

"We'll try to push them back," Evans replied. "Come on, let's get out of the LZ. This Chinook is about to depart and another one is on the way."

* * *

Evans was surprised. Rather than the uptight government manager he'd been expecting to meet, Lang was not only casual, but attractively so—and made the head-to-toe Levi outfit look good. As for the retro six shooter, was that an accessory? Or a tool? He looked forward to finding out. "Tell me about the ridge," Evans said, as he pointed west.

"We have lookouts up there 24/7," Lang replied.

Evans nodded. "Good. I'll put a squad up there, along with a drone team, and some comm gear. How's the water supply?"

"Adequate," Lang replied. "But just barely. What, if anything, can you tell me about the situation at the caverns? We were told to stay away."

"Not much," Evans answered. "Other than the fact that they were fumigated. Here's hoping the crew did a good job. I'd like to tour the camp if you're willing. Then we can drive to the caverns and check things out. Assuming they're habitable, I'll station a platoon in there. Hopefully that will keep the cricks at bay while we make the move."

* * *

Lang was impressed. So much so that she stole a look at the Marine's left hand. No ring. *Stop it*, Lang admonished herself. *You swore off men, remember? The last thing you need is more pain.*

"That sounds good," Lang replied. "Are you ready? If so, follow me."

* * *

The tour began in Uptown, and crossed into Tent City, as Lang explained the way the camp had evolved. Then they came to the common area which had changed a great deal over the last few weeks.

Evans paused to take it in. The open space was defined by a ring of old cars parked bumper-to-bumper and chained together. "There's a four-person fighting position under each vehicle," Lang explained. "If the Prax attack, our residents will pull back into the defensive circle."

"The cricks can't attack the fighting positions from above," Evans said approvingly. "Not as effectively anyway. It's a great idea! Who thought of it?"

"I did," Lang replied.

Evans turned to look at her. "Did you drain the gas tanks?"

"Yes."

"You're a smart cookie," Evans told her. "What about the residents who would be massed in the open area?"

"We have an ancient backhoe," Lang replied. "We were planning to dig bunkers and cover them with plywood and sandbags. Work stopped once we learned the move was about to take place."

"That makes sense," Evans agreed. "Now tell me about those shelters." He pointed.

"That's what the residents call 'Shantytown,' or 'The Ghetto,'" Lang explained. "In spite of repeated requests, I've been unable to obtain additional trailers or tents from FEMA. That's because they don't have any to give."

"Which explains the cavern plan," Evans suggested.

"Exactly."

"So, let's take a look at the caverns and make sure the plan is realistic," Evans said. "Can you provide transportation?"

"I can," Lang said. "But it won't be pretty."

"All it has to do is get us there and back," Evans assured her. "I need fifteen minutes to coordinate things. Where will we meet?"

"At the vehicle park," Lang said, as she pointed.

"Good. I'll bring a squad with me just in case. That means we'll need seats for ten people, counting the two of us."

Lang nodded. "Got it."

The second Chinook was in sight by then. Andy Yamada was the company's XO in addition to leading the 1st platoon. Evans found him near the LZ. "Hey, Andy... Ms. Lang and I are going to eyeball the caverns. We'll need a squad just in case.

"Plus, I'd like to establish an OP up on that ridge. Along with a drone team. And take a look at the open area at the center of the compound when you have time. If we can use the fighting positions under the cars, then so much the better. If not, we'll need a plan. I'll be back by 1300. Give me a holler if problems arise."

"Will do," Yamada replied. "I'll detail a squad from my platoon."

Thirty minutes later Evans led the squad to the car park where Lang was waiting. Three vehicles and three drivers were ready to go.

"Let's put the SUV up front," Sergeant Bovee suggested, "with the pickup in the middle and the van to the rear."

"That sounds good," Evans agreed. "I'll ride in the back of the pickup. I'll be able to see more from there."

***

Riding in the back of a pickup wasn't Lang's first choice. But it made sense to stay close to the Marine corps officer and get to know him.

* * *

The caves were located four miles southwest of the camp, in the Carlsbad Caverns National Park. The terrain was dry and rocky. The presence of hills, and the hardy shrubs that populated them, kept the landscape from looking like a desert.

Except for the abandoned cars, shot up signs, and post emergence graffiti, the highway looked normal. Evans had to raise his voice in order to be heard over the wind *rumble*. "How many residents will be able to walk? How many will have to ride? And how much gas do you have?"

"This is a guess, mind you," Lang replied. "But, since most of our residents are older, I'd say that roughly a thousand of them could complete the walk. The remainder, something like three hundred residents, will need to ride.

"As for gas, the answer is 'not enough.' Some of our folks have been willing to contribute fuel to the camp's reserve. But many haven't. So, we're in a bind."

"I'll try to get more," Evans promised. "Assuming I'm successful, you and I will dole it out."

* * *

So far, so good, Lang decided. *Evans could take control, or try to. And he hasn't. I lucked out.*

* * *

The parking lot was empty except for the blackened remains of a burned-out motor home. Crickets? Or an accident? Both were possible.

Sergeant Bovee approached as Evans jumped to the ground. "What have you got in mind, sir?"

"Let's leave three Marines here to guard the vehicles. Tell them to monitor their radios, and to keep their eyes peeled. If a squirrel takes a shit, I want to hear about it."

Bovee grinned. "Yes, sir."

"The rest of us are going in," Evans added. "The caverns are clear. That's what the briefer told me. But who knows? Tell your people to lock and load."

Evans and Lang led the way. It wasn't long before they found themselves on a paved path. It twisted down a steep slope and through the cavern's oval shaped entrance.

The path didn't end there. More switch-backing ramps led them into the cavern's interior where, much to Evans' surprise the lights were on!

There were all sorts of rock formations to admire, and Evans was just starting to process the scene, when Lang pulled her pistol and fanned it. The half-grown cricket was crouched between two stalagmites. Two out of three bullets hit the alien, blew half its head away, and knocked it over. "She-it," a Marine named Dobbs said. "That chick can shoot!"

"She certainly can," Evans agreed. "And some women don't like to be referred to as 'chicks.'"

"That's true," Lang said, as she took a moment to eject the empty shell casings. "But I'm not one of them."

"So noted," Evans replied. "All right, where there's one bug, there are likely to be more. Our job is to find out. Stay focused. Let's go."

The group followed the path through the auditorium, past the Devil's Den, and into the main corridor. It led to the Iceberg, and on into the Big Room, ending at the Bottomless Pit. "Damn!" a Marine said. "What stinks?"

"There's a dead giver down there," Lang replied. "That's what a seismologist told me. We'll rope it off."

"That makes sense," Evans agreed. "Come on, let's head for the parking lot."

After returning to the vehicles Evans and Lang held a short meeting. "So, except for the crick you shot," Evans said, "all we saw were dead bodies. That suggests that the fumigation was mostly successful."

"True," Lang allowed. "And, if there are more strays, we can handle them."

Evans nodded. "So, the move is on?"

"The move is on. I'll make a call and request the package FEMA promised me. We need MREs, tools, and wood for sleeping platforms."

"Good," Evans replied. "Assuming you're willing, I'm going to provide you with a two-person security detail."

Lang frowned. "*Why?*"

Evans grinned. "Because you might come in handy."

* * *

The statement could be taken in various ways. Which should she choose?

Don't try to make something out of nothing, Lang told herself. *And remember, men can't be trusted.*

* * *

Las Vegas, Nevada
Rather than a ringtone, Tully preferred "*I Heard It Through the Grapevine*," by Marvin Gaye. He rolled over, grabbed the phone, and thumbed the call. "Yeah?"

"My name is Mike," a male voice said. "Frank Barton suggested that I call."

Tully eyed the time. "At three-fucking AM?"

"I work odd hours," Mike replied nonchalantly. "And I understand that you're facing a short deadline. So, time is critical. How would you like to make two mil? That's what you need, right?"

Tully sat up. "What is this? Some sort of sick joke?"

"No," Mike said. "This is for real. I'm looking for a recovery specialist, someone who has a brain, and a pair of brass balls."

"I'm not an assassin."

"Of course, you aren't. I could hire a hitman for a couple of thou. Get dressed and meet me at The Martini thirty from now. That's on your side of town if I'm not mistaken. I'll be the guy with white hair." *Click.*

Three days had passed since Tully had delivered the hundred thousand to Samantha. It was enough for a downpayment and she was grateful. But that left two-mil unaccounted for. And try as he might, Tully had been unable to concoct a scheme to earn or steal the additional scratch. That meant Tully couldn't afford to ignore any possibility, even a late-night call from some dude named "Mike."

After a quick trip to the shared bathroom down the hall, Tully got dressed, and went out to his car. The beater had been towed, just as Tully feared it would be, but a fifty-dollar bribe had been enough to liberate the junker the following day.

Tully started the engine, pulled away from the curb, and was careful to stay under the speed limit. "Don't let the heat stop you for something stupid." That was the way Barton put it and he was right. The restaurant's parking lot was nearly empty. Tully parked near the front door, got out, and went inside. And there, in a booth in the back, was a man with white hair. Short white hair. Like a buzzcut. He was wearing sunglasses inside. An albino? Possibly.

Tully made his way back and slid onto a bench style seat. "Mike?"

"None other," the man said, as he raised his martini glass. "Thanks for coming on short notice. Shall I assume that you're interested?"

Tully nodded. "Yes. You spoke with Frank … So, you understand my situation."

"I do," Mike replied. "Here's the deal. The U.S. government would like to have an intact Mechan to study, and by 'intact,' I mean fully functioning in every way."

Tully frowned. "*Why?*"

Mike took a sip of his drink. "The Xyfors aren't going to give us one. And the freaks would go postal if they knew we snatched one. So, the brainiacs turned to my department, and I'm turning to you."

"And why is that?" Tully wanted to know.

"Because we're short-handed, you're deniable, and you're wanted. That gives us plenty of leverage."

Tully sighed. "Will I have any support?"

"I'll give you five thou for expenses, none of which can be spent hiring people. You will also receive an Intel briefing and a special stun gun. The good news is that a single shot will cause a Mechan to freeze up and shut down. The bad news is that you have only one shot. So, get close. Then you'll need to hide the body, and call me. I'll arrange for an extraction.

"So, what do you say?" Mike inquired. "Are you in or out?"

Tully was suspicious. "Why two million? I'm not complaining mind you, but that's a lot of money."

"It is a lot of money," Mike agreed. "But my boss assumed I would hire a team. So, she gave me a budget of five million. I however, believe that there's no need for a team, so I'm going to spend two million on you—and keep the rest for myself."

"So, I could have asked for more."

"Yes, but you didn't," Mike replied. "And a deal is a deal. So, what's the answer? Are you in? Or out?"

Tully was in a bind. He didn't want to participate in a crime, but Lea needed the money, and Mike could turn him in. Sure, he could tell authorities his side of the story, but who would believe it? Tully had no choice. "I'm in."

"Good," Mike said, as he produced a brightly decorated gift bag. "Here's the money, some Intel, and the stun gun. You have my number. Call when you're ready for a pickup. Oh, and don't forget to burn the Intel. Welcome to the federal bureaucracy."

* * *

Near Goodsprings, Nevada

Tully arrived in the tiny town of Goodsprings to find that the hamlet was deserted. It appeared that all 230 of the hamlet's citizens had elected to depart for safer locations.

As for the adjacent 800-acre Motorhead junkyard, the swinging gate was closed, and had a sign that read: "Closed for the Deration." By which the errant speller meant the duration of the war. Or, so Tully assumed.

All of which was fine with Tully, since the last thing he needed was to have someone summon the sheriff, and wind up back in prison. Which he now realized was where he would end up if he failed to please Mike.

Whoever owned the junkyard hadn't bothered to chain the gate, knowing that thieves could enter with a pair of bolt cutters. So, all Tully had to do was drive in and park his junker between a couple of other junkers. The next step was to remove the brand-new pack from the trunk, along with a five-gallon jug of water, and a wide-brimmed cowboy hat to protect him from the sun.

Then Tully shouldered the pack, took hold of the water bottle, and set off for the junkyard's tower crane. It had a cab and a horizontal arm long enough to access nearly every wreck in the yard. The crane was visible on the aerial photo Mike had given him, and the label said it all: "Observation Point."

A zigzag path took Tully through a maze of cars, and parts of cars, to the base of the crane. A sign read: "Employees Only." Tully tilted his head back to look upwards. He wasn't afraid of heights, but it was going to be a hellacious climb. *One rung at a time*, Tully decided. *Just keep on keeping on.*

With the pack on his back, Tully tied one end of a two-hundred-foot length of cord to the water jug, and the other to his belt. Then he began to climb. The first fifty-feet was easy, the second fifty was more difficult, and the last stretch was a bitch.

But finally, with his breath coming in short gasps, and legs that felt like lead, Tully arrived on a steel grating. He had a sweeping view of the junkyard and the hills beyond. So far, so good.

Tully entered the cab, shrugged the pack off, and went back outside to hoist the water container up off the ground. Then he returned to the cab and placed the jug on the floor.

Retro centerfolds wallpapered the interior and a pair of ginormous binoculars were sitting on a ledge. Tully had a pair of his own, but knew they wouldn't provide the same degree of magnification that junkyard glasses would.

After pouring some lukewarm water into a plastic cup, and taking a sip, Tully sat in the operator's chair. The binocs were wonderful. Everything Tully looked at was crisp and clear. Rather than let his gaze wander, Tully forced himself to examine the yard grid style.

He was looking for crickets and Mechans. But all Tully saw were occasional glimpses of a coyote that was skulking about. *Be patient*, Tully told himself. *According to the briefer, the robots arrive in the afternoon, and hike into the hills searching for cricks. And, since the area is riddled with old mines, they're guaranteed to find some.*

Hours passed. Tully did his best to stay awake but it was difficult. He would nod off every now and then, awake with a jerk, and feel guilty. Then he'd scan the yard and another bout of sleepiness would begin. It was during one such lapse that the Mechan transport arrived.

The *roar* woke Tully. And there, descending on the junkyard, was a flying box! Guns were mounted fore and aft, but had nothing to fire at.

Tully watched intently as a column of Mechans emerged from the vehicle and followed their leader toward the hills. *They're in a line,* Tully noted. *With about fifteen feet between them. And, as they wind their way through the wrecks, there are moments when they lose visual contact with each other. That's my opportunity. Be there, stun the last robot in line, and drag it away.*

But how? Tully wondered. *And to where? Because it won't be long before one of them notices that good 'ol Joe is missing. Then they'll start looking for him.*

In order to finalize my plan, I need to know if they follow the same route every day. Machines might do that. They're good at doing things over and over. Or not. Unfortunately, there's only one way to find out. And that's to wait for another visit.

A long wait began. Hours passed, and it was nearly dark by the time the transport returned from wherever it had been, and the Mechans trudged into the yard. They walked single file as they boarded the transport.

The vehicle took off two minutes later, turned to the west, and disappeared into the setting sun. That was Tully 's cue to exchange the binoculars for his night vision glasses. What, if anything, roamed the junkyard at night? He was about to find out.

The answer was a lot of things. Some of the heat signatures were too far away to identify. But during the next few hours Tully spotted what he believed to be coyotes, skunks, and rabbits—all of which were native to the area.

But what *wasn't* native were the five crickets that flew past the cab, no more than a hundred feet away. A hunting party? Tully thought so … And drew the nine-millimeter. Fortunately, there was no need to use it.

Thanks to how high the cab was, Tully felt quite secure as he laid his sleeping bag on the floor, with his pack as a pillow. The pistol was close at hand though, in case a flying bug decided to pay him a visit.

Tully awoke as the first rays of sunlight penetrated the cab. The floor was hard, he was sore, and felt a powerful need to pee.

After exiting the cab, Tully decided that it would be a waste of time and energy to descend the ladder, and climb back up again. So, he stood with his back to the morning breeze and let fly. Which, come to think of it, was what the operator probably did.

Tully had never been camping. So, the Jetboil stove was a revelation. And it wasn't long before he had hot coffee to drink and cinnamon raisin oatmeal to eat.

After breakfast Tully lowered himself to the ground where he went in search of the pink Cadillac he'd seen from the tower. For some reason the car was planted nose down in the ground. A whim perhaps. But it was a good landmark. And it was adjacent to the route the Mechans had followed the previous day.

The sun continued to rise, and shadows shifted, as Tully arrived next to the vertical Caddy. *Think*, Tully told himself. *And pay attention to what's around you.*

Tully saw donor cars stacked three high, an ancient boiler, and a cargo container. Tully went over to inspect it. The door on the left refused to budge. The one on the right produced a loud *squeal* as it swung open. The interior was dark. But, from what Tully could see, the back half of the container was being used to store car doors. Maybe two dozen of them.

He turned to peer outside. That was when he saw the way the path turned after it passed the container, and a plan began to take shape. *I could hide in the container,* Tully reasoned, *and wait for the column to pass.*

Then, just before the last Mechan enters the turn, I could step out and fire the stun gun. The Mech would collapse. What then? Those suckers are big! Could I drag the sonofabitch all the way to the container?

No, that seems doubtful, Tully decided. *So how 'bout a wheel barrow? Nope. I'd have to lift all that dead weight off the ground.*

How 'bout something lower? A mechanic's creeper? Like the one dad used at the garage? Maybe. But the ground is uneven. And larger wheels would be better. Like those on a furniture dolly! I could hide the dolly near the turn, pull it out, and roll the Mechan onto it. Then it would be a simple matter to tow the Mechan into the container and close the doors.

How far would the robots go before they realized that one of their units was missing? Would they backtrack? Would they check the cargo container? *They might,* Tully decided. *But, if it's locked, they'll move on.*

Tully went over to examine the doors. There weren't any internal locks. That sucked. But the problem could be solved. The next half hour was spent smoothing the ground between the curve and the cargo container to make moving the body easier. Something the Mechans were unlikely to notice.

Then Tully returned to the tower. He had a plan. But were the Mechans as predictable as he hoped they were? How long would it take for them to eradicate the crickets in the mines? Were they just getting started? Or were they finished? Lea's fate could depend on the answer.

Another long wait ended when the boxy transport arrived at the same time it had the day before. Tully felt a sense of vindication. The machines were acting like machines!

Once disembarked the Mechans followed the same path past the pink Cadillac and back into the hills. That was all the encouragement Tully required.

To purchase the equipment he needed, Tully had to drive back to Vegas, and pay wartime prices. His cash stash was quickly disappearing.

The sun was nudging the western horizon by the time he returned to the junkyard. And, assuming the robots were on schedule, they had returned to their base.

Tully knew he had to be careful however. Not only was there the possibility that the Mechans were working late, there were roaming crickets to consider, so he went armed. Not that the nine could stop a gang of Prax. *But I can shoot myself*, Tully reasoned. *And wait for Lea in heaven.*

So, with a headlamp in place, and a pack on his back, Tully towed the newly acquired furniture dolly into the quickly gathering darkness. It jumped, it swayed, and it had to be freed from at least a dozen obstructions along the way. But the effort would be worth it—assuming the plan was successful. Making use of the headlamp was risky. But getting lost was risky too.

The blob of white light played across old cars, trucks and, in one case, an aluminum fishing boat—before finally finding the Caddy and the container nearby. Tully wasted no time planting the dolly before starting work on the container.

The industrial strength drill, plus a new cobalt bit, were perfect for punching holes in the 0.075-inch steel. Once the prep work was finished it was a simple matter to mount two heavy-duty surface bolts on the inside of the doors and tighten the nuts.

Could the Mechans cut their way through? Or blast a hole in one of the doors? Yes, they could. But why *would* they? The missing Mechan wasn't going to hide in a container and lock itself in. So, the searchers would try the door, discover that it refused to open and turn their attention elsewhere. Or so Tully hoped.

One thing was for sure however … The locks made Tully feel better about the prospect of sleeping in the container.

After placing a call to Mike, Tully used the Jetboil to prepare a meal, followed by a mug of instant hot chocolate. Then it was time to turn in. The floor was hard, mysterious noises could be heard outside, and it took a long time to fall asleep. With sleep came a disturbing jumble of dreams. At one point Tully found himself back in Elly, listening to the mad rantings of a mentally ill prisoner, mixed with an acappella performance that a group called the Jail Birds put on every night.

When Tully awoke, he could see light through the cracks around the doors, and knew that the big day had arrived. He was outside, taking a leak, when the Mechan transport arrived. The Mechans were six hours early!

Tully's initial reaction was panic. Then logic took over. *It doesn't matter*, Tully assured himself. *Get the stun gun, hide, and be ready.*

Could the alien robots detect heat? Tully assumed that they could. Which is why he was careful to choose a hiding place where sun-warmed metal would help to camouflage his presence. Tully heard the *whir-whir-whir* of the lead Mechan's servos before he saw it. Then it appeared, head swiveling 360 degrees, with two weapons ready to fire.

More machines followed, each separated by fifteen or twenty feet—twelve in all. *Get ready*, Tully told himself, as he raised the stun gun. *Release the safety.*

A blue indicator light appeared as Tully pointed the gun at the last robot in line, waited for the rest to round the curve, and pulled the trigger. There was no recoil, and no report.

The Mechan fell like a sack of potatoes and lay inert on the ground. The carefully concealed furniture dolly was only yards away. The plan was working!

Tully emerged from hiding, and was halfway to his goal, when the crickets attacked. They too had been lying in wait.

And Tully could hear the *whuf, whuf, whuf* of their bioelectronic wings as they passed overhead.

Then the shooting began. And, with cricks circling above, the plan was off. Tully took his victim's weapons before entering the gap between two wrecked cars.

What looked like flaming ping pong balls stuttered down to explode among the Mechans, even as smart darts lashed up to strike the aliens above. Each dart carried an explosive charge, which were quite effective at blowing cricks out of the air.

Tully's brain shifted into high gear. *His* Mechan was down, so the airborne aliens weren't firing at it, and they couldn't eat it. Therefore, it made sense for Tully to fire on the Mechans, until all of them were down. Then he would turn his attention to the flying bugs.

There was plenty of cover and Tully made use of it to approach the area where the Mechans were gathered. Tully was equipped with what he believed to be a dart gun. The weapon was too large to be comfortable, and unexpectedly heavy, so Tully was forced to rest it on top of a car. The sight picture was excellent however, and once Tully put the crosshairs on a Mechan, he knew a dart would hit it. Except that it didn't.

Rather than strike the intended target, the self-guided dart angled upward, chased a cricket and hit it. *Shit, shit, shit.* It seemed that Mechan darts weren't allowed to target Mechans!

That forced Tully to switch to the second weapon he was carrying. The long gun was awkward to use. But when Tully fired, a stream of micro pellets struck a robot, and tore its head off!

That was the good news. The bad news was the fact that while Tully had been ignored previously, that was no longer the case, and he had to take cover in between stacks of flattened junkers. They shook and rattled as all manner of ordinance came to bear on them.

That was Tully's cue to target crickets with the dart rifle. His fire, combined with that of the surviving Mechans, brought the last bugs down.

Only two Mechans remained in the fight. So, Tully switched to what he thought of as "the shotgun," and moved from place to place, firing on them.

They fired back, and as they did so, Tully ran out of ammo. Fortunately, dead cricks and their weapons lay scattered about. And, when Tully spotted what resembled a human rocket launcher, he grabbed it. The robots were about six feet apart, so Tully aimed for the spot halfway between them. The launcher jerked, a rocket sped into the gap, and exploded. Both Mechans went down. With weapon raised Tully performed a slow 360. There were no targets left to shoot at. He placed the launcher on the hood of a car and fumbled for his phone. Mike answered. "Yeah?"

"I have it," Tully replied. "But come quick… The cricks ambushed the Mechans and reinforcements could arrive at any moment."

"We'll be there in ten," Mike promised. "Once you hear the helo, pop the flare I gave you." *Click.*

Tully picked up a shotgun and went to the spot where "his" Mechan lay. The sky was empty, and remained so, until he heard the distant mutter of helicopter rotors and a dot appeared. He lit the flare and red smoke billowed up into the sky.

The helo landed in a clearing, a crew equipped with a specially designed stretcher swept in to collect the "specimen," and carry it on board.

This is it, Tully thought. *The moment when Mike might double cross me.* The shotgun was ready as Mike got off the helo. He was wearing a flat brimmed hat and holding a manilla envelope. "Here's your pay. Take it straight to a bank. The check is written on a company you've never heard of. But don't let that bother you."

Tully felt a stab of fear. "I can't. They'll ask for ID."

"A righteous ID card is in the envelope. You work for me now. Unless you want to return to Ely."

"I work for you? Doing *what?*"

"Things I tell you to do. Are you in?"

Tully thought about it. A job. Samantha. Lea. He nodded. "I'm in."

CHAPTER TEN

FEMA TRC 1106 adjacent to Whites City, New Mexico

Night was falling, the stars were out, and a comet streaked across the sky. Or was it something else? Xyfor aircraft came and went as they pleased, could outmaneuver every plane the humans had, and were known for their hair-raising fly-bys.

Evans turned back to the trail that led up to the top of the ridge. It was home to a couple of cell towers, most of Charlie company's comm gear, and a drone team. Evans was breathing heavily by the time he topped the ridge.

Lang's lookouts were on duty, as were his Marines. A small fire *crackled,* and the smell of woodsmoke drifted through the air. Evans knew better than to enter the area unannounced. "Evans! Searching for hot coffee."

"Your timing is perfect," Lang said, as she emerged from the gloom. "A fresh pot is waiting." Her Marine bodyguards saluted.

After chatting with the lookouts, and visiting the drone team, Evans poured some coffee into the guest mug, and went over to join Lang. The team leader was sitting on a large chunk of limestone. "May I join you?"

"Of course," Lang replied. "My rock is your rock."

Evans smiled as he sat next to her. "Well, tomorrow's the day. Are your people ready?"

"Not really," Lang replied. "But there's no way to make them younger."

Evans nodded. "Yeah, it's only four miles. But that will be a long walk for many of them. How's their team leader holding up?"

"I'm bone tired," Lang confessed. "But that's okay."

"How did you wind up as a FEMA team leader anyway?"

Lang shrugged. "I felt lost after my husband left me. My life was organized around him. And I'm a people person. So, when a friend told me that FEMA had openings, I applied. And I was approved. Then the crickets emerged," Lang added. "And, well, here I am."

Evans couldn't help but take note of the fact that Lang was single. "The residents worship you," Evans told her. "One of them referred to you as a 'God Send.'"

"And others damn me to hell," Lang replied. "But that's how it goes.

"How 'bout you? Were you in the Marine corps when the cricks appeared?"

"I was a lieutenant stationed on the west coast."

"And you're a captain now."

"Yeah, a lot of Marines have been killed since the emergence," Evans said soberly. "Promotions come quickly."

Lang frowned. "I get the feeling that something bad took place."

Should Evans tell Lang about the silo mission? Or, tell her that everything was fine, and move on?

A confession could be seen as a weakness. But for some reason Evans felt he could trust Lang. So, he told her about how the Mechans went off on their own. And how he took a team into the underground complex to find them.

"I lost two Marines," Evans confessed. "Both of whom would be alive if I'd been more objective. The Mechans are machines, not people."

"I'm sorry," Lang said, as she placed a hand over his. "It's easy, not to mention natural, to anthropomorphize animals. Or, machines. My mother named her Audi, Gunther."

Evans smiled. "Otto would have been better."

Lang laughed. "That didn't occur to her. But here's the so-what ... We're human. And humans make mistakes. It doesn't make sense to organize your life around a single error. You've got to put it aside and move on. People are counting on you ... And I'm one of them."

Evans gave her hand a squeeze. "Thank you. So, who was the stupid jerk who walked away?"

"His name is Ken," Lang replied. "But I wasn't Barbie. So, he left, and took my sister with him. That's why I'm done with men."

"How 'bout sisters?"

Lang laughed. "Yes, I'm done with sisters too."

"I need to go down and make the rounds," Evans said. "Are you finished here?"

"I am."

"Then let's go."

Lang's security detail led the way. They paused at the entrance to the camp. "I enjoyed the talk," Lang told him.

"Me too," Evans replied. "Keep that six-gun handy. According to my drone operators a lot of crick scouts are out and about. And that's to say nothing of their micro drones."

"Watch your six," Lang told him. "That's military lingo, right?"

"It is," Evans answered. "And you do the same. Goodnight."

Lang watched the Marine walk away. How could she come to like a person so much in such a short period to time?

You're like a middle school adolescent with a crush, Lang told herself. *Grow up.*

* * *

The next morning dawned cold and clear. Orders were shouted as the refugees were herded into five identical blocks. Each formation was sixteen people wide, and twelve ranks deep, which added up to roughly 192 residents per unit.

Not open squares, like the ones Wellington used during the Napoleonic Wars, but closed formations. Each group included a Marine Corps fireteam who, along with civilian volunteers, would provide leadership.

Evans was responsible for the concept, and worried about whether it would work. *If the squares hold, we'll take minimal casualties*, Evans thought. *But, if they don't, lots of people are going to die.*

Marine instructors shouted until they were hoarse. "Obey orders to march, and obey orders to stop!"

"Memorize the faces around you!"

"Stay with the people you know!"

"Don't run!"

"Aimed fire only! One bullet, one kill. Remember to reload!"

"Move the wounded to the center of the formation, and leave the dead behind!"

Over and over until the Marines and the camp's residents were sick of it.

Those who couldn't participate in the march were to remain within the "arena" where volunteers would stand guard until all five blocks arrived at the caverns.

That entailed risk. But sending them first would be dangerous as well. Evans hoped that if the cricks attacked, they would assault the main column, which stood a better chance of defending itself.

Hollis blew a whistle, and "Block 1" began to march. If "march" was the correct word. There'd been no attempt to teach the residents to march in unison because Evans knew that would take a month. So, what the residents did was shuffle, much as zombies might shuffle, with packs on their backs and weapons in their hands. Marines sought to herd them. "Pick up the pace!"

"Keep your ranks straight!"

"Elevate that gun barrel!" And so on.

Hollis had a stopwatch and gave Block 1 a five-minute head start, before dispatching Block 2, and warning Block 3 to get ready. Otherwise, the civilians were likely to fire on each other during a firefight.

Meanwhile, Evans was at the wheel of a UTV occupied by his RTO and a corpsman. By driving up and down both shoulders of the road Evans hoped to reassure the refugees and keep the various blocks moving at roughly the same pace.

And that's what he was doing when a boulder came rolling down the adjoining slope, took a jump, and landed in the middle of Block 2. People screamed. Blood flew. And the square jerked to a halt. Evans braked the UTV, jumped out, and raised Lang's megaphone. "Don't stop! Restore the square! Keep moving! And prepare to fight!"

Slowly, uncertainly, Block 2 began to move—as another boulder tore through the ranks of Block 3. Shadows flitted over the scene, and guns began to fire, as crickets appeared overhead. A corporal shouted: "Step, aim, fire! Step, aim, fire! Step, aim, fire!"

Evans paused to take aim with his M27 IAR and opened fire. A cricket jerked, lost a wing, and corkscrewed into Block 3—where it knocked a woman over. Other residents lifted her up. "Here they come!" a man shouted. "Eyes right!"

Dozens of crickets were hopping, jumping, and skidding downslope. Miniature landslides preceded them. Evans opened fire as did the men with him.

Alien bodies tumbled while a noncom shouted: "Step, aim, fire! Step, aim, fire! Step, aim, fire!" And, much to Evans' delight, the people in Block 2 did as they were told! Some were hit and supported by those around them. Others were killed and left behind. A man knelt next to the body of his dead wife, and was holding her hand, when a crick shot him.

Revenge was swift as a man with a shotgun cut the alien in half.

As Evans drove back along the column he witnessed acts of self-sacrifice, craven cowardice, and stoic determination—as the men and women of Temporary Relocation Camp 1106 ploughed ahead.

And there, at the very tail end of the procession, was Cassie Lang. She was standing in the back of a slow-moving pickup with a lever action rifle at her shoulder. A crick flew at her, a shot rang out, and the alien went down.

Evans stared at the scene that stretched back toward camp. A scattering of dead bodies, feeding crickets, and lost belongings. He didn't know what to feel. Joy? Because the column was no longer under attack? Sorrow? Because at least two dozen people had been lost? Both emotions were appropriate.

Lang jumped to the ground and Evans went to meet her. Their eyes met. "You're alive," Lang said.

"And so are you."

"There's more to do."

Evans smiled. "Yes, there certainly is."

* * *

Washington D.C. The Oval Office, in the White House
"No fucking way," Secretary of Defense Morton Jones said. "I'm a hard 'no.'"

"Well, I'm an enthusiastic 'yes,'" Secretary of State Larry Bowes countered. "What? You're going to let the President of China meet with the Xyfor unopposed?"

"He's a warlord," Jones put in. "One of five or six. And we have a vice president," Jones put in. "We'll send him."

"You must be joking," Bowes countered. "He's a good man, but he was confirmed, what? Three days ago?"

"Okay," President Vanessa Seton said. "That's enough. There's some physical danger associated with a trip into orbit, I get that.

"But, since the heads of state for Great Britain, France, and India agreed to go, I have no choice. Whatever happens at this meeting will be a big deal, and will not only have implications for the war, but the international pecking order once it's over."

Seton looked from face to face. "So, I'm going. That's settled. Please respond to the invitation by informing the Xyfor that I will attend the conference.

"So, what do you think? Should I dress as Princess Leia?"

That got a laugh, just as it was supposed to, and the meeting continued.

Billions of Prax micro drones roamed the planet, but only one had been able to penetrate the Oval Office, and record the conversation.

Once the meeting came to an end the tiny device took refuge in Bowes' briefcase, and was still there, when the Secretary of State departed.

***

Joint Base Andrews, Maryland
Two days had passed since the decision to take part in the Xyfor conference. Seton had butterflies in her stomach as a pair of motorcycle cops led the so-called "Beast" through the main gate, and onto Joint Base Andrews.

Lights flashed as the motorcade made for the runways—both of which were temporarily closed. And there, surrounded by Air Force security personnel, was a sleek aerospace plane that bore a close resemblance a human B-21 Raider.

The stealth bomber had been unveiled well before the Xyfor dropped into orbit. That did nothing to stop the rumors however.

Had the Raider's design been influenced by top secret UFO images? Or was it inspired by a wrecked UFO?

Some conspiracy theorists believed that it was, citing remarks made by a Mechan leader, who acknowledged that UFOs were Xyfor scout ships.

But the Air Force said "No," and insisted that form follows function. Meaning it was possible for humans and the Xyfor to produce aircraft that had similar designs.

Seton was ready to accept that premise, but what about the flying boxcars that the Xyfors used to transport their Mechan troops? Form didn't follow function where those vehicles were concerned. So, did she know everything there was to know? Her team said "Yes."

The limo came to a stop, a secret service agent opened the door, and Seton got out. Each head of state was allowed to bring two "assistants." And Seton's assistants were bodyguards.

Not her preference, but a nod to the Secretary of Defense, who didn't trust the Xyfor *or* the other attendees.

Nick Omata, and Carlie Brown were regular members of Seton's security detail, and stood waiting next to a set of rollup stairs.

Seton turned to wave at the cameras. Her trip into orbit was big news because she was going to be the first president to enter orbit, and because of the high-level conference itself.

Reporters yelled questions which Seton studiously ignored, while a Mechan utility bot briefed her party. It had a slender build and two arms instead of four. It spoke in a monotone. "Leave your belongings here. They will be stored separately.

"Once on board enter an escape pod. In case of an emergency, your pod will be ejected from the plane and will return to Earth."

But *where*? Seton wondered. *What's to keep the pod from landing ten feet away from a bunch of cricks?*

"You will remain in the cube until the plane arrives on Warship 7865, where the pod will open, allowing you to disembark. Please board."

Omata grinned. "Ladies first."

Seton made a face and Brown laughed.

After climbing a flight of rollup stairs, Seton entered the space plane's dimly lit interior. Rather than seats, both sides of the center aisle were lined with what looked like closets, with their doors slightly ajar. There were no directional signs or labels so Seton took the first pod on the left.

A padded shelf was there for her to lay on. Seton rolled onto her back, and stared at the ceiling. She could see vents. Nothing more. What light there was seemed to ooze through the translucent walls. Where was the seatbelt? The door closed, Seton heard a click, and got up to try the handle. She was locked in.

Seton felt the first stirrings of panic, and immediately sought to smother fear with logic. *It's a safety precaution*, Seton assured herself, as the hull started to vibrate.

It seemed best to lie down, so she did. Seton felt the plane begin to move, and as she looked upward, she saw what looked like liquid ice cream begin to pour out of the vents, and ooze down the walls. Seton reached out to sample the substance and discovered that it was smooth. What the hell?

That was when actual panic set in. Seton got up again, banged on the door, and kicked it with her feet. But to no avail. The level of white goop was rising rapidly and soon over-topped her shoulders. The Xyfor were trying to kill her! No, that didn't' make sense.

Seton felt the white material touch her lips, and raised her head in a futile attempt to escape it, but couldn't. So, she held her breath. The goop wasn't warm and it wasn't cold. Room temperature was the best description.

Finally, as Seton's lungs threatened to burst, she was forced to capitulate. *What a horrible way to die*, Seton thought, as she took a breath.

But she didn't die. Because Seton could breathe the goo. Or was she breathing *through* the goo? Not that it mattered.

What was the stuff for anyway? *It's packing material*, Seton decided. *If they launch my pod the goo will protect me.*

That understanding made Seton feel better even if she didn't like the sensation involved. Or the fact that she couldn't read briefing papers or watch news summaries.

What Seton *could* do was take a nap standing up, or try to, although that seemed unlikely.

Seton awoke an hour later to discover that the white goo was flowing out of her pod via the same vents used earlier. She expected that everything, including her clothes would be wet, but that wasn't the case.

Seton's skin was dry, as was the military style jumpsuit she'd chosen to wear in lieu of business attire. And once the last of the goo disappeared the door popped open.

Seton wasted no time leaving the pod. Omata and Brown met in the center aisle. "No offense, Madam President," Brown said. "But that trip sucked."

"Yeah," Omata agreed. "I quit. Oh, wait, I *can't* quit, because I'm on an alien spaceship!"

Seton laughed.

A utility robot appeared. "Welcome to Warship 7865. The controllers are waiting. Follow me."

The robot led the humans out of the plane and onto what resembled a two-lane access road. Various pieces of machinery were parked on it, stacks of color-coded cargo modules were waiting to be loaded, and alien symbols glowed on the walls. An identical "road" could be seen on the far side of the vast hangar area.

The space plane was located between the elevated roads in a wide trench. Two planes were parked in front of it suggesting that other guests had arrived.

Further down an enormous hatch was visible—thanks to the flashing lights which encircled it. That was the moment when Seton became conscious of the fact that the fly-through hangar was pressurized, she could breathe, and she wasn't floating around.

Did the aliens have some sort of artificial gravity? If so, that was a prize well worth angling for. Seton was amazed by how large the ship was. Metal ribs curved up to meet their counterparts two hundred feet above. That left plenty of room for airborne maintenance bots to come and go, each marked by a strobing light.

The humans soon arrived in front of the brightly lit hatch. It opened to reveal a lock. They followed the robot in. Roughly a minute then passed before they were ushered into the corridor beyond. The brightly lit passageway was empty except for a couple of maintenance robots.

Seton caught glimpses of empty compartments to either side as the group passed a succession of open doors. Where was the crew? She assumed the ship was highly automated. But, if so, why make the vessel so large?

The trip ended in a spacious compartment dominated by a huge viewport. Earth hung like a multicolored gem in front of her. Seen from afar the wisps of cloud cover, the blue oceans, and the sprawling continents offered no hint of the war-torn misery below.

But maybe, with help from the Xyfor, and increased cooperation from world leaders, the planet could be pacified. Only one of the Xyfor controllers was there in person. His name was Ecor Rinn. After greeting each human, he introduced the rest of the Xyfor including Mezo Zork, Bak Fay, and Ka Non—all of whom were visible via holo tanks.

Though vaguely humanoid the Xyfor were notably different in appearance. Glowing skull implants signaled the emotions they were feeling and served to enhance interpersonal communications. Supraorbital ridges shadowed their eyes, feeding tentacles circled their mouths, and their hands were equipped with tentacles instead of fingers. Rinn was dressed in a high-collared robe. He turned to Seton. "You may recall that Controller Las Tith was killed by the Prax," Rinn said. "A painful reminder of how lethal the Prax are.

"I believe you already know our other guests? Including British Prime Minister James Chittick, French President Marie Brisson, Chinese President Pro Tem Yim Min, and Indian Prime Minister Gopal Vakar."

"That is mostly correct," Seton replied. "Prime Minister Vakar and I have spoken on the phone—we've never met face-to-face. And it's a pleasure to do so now.

"As for President Pro Tem Min, no, I haven't had the pleasure."

Seton shook hands with Vakar and Min, followed by the rest, with the exception of Brisson—who greeted the American with two air kisses.

Vakar was dressed in a business suit, Chittick appeared to be ready for a day in the country, Brisson looked chic in tailored leathers, and Min was dressed in an Army uniform minus any indication of rank. A semicircular table faced the holo tanks and each human took his or her seat on chairs clearly brought up from Earth. Which was a nice touch.

Rinn opened the meeting on a somber note. "Of the one hundred and ninety-five countries on your planet you are the only leaders who could come.

"Some felt an obligation to stay home and fight. But the vast majority made no reply to our invitation, suggesting that their governments are no longer operational, or that they are dead."

That elicited a startled "*Sacre' bleu*" from Brisson, and expressions of sorrow from the others.

"Fortunately, your governments still exist," Rinn said, "are fighting the menace, and cooperating with us. But, can more be accomplished? We believe the answer is 'yes.' And it's our hope that you will increase intelligence sharing, integrate your command-and-control functions, and do what you can to aid other countries."

All of which made perfect sense except for one thing: What Rinn was suggesting would require trust. Yes, the three NATO countries trusted each other for the most part.

But India? And China? Not so much. And that schism became ever more transparent as the conference continued.

It soon became apparent that what each human representative wanted was more support from the Mechans, with few, if any, strings attached.

And what the Xyfor wanted was for humans to do more of the heavy lifting via a web of multilateral agreements. Seton thought that Congress might approve some of the Xyfor proposals, excluding China, which according to the CIA was being led by warlords like Min.

Meanwhile the Indian government had extended special protections to Hindi citizens, leaving Muslims to fend for themselves.

So, by the time the three-hour conference ended, Great Britain, France, and the United States had agreed to strengthen their ties, while the other two countries made a vague promise "to review the situation and respond within thirty days."

There was no way to know how the Xyfor controllers felt about the gathering, but Seton assumed they were disappointed, as a Mechan led them back to the space plane. "Because the other shuttles arrived first, they will depart first," the robot informed them. "Please enter your pods."

The last thing Seton wanted to do was breathe white goo for a couple of hours. But there was no choice. Seton tried to appear nonchalant as she waved to her bodyguards, and entered the pod. Nothing happened for twenty minutes. There was no goo, and no sense of motion. But that made sense if the other planes were departing.

Then Seton felt a faint vibration, as if the shuttle was coming to life, and the first rivulets of goo appeared. The subsequent process wasn't any fun, but Seton managed to tolerate breathing through the goo, knowing she would survive.

Seton felt additional gees pile on as the plane accelerated down the short runway, followed by a feeling of lightness, as she entered zero gravity.

Damn, Seton thought. *It's been a long time since I ate anything. Ah well, I'll be in D.C. two hours from now. Time for a nap.*

That was the moment when the pulse from a Prax surface-to-space energy cannon struck the plane and destroyed it. Thanks to the onboard AI, the escape pods were launched even as the rest of the shuttle disintegrated, and emergency reentry rockets fired.

Seton felt the sideways acceleration, followed by a spinning sensation, and tried to scream. She couldn't.

CHAPTER ELEVEN

FEMA TRC 1106 adjacent to Whites City, New Mexico

The good news was that 937 of the 960 camp's residents had been able to complete the march to the caverns. Not a perfect score by any means, but vastly better than the number of casualties likely to have been suffered had they remained where they were, and most of them realized that. The bad news was that the more than 300 people still in the camp were too weak or frail to walk four miles while under attack.

So, the plan was to pack the evacuees into the remaining vehicles and drive them to the caverns. But the crickets would be waiting. And the convoy of cars and trucks would be extremely vulnerable. So, what to do? Other than request additional resources that wouldn't be approved.

After racking his brain, and conferring with his drone operators, Evans settled on an alternative that might work. And that was to send a feint down the road, while leading the actual column along a dirt track which, though longer, would theoretically circumvent the cricks waiting along the highway. There was no time to lose, since the camp was unlikely to survive another night.

It was two in the afternoon by then, and Evans was giving orders to Lieutenant Yamada. "Go far enough to make contact with the cricks and pull back. Make it appear as if we're trying to break out, but hesitant to run the gauntlet. Buy as much time as you can, and haul ass. I'll see you at the caverns. Got it?"

"Yes, sir," Yamada answered. "I like the 'haul ass' part."

Evans laughed. "Good! Get going. We're about to pull out."

As Yamada left, Evans turned his attention back to the convoy. Lang was in charge of the ragtag assemblage of cars, trucks, vans and motorhomes all loaded with people.

Yamada's platoon was going to bait the crickets, and Christou's platoon was guarding the caverns, so the 3rd platoon under Second Lieutenant Dawkins had orders to protect the convoy with help from the Marines in the headquarters platoon.

Evans had assigned himself to the 1st squad, which was at the head of the column, just behind Lang. The 2nd and 3rd squads were interspersed in the column, and ready to not only defend it, but to cope with the inevitable breakdowns. The 4th squad was in the six slot, and responsible for guarding the back door.

Lang gave the order. Engines coughed, sputtered, and roared as a cloud of exhaust fumes rose to partially cloak the convoy. Then, like a herd of turtles, the parade was underway.

Progress was slow, but steady. And it wasn't long before Lang's pickup turned onto a dirt road used by hunters and amateur prospectors.

It wasn't maintained, which meant there were pot holes, washouts, and rocks that had to be moved. That made for a rough ride as vehicles rocked, bounced, and wobbled along. *The road sucks, but it beats getting shot at,* Evans decided as he put his foot down and the UTV spewed gravel.

Low hills rose along both sides of the track as it followed the seam between them. And it wasn't long before problems began to surface. A car overheated, was pushed to one side, and left for dead. A boxy motorhome lost traction, had to be towed, and delayed the procession by fifteen minutes. And so it went.

Evans was eyeing the incline ahead when he heard Yamada's voice via his headset. "Charlie-Six, this is One. Over."

"This is Six actual. Go. Over."

"We're on the road to the caverns. The bodies disappeared. Over."

"No surprise there, over."

"True. But there's no sign of the enemy. They're gone. Over."

Evans took a moment to digest that. If the cricks weren't lying in wait along the road, and they weren't attacking the convoy, that left only one possibility: The Prax were massing for an assault on the caverns! "Charlie-Two, this is Six. Did you copy?"

"That's affirmative," Christou replied. "Over."

"Get ready. The bastards are going to attack you! Hold the parking lot... If they reach the ramp that leads to the entrance, they'll have the advantage of height. And if they get inside there'll be a blood bath.

"Charlie-One and I will attack them from two directions as soon as we can," Evans added. "But in my case that will take fifteen minutes. Over."

"Roger that," Christou replied. "Over." Her voice was flat.

After a quick conversation with Lang, Evans took two squads and raced forward. That was the plan anyhow. But the reality was quite different.

The dirt track was as rough as ever, and try as they might, the Marines couldn't make more than a painful 5 miles per hour. In the meantime, they could hear Christou and her Marines on the radio. "This is Eight," platoon sergeant Baxter said. "Here they come! Aimed fire only. Cut 'em down!"

"This is Two-Six," a female voice said. "We need a corpsman over here."

"Drone at twelve o'clock!" a Marine said. "Make that two drones. Pop 'em!"

Evans remembered the drones in the SubTropolis and swore. If allowed to, the machines would fire down on his Marines, and prevent them from taking cover.

He could hear the rattle of automatic fire by then, as well as the occasional *crack* of a grenade exploding, and loud chittering. "Dismount! On me! Let's kill the bastards!"

In order to reach the parking lot, and the Visitor Center beyond, the Marines had to scramble up and out of the arroyo. Scree slid from under Evans' boots as his legs pumped and his lungs sucked air.

Suddenly he was there, at the southeast corner of the lot, with the firefight spread out before him. The crickets were hiding behind the haphazardly parked cars they'd arrived in, and were firing at the Visitor Center. Automatic fire lashed back. A sedan exploded into flames.

A hand signal sent Marines to the left as Evans spoke. "Charlie-Two, this is Six. We're at the southeast corner of the lot."

"Welcome to the party," Christou replied. "Over."

"Six, this is Charlie-One," Yamada said. "We're about to turn onto Reef Top Circle, and will reinforce the Visitor Center from the north. Over."

"Roger that," Evans replied. "We're moving west to exit your field of fire. Hold five. Over."

The cricks were using the parked cars and smoke as cover while they shuffled ever closer to the Visitor Center, firing as they advanced. And they were getting close. *Too* close. Three cars were on fire by then, and one exploded, cutting some of the bugs down.

Traffic barriers lined the west side of the parking lot. Evans made the call once his detachment was in place. "This is Six... Stay off the southwest corner of the lot, and we'll stay off the building. Take 'em out. Over."

The arrival of more Marines tipped the balance. The aliens were blocked to the north, and the southwest, so they attempted to head east. But Christou had people on the Visitor Center's roof, two of whom were armed with 40mm grenade launchers.

The Marines took turns firing and reloading. That produced a continuous rain of fire. The crickets who tried to pass through it were blown to bloody bits. The rest fell to sharpshooters.

The battle ended minutes later. And just in time too, as Lang's pickup appeared, followed by carloads of elderly residents.

The sun was setting, and Evans had just completed the task of establishing a perimeter, when Lang appeared. "We lost thirteen people this morning, but none this afternoon," she announced. "That isn't good, but it could have been a lot worse. And it would have been, except for you and your Marines. Thank you. How many did you lose?"

"Seven," Evans replied soberly.

Lang could see the misery in his eyes. "We're at war," she said. "No one could have done better."

Evans forced a smile. "Someone could have. But they weren't here."

Lang nodded. "My folks want to mourn. And they want to celebrate. Alcohol could be involved. You're invited."

Evans smiled. "Thank you. Can off-duty Marines participate?"

"They can," Lang replied. "The wake will start at eight."

"Good," Evans said. "Will you save me a seat?"

"I will," Lang promised. "Right next to me."

***

In Earth Orbit

President Vanessa Seton was falling out of the sky and plunging down through the atmosphere to *what?* A hard landing? Or a soft landing? And, if the latter, then *where?* North America? Africa? China? *Shit no*, Seton thought. *Don't let it be China. Min will use me as a hostage.*

That's unlikely, Seton assured herself. *Something like 70 percent of the planet is covered with oceans. So, a water landing makes sense. Will this thing float? Or course it will. It's an escape pod. But, even if it floats, I'm screwed. No one will know where to find me... No, wait, the Xyfor will know! Odds are that the pod will broadcast a distress signal.*

Crap! Could the Prax follow the signal to the pod? Of course, they could. Assuming they could hijack some boats.

Seton knew she was traveling at thousands of miles per hour, but couldn't put a number on it, and wondered how long the process would take. Forever, was the answer. That's how it felt.

Seton found herself drifting from memory to memory, treasuring some, and regretting others. That's what she was doing, regretting the relationship with her mother, when the pod jerked. It felt as if Seton was floating up before falling again.

Parachutes? Yes! She thought so. Seton wanted to brace herself for the inevitable impact, but couldn't because of the protective goo. *Here's hoping it works,* she thought, as the pod hit, bounced, and landed. *I hit the ground instead of water,* Seton concluded. *That could be good or bad. I'm about to find out. Maybe I'm in New Jersey.*

Seton tried to open the door while the white goo was being sucked out of the compartment but it refused to budge. Then, as the final puddle disappeared into a floor drain, the latch gave. Cold air surged into the previously warm compartment as Seton pushed the hatch open. It was dark, but the moon was up, and the light was enough to see by.

Seton stepped outside. "Stay with your aircraft if you can." That was the maxim the Army taught her. And that made sense. First, because it was logical to believe that the Xyfor knew where the pod was. And second, because it would be more visible from the air than she would be, out wandering around the countryside. All of which was fine, except for the possibility that the Prax had seen the pod descend, or would stumble across the site by accident.

And that's what Seton was thinking about when she heard a familiar voice. "Don't shoot! It's Nick and Carlie. We're coming in."

Her secret service agents! Seton was astounded. And pleased. It seemed the pods were programmed to land near each other. Which, come to think of it, made sense.

Omata appeared first, quickly followed by Brown. And, thanks to the wan light provided by the moon, Seton could see that they were festooned with gear. "Wow! It's wonderful to see you... Where did you get all that stuff?"

"It was under our seats," Brown replied. "I suggest that you take a look. We're going to need everything we can lay our hands on. Xyfor weapons included."

Seton felt a stab of fear. "*Why*? Where are we?"

"We're in Russia," Omata replied. "And, correct me if I'm wrong, but the entire country was overrun." Seton felt stupid as she reentered the pod, found the release lever under the cushion, and pulled up on it.

Seton heard a *click*, followed by a *whir*, as the seat folded up and out of the way. And there, illuminated by interior lights, were Mechan weapons, gear, and other equipment. *Hell yes*, Seton thought. *Now we have a chance.*

Some of the equipment was going to be very useful, especially the rifle and pistol. There was a serrated combat knife too, plus a first aid kit, and what might have been Xyfor emergency rations.

Seton fastened a pistol belt around her waist, to which she added the clip-on knife, and first aid kit. Then, with the rifle cradled in her arms, she stepped out of the pod. "Do I look like Rambo?"

"Better," Brown replied. "The gun belt matches your eyes."

Seton laughed. "So, we're in Russia... How do we know that?"

Omata was facing out, scanning for danger. He turned. "We know, because my Garmin says so. It's the high-end model with satellite access. So, I can send and receive messages."

"Yeah," Brown put in. "And it'll tell your fortune too."

Omata ignored her. "We're about five miles south of the Khankala military airbase. And that's where I think we should go."

Seton's eyebrows rose. "Why would we do that?"

Omata had clearly given the matter some thought. "Because we might find human weapons there, and we're going to need an airstrip."

Seton realized that the secret service agent was right. A rescue would involve some sort of transport. "Should I message my boss?" Omata inquired.

"Tell me something," Seton replied. "What does it take to recharge your watch?"

"A USB connector."

"Do you have a connector? And a wall outlet?"

Omata frowned. "No."

"Let's conserve power," Seton suggested, "and report in after we reach the airbase.

"Were either of you in the military?"

"I served a hitch in the Navy," Omata offered.

"And I was an English major," Brown added.

Seton laughed. "Okay ... So, it looks like I'm the best qualified to lead this patrol. We'll head north per Nick's suggestion, stay off trails, and keep our eyes peeled. Watch your spacing. Fifteen or twenty feet should be about right. Oh, and since we don't know jack shit about our weapons, keep your fingers off the triggers. Let's go."

Moonlight glazed the land, most of which was flat, and cut by occasional streams. Seton didn't know anything about farming. But to her untrained eye it looked as if crops were rotting in the fields. There were no lights to be seen, which suggested a temporary power outage, or one that was ongoing. Curiosity led Seton to approach a farmhouse, even though doing so involved the risk of encountering a dog. But there was no dog. Just a scattering of gleaming white bones in the overgrown yard, and a human skull that was tipped on its side. It grinned as Seton toed it.

As president, Seton was quite familiar with what had transpired in Russia. The calamity began when the *byurokraty* (bureaucrats) failed to grasp the full extent of the Prax threat.

And by the time they came to their senses, Moscow was surrounded by ravenous aliens who were willing to take heavy casualties in return for a city full of meat.

The Russians fought, and fought hard. But Moscow fell. And, when it did, the bugs ate their fill. As for those who weren't lucky enough to die, they were forced to work in Prax factories, or marched into underground nests and placed in "live storage."

Later, in the town of Kozelsk, crickets captured an SS-18 Satan silo, and coerced personnel stationed there to launch an ICBM at Washington, D.C. It was, according to the Intel community, an attempt to kill *her.*

Fortunately, the National Advanced Surface-to-Air Missile System was operable and launched PATRIOT missiles, which blew the incoming ICBM out of the air. And did so without detonating the incoming weapon's nuclear warhead.

That was good, but some sort of measured response was necessary, lest the Russians attack again. So, Seton gave the order to launch a single ICBM carrying Multiple Independent Reentry Vehicles, all targeted on Moscow.

There was no way to know how many Russians, civilian *and* military, had been killed. The sorrow associated with that decision still troubled her.

Seton felt cold. She looked around. "How far is it?"

"About two miles," Omata answered.

The sky was starting to lighten in the east. "Let's go," Seton said. "Let's find a place to hide before the sun rises." There were lots of homes and businesses to avoid as the party entered the outskirts of Khankala. And that was where Seton spotted the cricks. Sixteen of them. She motioned for the others to kneel.

The aliens were directly ahead, crossing the line of march from left to right, with three human prisoners in tow. The Russians were dressed in ragged clothing, and roped together, as they stumbled along. Seton's first impulse was to attack the bugs, and attempt to free the prisoners. But she knew that would be suicidal and therefore pointless.

The horror of it distressed Seton, as she waited for the Prax to pass before leading the others forward. It wasn't long before they came to a two-lane road, crossed it, and entered a dense housing complex. A wary dog watched from a safe distance, while they hurried along a deserted street to a large parcel of farmland that bordered the south side of the base. There was no cover to speak of.

Seton could see a clutch of buildings and felt sure they were part of the base. She turned to her companions. "Come on! Let's cross the field as quickly as we can." They started to run.

* * *

Praporschik (warrant officer) Dimitri Gribov was lying prone on a rooftop, and peering through a telescopic sight. Three humans were running straight at him. Survivors? Resistance fighters? The details didn't matter. No, what mattered were the supplies they might have, and the strange looking rifles clutched in their hands. Not Russian, not western, and not Prax. What then? He wanted to know.

Plus, there was the fact that two of the three were female, and Gribov was horny. Should he kill the man? The Lobaev sniper rifle was accurate out to 2000 meters.

No, Gribov reasoned. *If I kill him, the women will turn and run away. I'll befriend them instead, and wait for my chance.*

CHAPTER TWELVE

The National Military Command Center, the Pentagon, Washington D.C.

The Command Center was located in a large room with flat screens on the front wall, and rows of desks with chairs, all of which were occupied. As were the seats provided for observers and staff at the back of the room.

Those present knew what the public didn't know: President Vanessa Seton, and two members of the Secret Service, were missing. The gabble of conversation ended as an officer yelled, "Atten-shun!" The participants stood as General Arthur Fenwick entered, closely followed by Secretary of Defense Morton Jones, and half a dozen aides.

Fenwick went to the front of the room and stood at the podium. Conversation stopped and every eye was on him. Fenwick was known for his no-nonsense manner, and got straight to the point. "The Prax attacked the space plane carrying the president and her bodyguards shortly after it cleared a Xyfor warship and was destroyed."

Fenwick's statement elicited gasps of surprise, expressions of horror, and a lot of profanity. Fenwick raised a hand. "There's reason to be concerned, but there's also reason to hope. The Xyfor assure us that our people were in escape pods when the plane was attacked. Those pods were ejected, and made successful landings. Colonel Harper has more. Colonel?"

Harper was tall, rangy, and in need of a shave. As he made his way over to replace Fenwick at the podium new imagery appeared on the wall screens. An aerial shot of a town and airstrip could be seen. Harper eyed the audience "The pods landed near the Khankala airbase, in Russia."

Harper's statement produced a chorus of groans. Every person in the audience knew that Russia had been overrun. So, even if the Americans had survived the landing, they were in deep shit. "Yeah, I feel the same way. However, we do have this."

The image on the center screen grew larger in a series of jerks revealing three different escape pods, with hatches open, and parachutes puddled around them. More shots followed. "These images were captured by a drone launched off the carrier USS Gerald R. Ford in the Black Sea," Harper said.

"As luck would have it," Harper added, "the Ford and her escorts are there searching for Prax artifacts. That means we have an excellent platform to work from.

"There's a lot we don't know however," Harper added. "As you can see all hatches are open, suggesting that the president and her bodyguards survived impact, and left the scene.

"Or, and this is the possibility we fear most, they were captured by Russians or cricks.

"Unfortunately, Khankala is outside of helicopter range. So, we can't drop SEALS in, nor would we, without better Intel. But remember this, President Seton saw combat as an Army officer ... So, this ain't over till it's over."

An Army officer shouted, "Hooah!"

And everyone, regardless of branch, repeated the call. "HOOAH!"

* * *

Khankala Airbase, Russia

President Vanessa Seton could see the chain link fence up ahead, and the ragged hole that someone or something had cut in it. Her goal was to reach the fence, and pass through the opening, without getting shot.

Her legs pumped, her heart pounded, and her breath came in short gasps. Finally, Seton was there, diving through the gap and landing on her chest.

The impact drove the air out of her lungs. Seton was still trying to recover as the others arrived. No shots had been fired. And for that she was thankful.

Seton stood, heard a noise, and whirled. A scarecrow raised his hands. One of which was holding a rifle. "*Privet! YA praporshchik Dmitriy Gribov. Dobro pozhalovat' v Khankalu, na aviabazu.*" (Hello! I am Warrant Officer Dimitri Gribov. Welcome to Khankala, Airbase.)

Seton was somewhat reassured by the man's welcoming tone, but well aware that there could be more Russians, and they would almost certainly see the newcomers as a threat. "Do you speak English?"

"Yes, of course," the man replied. "I am Warrant Officer Dimitri Gribov. Welcome to Khankala, Airbase. And you are?"

"Vanessa Kirby," Seton lied. It seemed best to conceal her actual identity. Kirby was her mother's maiden name. She pointed. "That's Brown, and that's Omata."

"Americans?" Gribov inquired incredulously.

"Yes," Seton admitted.

"How you get here?"

"We were on a plane, and the crickets shot it down," Seton replied simply.

"Crickets? You mean bugs?"

"Yes."

The Russian frowned. "I know American weapons. And alien weapons too. Your rifle is something different."

"It's a Mechan weapon."

"Mechan?" Gribov inquired. "What is Mechan?"

"The Mechans are robots that serve an alien race called the Xyfor," Seton explained. "The Xyfor are at war with the Prax, meaning the bugs, and came here to find them.

"But, before we get into that, please tell us about the situation here at the base. How many troops are there?"

"Only one," Gribov answered. "Me! Imagine, a warrant officer in command of an airbase! The dead colonels are jealous."

Seton was relieved to hear it. But could Gribov be trusted? Time would tell.

"You hungry?" Gribov inquired.

"Yes," Seton answered honestly. "And we need to clean up."

"Clean up? With water?"

"Yes," Seton said. "And go the restroom."

"Ah, yes, the *tualet* (restroom). Follow me." The Russian turned away

Seton turned to Omata. "Use your time in the restroom to send a sitrep. Keep it short to conserve power. We're in good shape, we're armed, and we're at the Khankala base. Got it?"

Omata nodded. "Will do."

"Good. Keep your eyes peeled."

Seton hurried to catch up with Gribov. She followed him into a maze of one-, two-, and three-story buildings. Seton noticed that each structure was labeled with a Cyrillic letter followed by a number. The kind of arrangement favored by military minds everywhere.

Gribov paused in front of a ladder, and turned to glance over his shoulder, before starting the climb. Seton followed. The fact that the alien rifle lacked a sling made the task more difficult than it should have been.

Once on the flat roof the Russian paused to let Omata and Brown catch up. "Is safer here when bugs come," Gribov said. "So, I stay off ground."

"What about the flying bugs?" Seton inquired.

"I have MON-50, command-detonated mines," Gribov replied, as he pointed to a small box perched on scissor legs. "Like American Claymore," the Russian added. "Bugs land, I press button, and *BOOM!*"

So, there's a weapons locker somewhere, Seton concluded. *And what about the humungous key hanging around his neck? Will that open the stash?*

* * *

Gribov watched Brown follow Omata onto the roof. The woman was young and pretty. He would strip her, chain her to a bed, and fuck her twice a day. He would have to feed her, and haul her *der'mo* (shit) out of the cell, but the rewards would be worth it.

* * *

"You follow," Gribov instructed, as he crossed the roof. "Watch step."

The reason for that became apparent as Gribov stepped onto the wooden plank that led to a second building. MON-50 wires followed the foot bridge across the gap.

The piece of lumber was nine-inches-wide max and gave slightly under Seton's weight. Gribov was waiting to greet her. "Can pull planks," he explained. "Make air moats."

Seton did the best she could to memorize the route Gribov followed as he led the Americans from roof-to-roof, eventually arriving at what looked like a concrete pillbox.

Bright scars marked the places where Prax projectiles had flattened themselves on the steel door. Hinges *squealed* as Gribov pulled the barrier open. "Come ... Lavatory and food."

Metal stairs led down to a steel door with Cyrillic writing on it. And, when Gribov pulled it open, Seton noticed the brackets for a drop bar on the inside.

Was this the Russian's safe room? The place where he could take refuge if all else failed? Seton thought so ... And what she saw beyond the entryway seemed to confirm the theory.

The windows were covered with sheets of metal. All manner of boxes were stacked against the walls, and a cot with sleeping bag sat atop a beautiful Persian rug.

That was when Seton realized the room had been an office before Gribov moved in. The base commander's office? Probably. *Watch for a door with a big keyhole*, Seton told herself. *That's where the weapons will be.*

"You have electric lights," Seton observed.

"Da," Gribov replied. "I take solar panels off weather station. Don't tell anyone." He *cackled* loudly.

A few minutes later, when it was Seton's turn to follow a short hall to the lavatory, she saw it. A side door with a retro lock! A file room perhaps ... Which Gribov converted to an arms locker.

Lunch consisted of Russian 24-hour IR (Individual Rations), which proved to be better than MREs. In Seton's opinion anyway. Of course, the fact that she was ravenously hungry, could have influenced her opinion. Seton's box included crackers, veggies, a variety of canned meats, candy, multivitamins, and an alcohol fueled heater.

When Gribov left to use the lavatory, Seton turned to Omata. "Did you get the message out?"

"Yes, and I received a reply," the agent answered. "'Stay put, and standby.'"

"Excellent! Tell Brown. What we need is a look at the airstrip."

"Thanks for lunch," Seton said, when Gribov returned. "We're going to inspect the runway."

"*Da*," Gribov replied. "I take you to control tower. Good view from there."

Seton didn't want the Russian's company, but thought it best to humor him. "Thank you. Please lead the way."

Gribov led them to stairs that descended to ground level and more steel doors. It was necessary to remove a crossbar to open them. A battered UAZ-452 van was parked outside. Judging from appearances the boxy vehicle had been shot at.

But, despite the damage, the wreck started up. And Gribov invited the Americans to get in. "The control tower is at the other end of the field," he announced apologetically. "We go now."

Seton was sitting next to Gribov in the front. And even though the windscreen had cracks in it, not to mention a couple of bullet holes, she could see the wreckage on the main runway. Gribov had to swerve in between the burned-out carcass of a fighter plane, a shot-up bus, and a mangled helicopter before arriving at the spindly tower.

Seton knew the airfield was unusable by then, but wanted to get a wider perspective, and followed Gribov up spiraling stairs to the observation deck.

That was when Gribov removed the chain from around his neck and pushed the key into an oversized lock. *Well, I'll be damned*, Seton thought. *The key is for the door to the control tower! Not a weapons stash.*

Gribov opened the door with a flourish, and gestured for Seton and Omata to enter, which they did. Then he slammed the door closed and locked it.

Gribov could hear muffled shouts, and a thumping noise, as one of the Americans kicked the door. But they could wait. The Russian's attention was on Brown, who had just arrived on the platform. He saw her eyes widen as he pointed the pistol. "Drop rifle."

Brown laid it on the deck. Gribov nodded. "Good. Put these on."

Brown accepted the open cuffs and appeared to examine them. Then the agent drew her right arm back and brought it forward. The cuffs struck Gribov's face and caused him to stagger backwards. That was when Brown kicked him in the balls.

Gribov uttered a grunt of pain as he bent forward. That exposed his back. Brown drew the Xyfor knife and plunged the blade in as far as it would go. Gribov jerked convulsively, and collapsed face down.

Brown bent to jerk the knife free and proceeded to wipe the blade on the dead man's jacket before returning the weapon to its sheath.

When the agent went to open the door, she saw the key in the lock, and turned it. Omata burst out of the control room pistol, at the ready. His eyes went to the body. "What the fuck happened?"

Brown shrugged. "He tried to handcuff me."

Seton joined them. "Holy shit, Carlie... You're a serious badass!"

Carlie nodded. "As are all the women of Delta Sigma Theta."

Seton laughed. "Okay, we're losing the light. Let's go back to Gribov's hideaway, and lock ourselves in. We'll work on clearing the runway in the morning."

The airbase had a spooky feel as night fell. Omata was forced to turn the headlights on, or risk a collision with one of the obstacles on the tarmac, even though cricks could be watching.

Seton waited for the cricks to fire on the van, and was thrilled when they didn't. Once inside what Omata called Gribov's "crib," Seton felt reasonably safe.

A number of messages were waiting for Omata, all of which added to Seton's sense of well-being. A MQ-9A Reaper Drone would be loitering over the airbase 24/7, ready to smoke the cricks, should they attack.

Secondly, a carrier-based Navy C-2A transport was on standby, ready to pick the party up once the runway was clear.

Last, but not least, the Air Force was going to drop a large loader onto the field early the next morning. And Omata assured Seton that the machine could clear the strip "In no time at all."

Seton frowned. "Really? Are they dropping an operator too?"

"No need," Omata replied. "I was a Seabee."

Seton was well aware of the combat record the Navy's "fighting Seabees" had amassed over more than 75 years of service, and looked at Omata with a newfound sense of respect. "Enough said. We're good to go."

Gribov's bathroom was far from clean, but something was better than nothing, and Brown drew the short straw. So she was in the shower, enjoying the tepid flow of water, when Seton tried the door she'd noticed earlier. It opened smoothly, revealing a mini armory.

Seton wasted no time trading her awkward Xyfor rifle for a Russian KS-23, pump-action shotgun, fitted with a 7 round, detachable magazine.

A number of pistols were available, and Seton chose a 9mm P-96S with hip holster, plus 2 extra magazines. It felt good to hold something designed for a human hand.

Once Seton was finished, she urged Omata to visit the armory, which he did.

Brown emerged from the bathroom with wet hair, and wearing the same dirty clothes. "That felt good!"

After eating most of a Russian ration, Seton volunteered to take the first watch, while the others made beds for themselves on the floor. None of them wanted to sleep on Gribov's rumpled cot. Omata and Brown fell asleep quickly, as evidenced by their breathing, and an occasional snore from Omata. Seton passed the time by cleaning her newly acquired weapons and searching the rooms for Intel. But, since she didn't speak Russian, Seton didn't learn much.

Meanwhile, what initially felt like a safe place was beginning to close in on her. And Seton knew why. *I can't see out*, she concluded. *What's going on out there? Is the base deserted? Or are the crickets about to attack?*

It's likely that the cricks don't realize the Reaper is overhead, circling above the base, so there's no reason to be afraid, Seton thought. *And, it's safe to assume they know four humans are hiding in this building. Especially since they've had previous run-ins with Gribov.*

Seton's watch ended, and Brown's began. Seton chose the saggy couch over the floor, and used an Army blanket for a throw.

Sleep came quickly. And Seton was chairing a meeting about a subject she couldn't put a name to, when something hit the door with a loud *thump*. "I think it's a battering ram!" Brown exclaimed. "Get ready to fight!"

Then a series of muffled explosions rocked the building. Dust showered her from above, and Seton heard *another* thump, as the door began to bulge.

Seton was standing there, shotgun at the ready, as *more* explosions were heard. *Why?* Destroying what remained of the base wouldn't help the crickets access the humans. Then she realized the truth. *Holy shit! The cricks are swarming the area, and the Reaper operator is trying to kill them.*

The brackets supporting the drop bar gave way at that point, the steel rod hit the floor, and a battering ram appeared. It was protruding though a piece of steel plate which functioned as a shield. "Fire low!" Seton shouted. "Aim at their feet!"

The shotgun produced a loud *BOOM!* and a heavy recoil as Seton fired it.

Her buckshot went in under the shield to amputate crick feet and dump bugs on the floor. Others charged forward, but were blocked by the bodies of wounded comrades, and by a hail of bullets. Seton yelled, "Grenade!" and tossed an RGN hand grenade through the doorway. There was a bright flash, followed by a *bang*, as more Prax fell.

Seton reloaded the shotgun while she waited for the next wave. There was none.

The exterior explosions had ceased as well. *The drone ran out of ordinance*, Seton reasoned. *I hope another Reaper is on the way.*

None of them could sleep. Not with the possibility of another attack hanging over them.

A message came assuring the party that a fully armed Reaper was on station.

Now that the cricks knew that death could fall from the sky, the aliens would be less likely to attack. Or so Seton hoped. The hours dragged by. Finally, when the sun began to rise, a new message came. "Merry Christmas! Santa's on his way."

Seton felt her spirits rise as she drank a mug of instant coffee, and paid a visit to the closet, where she appropriated a submachine gun for personal protection, along with an SV-98 sniper rifle. Just the thing for keeping the Prax away from the dozer.

Seton placed two bottles of water, some candy bars, and extra ammo in a backpack. Then with the rifle slung, and the SMG ready to go, she followed Omata out into the hall.

Crick bodies were sprawled this way and that, there were puddles of dark ichor to avoid, and the combined odor of formic acid and fecal matter made Seton nauseous.

And, if that was bad, the situation outside was even worse. Hundreds of cricks had been slaughtered by the Reaper's Hellfire missiles and bombs. Their bodies were covered by a seething mass of crows, all cawing and eating their fill.

Unfortunately, while the drone attacks had taken a serious toll on the local Prax population, they had also done additional damage to the runway. Could the three of them clear the strip, *and* fill the bomb craters, before the aliens attacked again? Seton hoped so.

Seton's musings were interrupted by the sound of jet engines, as two F-35C fighters appeared from the south, and immediately opened fire with GAU-22/A rotary cannons and missiles. One fighter roared down the east side of the base, while the second paralleled it to the west, as part of a concerted effort to eliminate any crickets hiding near the airport.

A plan that Seton heartily approved of as cannon shells ploughed fallow ground, trees keeled over, and explosions marched north.

The jets pulled up and began to circle as a C-17 transport appeared from the south.

Seton had seen vehicles dropped from planes during her time in the Army, but never loaders. It shouldn't make a difference though ... Construction equipment was tough.

But would the package land on the airfield? Seton hoped so ... Because if the three-person team had to retrieve a piece of equipment from the boonies, it would be extremely vulnerable. However, it soon became evident that Seton's fears were baseless.

The package left the plane smoothly, the chutes deployed, and the loader landed yellow side up. The C-17 waggled its wings before executing a wide turn and heading south.

Where was the transport from anyway? Not the carrier in the Black Sea. It wasn't designed for that. A temporary base most likely. Or it could have been flown in from the U.S. thanks to in-air refueling. The fighters followed. And a good thing too. The Prax didn't put fighters up often, but the C-17 would make a tempting target.

"All right," Seton said. "Let's head out, crank that puppy up, and get to work. Mama wants to go home."

Omata was at the wheel as the van bumped over crick bodies and crows flapped into the air. Omata got out the moment they arrived and rushed to claim his new toy. "She's beautiful!" he proclaimed. "I'm in love!"

"We'll see if it starts," Brown said cynically. "Then we'll celebrate."

"Here's something for you, Madam President," Omata said from the driver's seat, as he dropped a sat phone to Seton. "I'll bet they want to talk to you."

A package containing three tac radios followed. Seton knew they would be critical for coordinating the team's efforts, and put her headset on. Various people *would* want to speak with her. But first things first.

Did the loader have a winch? Yes, thank God. Someone was thinking.

Seton turned to Brown as the Cat roared to life. She had to shout. "Work with Nick! Hook the winch cable to whatever he wants to pull."

Brown nodded and went to confer with Omata.

What I need is a vantage point, Seton decided. *A good overlook. And the control tower is the obvious choice.*

After arriving at the control tower, Seton hurried up to the observation deck. The Russian's body was gone. No surprise there.

Following a scan of the area for cricks, and seeing none, Seton brought the rifle's telescopic sight to bear on the area around the loader. It was in motion by then, backing and filling to get the right angle on a piece of fire-blackened wreckage. There were no bugs to be seen.

So, Seton dialed the number taped to the sat phone, and waited for an answer. It came quickly. And rather than an AI there was a woman on the line. "What's your favorite alcoholic beverage?"

"A gin and tonic. With lots of ice."

"How many pets do you own?"

"None."

"Who won the last Army-Navy game?"

"The Navy. They cheated."

The woman laughed "Please hold the line, Madam President... Secretary Jones is holding."

Seton heard a click followed by the familiar sound of Jones' voice. "Hello, Madam President, I understand you're hard at work refurbishing a Russian airbase."

"Omata and Brown are clearing the runway now," Seton replied. "Thanks for the loader."

"Anytime," Jones replied, "Although..."

"Yeah, I know. You told me not to go."

"I did," Jones agreed. "But that was then, and this is now. Assuming you manage to clear the runway, we'll pull you out of there today."

"What about Chittick, Brisson, Vakar and Min?"

"All of them arrived home safely," Jones told her. "Their planes weren't fired on. There's no way to be sure of course, but we think the Prax targeted you in particular, just like they did with the Russian ICBM."

"I'll bet the cricks have micro drones on some of the Xyfor ships," Seton replied. "What about the American public? Do they know?"

"Nope. The Vice President ordered us to keep the lid on. 'She'll be back soon.' That's what he said."

Seton saw movement on the opposite side of the field. "He's a good man, Morton. I have to go."

"Call two hours before you want a pickup," Jones told her. "We have to launch a Greyhound and fly it up from the Black Sea."

"Will do. I'll talk to you soon," Seton promised, before putting the phone in her pack.

A loud scraping noise was heard as Omata towed the remains of a helicopter toward the west side of the strip. And as Seton peered through her scope, she could see that three cricks were hiding in the bushes that lined the runway. *They're waiting for Omata to come closer,* Seton realized, as her heart began to beat faster. *Three targets, with a bolt action rifle, at something like a thousand yards. This could go badly.*

CHAPTER THIRTEEN

Khankala Airbase, Khankala, Russia

Seton's heart was pounding like a triphammer as her crosshairs floated over "Alien 1." A name she'd assigned to one of the three cricks hidden in the bushes lining the runway.

Judging from the airport's windsock, the breeze was blowing west to east, which meant she'd be firing straight into it. It was a long shot, from up high, so there was bullet drop to consider. Seton thumbed her radio. "Nick... Be advised that three cricks are hiding directly in front of you! I'm going to kill one, or try to, and the rest will probably shoot at you. Over."

"Roger that," Omata replied. "Isn't this relationship supposed to work the other way around?"

Seton couldn't help but smile, as she brought the crosshairs down to a point just above Alien 1, and took a deep breath. The rifle seemed to fire itself. She heard a loud report, the rifle thumped her shoulder, and the crick went down. Seton worked the bolt. A casing flew to the right. So far, so good.

But the process of working a second shell into the chamber pulled the weapon off Alien 2, and Seton was attempting to recenter it, when she heard two bursts of automatic fire. The remaining targets staggered and fell.

Seton moved the scope to the right and there, holding a drum-fed, light machine gun, was Carlie Brown. Ex-cheerleader,

English major, and sorority girl. The agent was standing next to the loader, scanning the area in front of her.

"Nice shooting, Carlie. Over." Brown clicked her mike twice.

As the agents returned to work Seton made it her business to scan the runway, start over, and do it again. Meanwhile Omata managed to complete the clearing effort by pushing the bullet riddled bus off the runway. Then he turned his attention to filling bomb craters with gravel from a bunker on the east side of the strip. There was a pile of sand too... For use during snowy winters.

Seton heard the eerie scream of engines, wondered why she hadn't been notified that fighters were incoming, and turned toward the sound. There were two aircraft. They had a tubby appearance. Like in a cartoon. But they weren't cartoons! They were Prax fighter planes, armed with energy weapons! The aircraft came in low, no more than a couple hundred feet off the ground, and fired orange-red blobs at the loader. A line of explosions marched by the yellow machine as the jets screamed past and began to turn. Seton yelled into her mike. "Drive the loader off the runway! Then run like hell!"

Seton's first fear was that Omata would be killed. Her second was that, if hit, the loader might block the strip. Seton was on the sat phone, waiting for someone to answer, when the Prax made a second approach. One was firing at her! *Holy shit*, Seton thought. *The cricks can see me via one of their drones, and they know who I am!*

Seton made for the stairs, and was racing down them, as blobs of plasma hit the top of the tower and slagged the com center. Pieces of fiery debris rained down as Seton circled the tower, tripped, and took a tumble. The ground came up hard. Pain stabbed Seton's right knee as she lurched to her feet. She tried to run but couldn't. So, she hobbled toward a revetment, and the plane parked there.

She had a minute, maybe two, in which to cross open ground and reach the relative safety of a concrete divider. Her breath came in gasps, the pain was excruciating, and the cartoon planes were only seconds away. *What a sad ass way to go,* she thought. *I had something less traumatic in mind.*

* * *

Creech Air Force Base, Nevada
Drone Pilot Rusty Richards, and his Sensor Operator Jan Olson, were bored. And no wonder. Their MQ-9 Reaper had been circling a Russian airbase for more than hour as three Americans cleared the runway.

Who were they? Richards didn't know. Why were they in Russia? Richards didn't know. But one thing was for sure, they were some tough motherfuckers. Cause no one else would be running an op in crick-occupied Russia.

Richards and Olson were seated side-by-side in high-backed chairs, with monitors to the left, right, and center of their U-shaped alcove.

"So," Richards said, as his eyes scanned the screens. "That's why we chose a pickup instead of an SUV. Just try cramming your dirt bike into an SUV."

Olson frowned. "I have one, no *two,* fast movers, approaching from the north."

Richards' heart began to beat faster. "Fast movers." Whose? Not Russians certainly … So, they must be American. Navy pilots off the *USS Gerald R. Ford* perhaps.

If so, he was definitely going to give them some shit, because the area around Khankala was a "no go" zone.

"They aren't ours," Olson announced. "The IFF (identification friend or foe) system doesn't recognize them."

That was the split second when the possibility of Prax planes first surfaced in Richards' mind. Sightings, never mind air-to-air combat with the cricks, was rare but not unknown.

"They're diving," Olson warned, "and opening fire."

Shit, shit, shit! Richards thought. *Something's going on…Something above my paygrade. But that doesn't matter. What matters is protecting the people on the ground.*

And Richards had the means to do that. Theoretically anyway, because the loadout on his included two Air-to-Air (ATAS) Stinger missiles. That was pure luck insofar as Richards knew, because Stingers were the exception, rather than the rule for recon missions. "Get on the horn," Richards instructed. "Give the chain of command a sitrep. Tell them that we're about to engage two Prax planes. Meanwhile, I'm going to line up for a shot."

As far as Richards could tell the crick pilots were unaware of the Reaper's presence. If so, that was at least partly due to the fact that the drone was circling at 15,000 feet, while the alien fighters were almost on the deck—lining up for another attack.

The standard ATAS had the same characteristics as the famous shoulder launched version, which was to say a fire and-forget guidance system, a 6.6-pound warhead, and a range of 5 miles. And that distance was, in Richard's judgement, his biggest challenge. Five miles was perfect for ground troops. But not in the air.

Richard's Reaper had a leisurely cruise speed of 194 mph, which was nothing, compared to the Prax fighters. But what was, was. Richards could hear Olson's voice in the background but tuned it out. His plan called for a spiraling dive, that would put his drone near the Russian base, just as the Prax planes passed from north to south. That was their pattern so far.

Hopefully the Stinger, which would be traveling at a speed of 1,700 mph, would lock onto the alien aircraft—and fly up its ass. *Boom!*

The plan worked. The spiral put the Reaper where Richards wanted it to be, the enemy plane arrived, and the Stinger took off. Then the Prax plane launched chaff, the dumb-assed Stinger chased it, and *blam!* One ATAS gone, with one remaining.

Richards felt a sense of despair. Even if he nailed one of the Prax fighters, the other one would be free to hunt the people on the ground, not to mention his Reaper. Which would be easy pickings. But Richards could turn a tighter circle than the fighters could, and attacked one of them head-on. And it was a good decision, because the oncoming fighter was hotter than the chaff trailing behind it, and the Stinger scored a direct hit!

Richards uttered a whoop of joy, as the Prax plane was suddenly transformed into a ball of orange-red flame, and a wing whirled through the air.

But the joy was short lived. Richards was out of ammo, plane number two was coming for him, and the people on the ground were vulnerable.

* * *

After a long, zigzagging run, Omata was almost to the building that housed Gribov's hideout, when a Prax plane exploded, creating a fireball over the south end of the runway.

What the hell? Who shot the fighter down? Or did it self-destruct?

There were no American aircraft to be seen or heard. Just the eerie scream of alien engines as the remaining fighter began another run.

Focus, Omata told himself, as he climbed the ladder and hurried from roof to roof. Where was POTUS? He didn't know. He could try the radio of course, but that would take time. Something Omata had very little of.

The crick bodies were still in the hall, and so was the smell as the agent entered the hideout, and went straight to the weapons closet. *Yes!* His memory was correct. Two shoulder- launched missile launchers were leaning in a corner.

But, were they loaded? Omata hoped so, and thought they would be, because a guy like Gribov would want to be ready. As for the rest of it, he'd have to rely on the Seabee motto: "Can Do."

With a launcher slung over each shoulder Omata returned to the roof, put the weapons down, and forced himself to concentrate. *If an eighteen-year-old conscript can fire one of these things, so can I,* Omata assured himself. *Take the end cap off. Fold the antenna up. A power supply? Check. A green indicator… That's promising. This control opens the sight. And that's the safety. As for this thing, that's the trigger, so be careful.*

Omata stood, took what he hoped was the right stance, and thumbed the safety. The screen lit up, and scenery appeared as he swiveled to the north.

"There you are," Omata said, as the Prax fighter entered his sight. "Eat this… From Russia with love."

Omata lurched as the missile took off, found what it was searching for, and homed in. There was a momentary blink of white light, followed by a *BOOM*, and an orange-red fireball. Fiery debris rained down on a housing development and set it ablaze.

Omata dropped the launcher and stood mesmerized by the extent of the damage he'd done. He looked up as two Navy F-35C fighters screamed overhead. The ex-Seabee nodded. *Airdales. Where the hell were you five minutes ago?*

* * *

Seton was leaning against a concrete divider. Her knee hurt like hell. She put the sat phone down. Brown was standing guard. "What did they say?"

"A Navy transport is 22 minutes out. Say what you will, but sailors come in handy at times."

Brown nodded. "That's right, especially if they're tall, dark, and handsome."

Both women laughed.

* * *

Portland Air National Guard Base, Portland, Oregon
Captain Lester Evans, and half of Charlie company, were on a C-17 and about to land in Portland, Oregon. *Why?* "Because you're in charge of weird shit missions."

That's what LT. Colonel Brock told Evans, prior to his departure from Holloman Air Force Base in New Mexico.

Being in charge of "weird shit missions" was a dubious honor, but indictive of the trust earned during the successful Carlsbad Cavern relocation.

Had Evans put the disastrous Silo Mission behind him? Yes, in the minds of others. But not in his dreams. So, what sort of challenge awaited him? He was about to find out.

There was a solid thump as the C-17 put down, followed by the usual chatter from the cockpit, and a fifteen-minute wait before the transport could taxi to the military part of the dual-purpose airport. The base was home to the 142nd Fighter Wing, better known as the "Redhawks," and didn't have transient quarters capable of handling a company of Marines. So, a hangar had been equipped with porta-potties, cots, and folding tables.

The balance of the day was spent moving in, and moving in *again*, as the rest of the company arrived. Dinner was supplied by three food trucks. An arrangement the Marines heartily approved of.

When morning rolled around the company's platoon sergeants put the Marines through the usual PT routine, followed by "preparations for a week in the field." Marines asked why, but no explanation was given. So, rumors flew.

Meanwhile Evans, his platoon leaders, and Gunny Ralph Hollis were loaded into a van and driven to a low-slung building. There the Marines showed their IDs to a man in civilian clothes, and passed through an EMP "toaster," which was supposed to kill Prax micro drones. Evans wondered how many he'd been carrying.

A young woman, also in civilian clothes, introduced herself as "Linda," and led the group down a gleaming corridor to "Conference Room C."

It was a medium-sized room set up theatre style with a flat screen, podium, and two rows of chairs. Three people were waiting to introduce themselves: Louis Orting, a professor from the University of Oregon, Dr. Sandra Fenton, an "Investigator" with the United States Geological Survey Department, and Army "Advisor" Colonel Homer Lasky.

It made for an interesting cast of characters, and Evans couldn't imagine what they were up to, or how they were connected. "Please have a seat," Professor Orting said, once the introductions were complete. He was dressed in sweater and slacks. A pair of glasses dangled from his neck. "Welcome to Oregon. I work for the University of Oregon's Department of Earth Sciences, and my specialty is geology. Please bear with me as I provide you with background information about Crater Lake."

Orting aimed a remote in the direction of the screen and a photo appeared. The image had been taken on a clear day, with snow-covered trees in the foreground, and a beautiful lake beyond. "You're looking at Crater Lake," Orting announced. "It's located in south-central Oregon. And it's famous for both its clarity and depth.

"The lake was formed about 7,700 years ago, by the collapse of a volcano called Mount Mazama, which created a 2,148-foot-deep caldera. A bowl if you will, which gradually filled with water. No rivers flow in or out of the lake. But snow and rain are sufficient to replace the water lost to evaporation."

What the heck? Evans felt as if he was back in college. Where was the presentation headed anyway?

"Finally," Orting added, "the lake is 1,949 feet deep, which makes it the deepest lake in the United States. It's home to a couple of small islands, neither of which is inhabited.

"And with that, I will hand the presentation off to Doctor Fenton."

Fenton had a pretty face, a shapely figure, and mocha colored skin. She smiled. "I'm going to share more facts, plus some theories, which I will identify as such.

"In the weeks following the crick emergence, scientists recovered the well-preserved body of a native American from a Prax meat locker. They named him Harry.

"Based on Carbon 14 dating, we know that Harry died about 12 thousand years ago, give or take. And that's the approximate time when modern humans arrived in the Americas.

"So, in order for Harry to wind up in a crick meat locker, the Prax had to be present 12,000 years ago. That's a fact."

Now we're getting somewhere, Evans thought. *But where does Crater Lake come in?*

"Based on drone surveillance," Fenton added, "we know that a Crick nest exists adjacent to, or possibly under the lake.

"We also know that a surface-to space (STS) plasma cannon located on or near the lake fired the bolt that struck President Seton's plane as she left a Xyfor warship. If you follow the news, you know that the president survived, landed in Russia along with a couple of Secret Service agents, and barely made it out.

"Three satellites observed the attack, and our friends at the NRO (National Reconnaissance Office) managed to get a fix on the cannon's location.

"Those are things we know," Fenton said. "What we *don't* know is whether the cricks were already in residence when the volcano erupted, or arrived thereafter, and hid themselves away. The second possibility seems more likely, but in the absence of proof, it remains a theory.

"Okay, now it's Colonel Lasky's turn. He'll be your link with the Army Special Operations Command. Colonel?"

Lasky reminded Evans of the Skeletor character from Masters of the Universe. The officer was tall, gaunt, and somewhat foreboding. He nodded to the Marines. "Good morning. By now you've concluded that you're here to deal with the Prax energy weapon, and whatever crickets happen to be in the area. That impression is correct.

"But understand this, the mission is to *capture* the cannon, not destroy it. *Why?* So, we can reverse engineer it. Something the Xyfor aren't likely to approve of, since we could use the technology to attack them."

Lasky's eyes roamed the faces in front of him. "Let me be clear ... We have no desire to fire the Prax cannon, or any other weapon, at the Xyfor. Rather, our goal is to protect Earth from any hostile species that might drop into orbit. And, after contact with *two* alien races, it's reasonable to assume that others exist."

Lasky said that for the Xyfors, Evans reasoned. *In case they managed to get a micro drone into the meeting. Here's hoping that they didn't.*

"Exactly how you accomplish the mission is up to you," Lasky added. "But consider this: The bastards are dug in, they have good Intel, and they know the terrain. So, it will be difficult if not impossible to sneak up on them. Okay, I'm sure you have questions. Shoot."

Lieutenant Riley raised his hand. "What, if anything, is at the bottom of the lake?"

"I'll take that one," Orting said, as he got to his feet. "During the summer of 1987 scientists spent 20 days studying Crater Lake's chemistry, biology, hydrology and geology.

"And while they collected all sorts of interesting data, they didn't report the presence of STS cannons—or any other artifacts for that matter."

Riley persisted. "Did they search the entire lake bottom?"

"No," Orting replied. "They didn't."

Evans raised his hand. "What about the surveillance mentioned earlier? Do we have a heat map? Showing clusters of activity?"

"Yes, we do," Fenton answered. "And that will be made available to you."

And so it went until all questions had been answered, and the meeting broke up. Evans took the opportunity to have a word with Colonel Lasky. "Sir, what kind of transportation will be available?"

"Whatever you need, son."

"How about a Black Hawk for starters? I'd like to insert a small team in, including myself, to reconnoiter."

Lasky grinned. His teeth looked like tombstones. "So, a team can follow some cricks home? And return with the rest of your company?"

"Yes, sir."

"That's a good idea. Colonel Brock is right. You *are* good at the weird shit."

***

Crater Lake National Park, Oregon
It was dark and thready clouds drifted across the face of the moon as the Sikorsky UH-60 Black Hawk helicopter came in low over the south end of the lake.

The helo's navigational lights were off, but nothing could conceal the roar of two turboshaft engines, and the distinctive *whop, whop, whop* sound that the Black Hawk's rotors produced. Evans and his six-person team were strapped in, amped up, and well aware of the risks. What was it Lasky said? "The bastards are dug in, they have good Intel, and they know the terrain."

That meant the cricks knew that a "meat" helicopter was in the area. But Evans had what he believed to be an app for that, which was to make an actual landing, followed by three more at various locations along the curvy 33-mile-long road that ran around the caldera.

Although he'd never used the tactic himself, Evans had read about it, and knew that fake landings were used to confuse the Viet Cong during the Vietnamese War.

"We're three out," the pilot announced, as the helicopter continued its decent. "Standby."

Evans said, "Let's make it quick...Ranger Canby will be on point."

Tom Canby was the sixty-something National Park Ranger, and retired Army noncom, who had volunteered to serve as their guide.

After working at Crater Lake for five years, and having studied the relevant Intel, Canby was well qualified to lead the team to the locations he thought were most promising. All of which were clustered along the south side of the caldera.

The gear touched down, and Canby was first out, quickly followed by Evans, Perez, Quigly, Sato, Owen and Gunnery Sergeant Hollis. Each member of the team was equipped with night vision gear, a radio headset, and two suppressed weapons. The goal was to reach three heat targets, evaluate each, and exfil without making contact. Assuming the team was successful, the Intel would be used to plan a company strength attack, with the goal of capturing a functional STS cannon.

Gunnery Sergeant Hollis' boots were barely on the ground when the helo started to rise. It passed in front of the moon, before speeding east, and the first fake landing.

Canby led the team off the highway, over a knee-high rock wall, and into the scrub beyond. Trails were dangerous for all sorts of reasons, including the possibility of encountering a crick patrol, or triggering an IED.

It made sense to go slow and use GPS devices to navigate. There was very little conversation and that was no accident. "Keep your eyes open and your mouth shut." That's what Hollis said, and it was good advice.

Moonlight reflected off the lake and shimmered as gentle swells rolled in from the west. That was when Evans noticed a large bird, with its wings spread, riding the wind. Except it wasn't a bird. It was cricket! A lookout? Triggered by the helo? Evans thought so. "This is Six. Airborne scout at ten o'clock! Down. Over."

The team went prone. And remained in that position for five long minutes before the alien banked toward the north and disappeared. Evans felt a sense of relief. "This is Six. On your feet. Move out. Over." It took the better part of ten minutes to reach Objective 1, which was adjacent to Chaski Bay, and not far from the tiny island called the "Phantom Ship."

"This is Four," Canby whispered. "We're close. Be careful. We're going to traverse a steep slope. If you lose your footing you'll wind up in the lake. Over."

A flurry of double clicks served to acknowledge the transmission.

Rocks *rattled* as the team traversed the slope. "There," Canby whispered. "The heat source is straight ahead." That was fine, except for the fact that Evans couldn't see any sign of heat through his thermal imaging binoculars. He lowered them. "Five will set security while I go forward to take a closer look."

Evans knew that would piss Hollis off, because it was something a private could theoretically do, but he felt the need to assess the situation himself.

The officer placed each boot with care as he crept forward. A ledge appeared, with evergreens all around, and a dark spot centered between them. What was it?

Evans was about to investigate when he heard the *whup, whup, whup* of wings, and a cricket landed on the ledge. A hatch irised open, heat blossomed, and the alien shuffled forward. Then it disappeared.

CHAPTER FOURTEEN

Crater Lake National Park, Oregon

Evans felt a rising sense of excitement. The cricks were there, right where they were supposed to be, which meant the cannon was nearby. But *where?*

It certainly wasn't out in the open where drones, planes or satellites could "see" it. That suggested the weapon was underground, and possibly co-located with a nest.

Or, as Fenton had suggested, the cannon could be at the bottom of the lake. However, that would require firing up through nearly 2,000 feet of water. And, according to what Evans had been able to find online, shooting bolts of plasma up through the lake was likely to be ineffective, or even dangerous. Although human scientists didn't know for sure.

As Evans began to back away, he was careful to find solid footing. He was halfway to the rest of the team, when *another* flying crick landed on the ledge. Evans waited for the alien to enter the hab before resuming his slow-motion journey.

Once back with the team, Evans delivered a terse summary. "We're right on top of, or next to, a nest. It's time to eyeball Objectives 2 and 3. Four has the point."

Canby led the Marines up-slope. Their movements triggered miniature landslides. And, as loose scree slid away from under Corporal Quigly's boots, he fell. The marine was skidding toward the lake when Hollis grabbed him. "You owe me a cold one."

"Roger that," Quigly replied. "Over."

Hollis would have stepped on that sort of exchange had someone else been guilty of it. But RHIP. Evans grinned.

"This is Four," Canby announced. "We're getting close. Whoa! I think we're there…I can feel warm air coming up out of the ground."

Evans made his way forward, and sure enough, a column of warm air was flowing up through a pile of rocks. He knelt, and with help from Canby, cleared the loose rocks off a metal grate. An air vent was revealed. And that made sense. A nest would require ventilation.

"Give me a hand, Tom," Evans whispered. "Let's see if we can remove the grating."

By working together, the men managed to lift the grating out of its frame and put it aside. Once that was accomplished Evans asked Sato to come forward. "Send your toy down the shaft, Private. Let's see what's down there."

The Black Hornet Nano drone was small enough to sit on the palm of Sato's hand, and could feed live video to an iPad-sized display.

The drone produced a *whirring* noise as it took off, hovered over the vent, and disappeared. Evans crouched next to Sato. The drone had three cameras. One looked forward, one was pointed down at 45 degrees, and the third peered straight down.

That was the one that produced the most useful information, and allowed Sato to avoid the walls. A greenish glow could be seen, and it grew brighter, as the Hornet dropped toward a second grating. Was it secured? Evans couldn't tell. For planning purposes, he would assume that it was. A corridor was visible below the grating, and Evans watched as cricks passed in both directions. "Okay," Evans said. "Bring it up. We have what we need."

After retrieving the drone, and replacing both the grating and the rocks, the team followed Canby north. The slope was steep, and it was necessary to navigate around two clusters of trees before approaching Objective 3.

Like Objective 2, three consisted of a grating through which warm air was passing. Rather than spend the time required to remove the grate, and send the drone down, Evans opted to start the exfil. The sky had begun to lighten in the east, and he wanted to get the team out before the sun rose.

Canby led the Marines east, zigzagging back and forth, as they climbed the steep slope. Evans knew the highway was up there waiting for them, and was tempted to summon the Black Hawk. But caution won out. *Don't assume*, Evans told himself. *Secure the LZ. Then call for the helo.*

Canby was near the top when he spoke. "This is Four. I see four crickets, no, make that three humans and a cricket. All headed north. The cricket is on a leash. Over."

What the hell? Evans hurried to reach the top, and arrived just in time to watch three humans pass by, the last of whom was towing a cricket tied to a rope! The alien's shuffling gait made it hard for it to keep up. That was when Canby stood. And, like the cop he was, gave an order. "National Park Service! Drop your weapons and raise your hands!"

The humans turned toward the sound of Canby's voice, raised their weapons, and opened fire. The rest of the team was present by that time. "Don't kill them!" Evans shouted. "Take them alive!"

But his words came too late. Two humans went down. The third dropped the rope and tried to run. Canby jumped over the side rail that marked the edge of the road and gave chase.

Evans went after the cricket. The last thing they needed was for the bug to reach the local nest and report in. The cricket couldn't run, not the way humans did, but it could hop! And, each time Evans was about to grab the trailing rope, the leash was jerked beyond his reach.

Finally, knowing that the Prax was going to escape, Evans raised his M27 and fired a burst. The weapon's suppressor reduced the sound of gunfire to a clacking sound. The crick stumbled and fell. Evans went forward to fire another bullet into the alien's head prior to calling for the Black Hawk. Then he went looking for Canby. The Ranger had a scruffy looking man in custody, and was reading his rights. A courtesy which earned Canby a "Fuck you!"

Evans ordered Sato to guard the prisoner and took Canby aside. "What the hell were you thinking? I thought you were in the Army."

"I *was* in the Army," Canby said defensively. "But I'm a Ranger now … And Rangers are law enforcement officers."

The Marine shook his head in disgust. "Stay away from the prisoner. Keep your mouth shut. And do as you're told."

Evans wanted to interrogate the prisoner, but knew he didn't have time, as the roar of helicopter engines was heard. The Marines used wands to guide it in.

Once the Black Hawk landed, there was a rush to load the dead crick and human prisoner, prior to takeoff. Evans heaved a sigh of relief. The team had gone in and come out without losing any lives, or making contact with the Prax.

Yeah, his inner voice said. *But that was nothing. The hard part is up ahead.*

***

The White House, Washington D.C.

"A mild dislocation of the knee cap." That's what the doctor on the *USS Gerald R. Ford* called it, and the staff at the Walter Reed National Military Medical Center in D.C. agreed.

So there Seton was, sitting in a wheelchair with one leg extended, as a military aide wheeled her into the Situation Room.

Everyone stood and clapped. "Welcome back, Madam President," Secretary of State Bowes said. "We missed you."

"Please be seated," Seton replied. "I'm sorry about all the fuss. How are my heroic Secret Service agents doing?"

"They're fine," Chief of Staff Roy Jenkins answered. "And, according to them, you walk on water."

"Fall down stairs is more like it," Seton said, as she patted her leg. "So, what have you got for me?"

"A super-sized version of the PDB (President's Daily Brief)," the Director of National Intelligence replied. Reardon was short, balding, and had a fondness for bolo ties.

"Good," Seton said. "Lay it on me."

Reardon nodded. "Let's begin with the big-big picture. The planet's pre-Prax population was roughly 7.8 billion people. The estimated post emergence population is presently somewhere in the neighborhood of 5 billion. Exact figures are impossible to come by.

"The CIA believes that as things stand now, and with continued assistance from the Xyfor, humanity has a 53.2 percent chance of survival."

"That's good," Seton commented. "I thought we might be in trouble."

That produced some chuckles and Reardon smiled. "Fifty-three point two beats the hell out of forty-eight point nine, which is where we were a few weeks ago. So, the trend is in the right direction. Now, let's go to Mexico."

Drone video rolled on the main screen. Crickets flying over a town somewhere in Mexico. As the aliens fired down, humans fired *up*, and a bug lost a wing. It spiraled out of control, and landed in the middle of a street, where men with machetes hacked it apart.

"What you're looking at," Reardon said, "is a battle between the Prax, and members of the Guadalajara Cartel. As far as the cartel is concerned the cricks are just another gang trying to muscle in on their territory. Other gangs are battling the bugs too… And, taken together, they're helping to keep the lid on south of the border."

"That isn't the case in Central America," Reardon added, as the battle footage dissolved to a map of Central America. The countries of Guatemala, El Salvador, Costa Rica, Honduras, Nicaragua and Panama have all been overrun. And based on computer projections, we believe the crick population is growing, which could force a break out."

Reardon's eyes swept the faces around him. "South America is next on the list. For the purposes of this briefing, I'm going to focus on Brazil, which is home to half the continent's population." The map was replaced by drone footage of the Amazon River.

"Even though Brazil has suffered heavy casualties," Reardon continued, "the situation there is better than one might expect. It's important to remember that just under three million square miles of the Amazon floodplain is submerged each year.

"And, because the cricks aren't physiologically equipped for aquatic environments, they've been forced to nibble around the edges—no pun intended. That has encouraged millions of Brazilians to seek refuge in the jungle.

"That's the good news. The bad news is that the refugees are doing irreparable damage to the Amazonian ecosystem."

"And this isn't the only place where climate and the environment are helping us out," Reardon added. "In the same way that the Prax aren't adapted to watery environments, they aren't adapted to cold weather either, so people in the Nordic countries are under less pressure than would otherwise be the case. That said, predation tends to spike when the weather is good, and the bugs attack from every direction."

Reardon turned to look at Seton. "Regarding Russia, well, as the president can attest, the population has been decimated—leaving partisans and bandits to battle over scraps. Even if we manage to defeat the Prax, it will be a long time before Russia can reconstitute itself."

A map of Europe appeared on the main screen. "As for Europe," Reardon said, "I'm happy to report that thanks to the EU and NATO, our European friends are functioning on a par with the U.S. "Meanwhile," Reardon continued, "thanks to its small footprint, and it's forceful response to the Prax awakening, Israel is nearly crick free."

Drone footage of Jerusalem dissolved into a vast vista of rolling dunes. "That brings us to North Africa," Reardon told them. "And the Arab states. Even though the Prax can tolerate extreme heat, deserts are lightly populated, and make for poor hunting grounds. So, most of the predation occurs elsewhere. Countries like Egypt, Nigeria, Ethiopia, Congo, and South Africa are examples of that."

The video dissolved to footage of war-torn China. Seton saw the National Stadium, as the drone cruised over Beijing, A facility she had visited years earlier. There was nothing but devastation all around it. "Like Russia," Reardon said, "China's top-down authoritarian government was slow to respond to the crick emergence, and the country's citizens paid a horrendous price. But, unlike Russia, islands of humanity exist, all controlled by self-appointed warlords.

"India is a different case entirely," Reardon announced. "India's population is in excess of one-point-four billion people. And rather than attack the country, the Prax treat India like a farm from which they harvest an estimated 65,000 people a day. That's roughly equivalent to the country's birthrate. And we believe that's the model the bugs hope to duplicate worldwide."

Seton could imagine the fear, the chaos and the sorrow. She spoke for the first time. "We must win! For them and for ourselves." Faces were grim, and heads nodded.

"Bear with me," Reardon said. "We're almost done. As many of you know the North Koreans saw the emergence as the perfect opportunity to attack South Korea.

"But the Prax had plans for South Korea's fifty-one million citizens, so they launched a counter attack, and slagged every missile silo the north had. There was no point in fleeing north into Russia, or west into China, so the North Koreans had to stay and fight.

"Meanwhile, down south, the South Koreans, with help from our troops and the Mechans, are holding their own.

"Finally, in what can only be described as an ironic twist, Brunei, Myanmar, Cambodia, Indonesia, Laos, Malaysia, Singapore, Thailand, Vietnam and the Philippines found a way to stymie the Prax. Their cultures embrace foods considered to be exotic elsewhere, including scorpions, tarantulas, and grasshoppers. So, adding cricks to the menu wasn't much of a stretch."

That produced nervous laughter and expressions of disgust.

Reardon smiled. "Yeah, me too. But, according to the experts, chitin is a good source of insoluble fiber, and provides prebiotic properties to the gut flora.

"And although insect muscle tissue has an astringent quality, all it takes is some sweet and sour sauce to cover that up. That's why every man, woman and child in Southeast Asia is eager to find crickets and kill them."

Seton frowned. "What would happen if we encouraged citizens to kill and eat Prax? Would it shorten the war? Or cause additional problems? It seems to me that plenty of things could go wrong if civilians hunt cricks en masse. Let's assemble a multidisciplinary team to look into it."

Jenkins nodded. "I'll get to work."

"That's a wrap," Reardon said. "Except for one thing... We have a fix on the Surface-to-Space energy cannon the enemy used to destroy the president's plane. And we're going to capture it."

Seton's eyebrows rose. "And copy it?"

There was no humor in Reardon's smile. "Yes, Madam President. And we're going to copy it."

* * *

Crater Lake National Park, Oregon

"About a week ago I saw a flash of light, followed by what sounded like the crack of doom. That's the sound my daddy said we'll hear on Judgement Day! I damned near shit my pants."

That's what bounty hunter Jessie Elias told investigators, after being arrested, and flown to Portland. According to Elias he and his companions were licensed bounty hunters who, for five hundred bucks per head, were willing to go where most people wouldn't, which was "straight into Crick Town." Except that now, after resisting arrest, and firing at Canby—Elias was going to jail.

Had Elias and his buddies been witnesses to the attempt on Seton's life? Not to mention those of her bodyguards? Evans believed they had.

But where was the STS cannon? The obvious answer was somewhere adjacent to the nest at or near the south end of Crater Lake. So, with permission from Colonel Lasky, Charlie Company was going to land on the highway that circled the lake. That would put one hundred and ten Marines on the ground.

Three platoons would attack. The 1st platoon was going after the entrance identified earlier, while the 2nd and 3rd platoons were slated to enter the nest via the heat vents. All three had identical orders: "Kill the cricks, find the cannon, and secure it."

Meanwhile the headquarters platoon was to secure the LZ—and serve as a quick reaction force if necessary. Additional protection was available from a Reaper drone circling above, and the F-15 Eagles flying top cover, in case Prax planes came out to play.

Evans felt the gear touch down, heard the Chinook's crew chief yelling "Out! Out! Out!" and followed the 1st platoon down the ramp. Since there hadn't been any groundfire thus far, Evans wasn't expecting any resistance on the road, and that assumption proved to be correct. A sure sign that the Prax had no advance knowledge of the attack. That was a big break.

But given all the noise, it was logical to assume that the bugs knew about the landings and were on the way. Each platoon included a Marine who had taken part in the scouting mission.

Quigly was in the two slot, right behind the point man, as the 1st platoon left the road and headed downslope. Evans was six Marines back. He thumbed his radio. "Bandanna, this is Six. It's time to knock on the door. Over."

The Reaper operator was more than a thousand miles away, sipping coffee. She put the mug down. "Roger that, Six. Standby… Over."

The plan was to hit the entrance to the nest with an AGM-114 Hellfire missile, destroy the hatch, and kill any cricks who happened to be there.

But because planners feared that explosions might cause the heat vents to collapse, they were left untouched. Evans heard a loud *BOOM*, and saw a flash of light downslope. "No need to say thanks," Bandanna said. "You're welcome. Over."

Blobs of fire shot up from the rocky area below and a Marine went down. Revenge came swiftly. The Marines were wearing night vision goggles, which meant they could see the alien heat signatures, and target them.

Bugs began to die as grenades rolled, bounced, and exploded. Shrapnel flew in every direction. The explosions caused the defensive fire to slacken, but put the Marines at risk too. "This is Charlie-Seven," Yamada yelled. "Belay the grenades!"

Evans wanted to see the entrance. Had the air to ground missile done enough damage for the Marines to enter? He hoped so. The faster they could get inside the better. Any pause, even for sixty seconds, would give the Prax time to strengthen their defenses.

Rocks slid and clattered as the Marines turned north and began to cut across the slope. Firing could be heard in the distance, as the 2nd and 3rd platoons began to close on the vents, and prepared to rappel down.

Someone yelled, "Take cover!" when an automatic weapon fired from the entrance. The barrier was gone, and a tripod-mounted plasma gun had been positioned there to defend the entry and the nest beyond. "This is Six," Evans said, "Put a LAW rocket on that weapon! Over."

The shoulder-launched, anti-armor weapon was ideal for the short-range situation. The rocket flew straight and true, hit the pulse weapon, and blew it to smithereens. Evans led the charge. "Follow me!"

Evans felt light headed, as he ran uphill and scrambled onto the ledge. Cricks were elbowing each other out of the way in their eagerness to go forth and harvest some fresh meat.

Evans fired his M27 IAR and killed one of them. A second alien tripped when a round severed its left leg, and it collapsed. Evans fired again.

A Marine yelled, "Grenade!" as he fired a round from his M32A1 rotary grenade launcher. It flew through the entrance to explode in the chamber beyond.

Evans saw a flash followed by a muffled explosion, and marched forward, shooting every crick he saw living or dead. The officer heard chitin crack as he stepped on a body and kept going. The entrance was connected to a tunnel whose walls were covered with patches of green slime. Someone yelled, "Tunnel Rats!" And another voice responded with, "Oorah!"

Things were going well thus far. But then the Marines entered a chamber that reminded Evans of the Big Room in Carlsbad Cavern. The ceiling was so high that there were galleries above. Spots sent beams of light back and forth cross the space.

Some were positioned to light a huge artifact that was partially embedded in what had been a lava flow thousands of years earlier. At first glance Evans thought the object was a plane. But where were the wings? Could it be a spaceship?

Suddenly all extraneous thoughts were washed from the officer's mind as flying cricks launched themselves off rocky balconies, snipers fired from ledges, and other bugs dropped plasma grenades from the galleries. A Marine danced inside a column of fire, his mouth open, as he attempted to scream.

Evans dropped to the ground and looked for cover. The possibilities included an outcropping that would offer protection from the fliers, a pile of cargo containers that could be used as a fortress, and a stationary tunneling machine.

To Yamada's credit, he saw the same things, and gave the necessary orders. Marines ran, and in many cases crawled, as they sought to reach cover.

Evans saw at least half a dozen members of the 1st platoon fall, and knew that if he called for reinforcements, the other platoons weren't likely to arrive quickly enough.

There was one possibility however, and that was the double-barreled pulse weapon which was positioned to fire on the entry, but was currently inactive. And no wonder, because based on appearances, the cannon's gunner had been killed while trying to reach its weapon.

Confident that Yamada was providing the right kind of leadership, Evans lurched to his feet, and ran a zigzag course toward the gun. Projectiles kicked up puffs of dust all around him, as Yamada yelled, "Covering fire! Protect the captain!"

M27s clattered as they fired short bursts, and Hollis yelled, "Smoke! On that cannon!" Smoke billowed as grenades arced through the air, landed, and rolled.

The artificial fog made all the difference. The Prax had to fire blindly as Evans skidded to a stop. Was the gun operational? Could he figure out how to fire it?

Those were the questions Evans pondered as he sat down on the awkward T-shaped seat, and eyed the controls. It appeared that extra-large foot pedals were used to traverse the weapon.

After reaching forward to grab two pistol grips, Evans discovered that he could elevate and depress the energy cannon's power-assisted barrels by tilting the hand controls up and down. Strands of gray smoke drifted past him as Evans pulled both triggers. He felt the weapon tremble when parallel lines of blue energy shot out and carved glowing red lines across a rock face.

But equally important, if not more so, was the shimmering, bubble-shaped force field which sprang into existence around him!

It produced a *buzzing* sound. And what looked like sparks flew, as enemy projectiles struck the protective dome. Evans uttered a war whoop then went to work.

By tilting the grips, he was able to point the twin barrels up toward the cavern's ceiling. Each flying crick was represented by a blob of green light on the oval screen in front of him. All Evans had to do was place the electronic crosshairs on a target and press both triggers to destroy it.

Evans heard a reedy cheer as dead cricks began to rain down, each landing with a *thump*. Then it was time for the officer to switch his attention to the galleries, and the cricks firing down from up there. The cannon began to traverse as Evans stepped on the left pedal, and blue death probed the nooks and crannies above.

Dozens of aliens directed their fire at the captured cannon. The force field shimmered, but held, so Evans continued to fire with impunity. *Thank God they weren't able to turn this thing loose on us*, Evans thought. *First the spaceship, now this. The nerds will have a field day.*

All of which was fine except for one thing... Their actual mission was to capture the STS cannon used to fire on the president of the United States. That meant the job wasn't done.

The 2nd and 3rd platoons arrived through lava tubes shortly thereafter and slaughtered the aliens on the ground level. Evans was about to have a face-to-face with his direct reports when a breathless radio operator arrived. "Captain! Did you get the message?"

Evans frowned. "*What* message?"

"The STS cannon, sir. It blew the Reaper and the F-15s out of the sky!"

***

The Candelaria Caves, in Guatemala

Prime didn't have emotions as such. But it could process a sense of completion. And in this case that was the capture of the new Terrorism Confinement Center in Tecoluca, El Salvador. The country with the highest incarceration rate in the world.

In fact, according to information provided by the meat media, almost 2 percent of El Salvador's population were being held in various prisons—or what Prime thought of as "meat lockers."

But the older prisons were nothing compared to the *new* facility which was home to 40,000 inmates. And now, after a well-executed assault, the confinement center's human staff had been replaced by Prax soldiers—thereby converting the prison into a farm.

So long as a steady stream of breeder females were introduced into the largely male farm, the Prax would be assured of a reliable source of protein for years to come. Similar to India, only on a smaller scale.

That was important in and of itself. But it was also part of a larger plan. After establishing food security for the region, Prime was increasingly free to focus its attention on North America. That was the area in which thousands of Prax had already been killed each day *before* the Mechans landed. Even more were dying now as a result of the Xyfor-Human alliance.

Initially it had been Prime's intention to selectively assassinate the north's leaders. A strategy which had been successful elsewhere. But that plan had been repeatedly frustrated. Vanessa Seton was still alive. So now, rather than continue to make the same mistake, Prime was going to use brute force. And, thanks to the givers, the bioelectronic computer had the hundreds of thousands of soldiers required to implement the new strategy.

In order to overwhelm the North American meats, Prime had to move its horde into position. But *how*? The meats and their robotic allies controlled the sky.

The answer was *La Bestia* (The Beast), also known as *El Tren de la Muerte* (The Death Train). Pre-emergence Guatemalans had used the train to reach the U.S. border.

By adding engines and cars sourced from Mexico, the new Prime calculated that it could move five thousand soldiers and functionaries a day up into the contested zone. And that, the Prax leader concluded, would be more than sufficient to turn the tide.

Would the drug cartels try to stop the trains? Not so long as Prax soldiers stayed aboard them. In fact, it was possible that the

Mexican gangs would approve of the invasion, hoping that the Prax assault would weaken the United States.

Prime allowed itself to sink thereby exposing its permeable surface area to the liquid nutrients it thrived on. A decision had been made. Victory would follow.

CHAPTER FIFTEEN

Crater Lake National Park, Oregon

The stench of formic acid permeated the air, isolated gunshots signaled the "cleanup" that Gunny Hollis insisted on, and a Marine babbled nonsense while a corpsman bandaged his leg.

Evans struggled to focus his thoughts as a radio operator stared at him.

According to the message just received from the headquarters platoon, the STS cannon had surfaced at the south end of the lake. That meant the weapon had been there all along, sitting on the bottom, ready for use. "Go outside Corporal, get a Chinook pilot on the horn, and tell 'em to standby for takeoff. Go."

"Yes, sir!" The operator took off at a run.

Evans hollered, "Hollis!" and the gunny appeared.

"Sir?"

"Give me your best squad. We're going to capture a cannon."

Hollis grinned. "Yes, sir!"

Evans gave hurried orders to the company's XO, First Lieutenant Lester Russo. "Set up your HQ here, send patrols out to explore the tunnels, and tell them to collect any Intel they come across. Oh, get lots of photos of whatever that big thing is. I have a feeling the nerds are going to love it. I should be in touch soon. If not, take command, and do whatever you can to complete the original mission. Understood?"

Russo nodded. "Got it."

Evans turned to Hollis. "Lead the way, Gunny ... And hurry."

After exiting the nest, they battled their way upslope, to the road where a Chinook was waiting. Engines roared as the rotors turned. Evans went forward to speak with the pilot. "A Surface to Space cannon is out on the lake. Take us there, and hover while we rope down. Go in low or that thing will blow us out of the sky."

"Roger that," the pilot replied. "Weapons free? Or gunners tight?"

"Tight," Evans answered grimly. "We have orders to capture the damned thing, not destroy it." Evans returned to the cargo area to find that his Marines were preparing to rappel. Hollis was moving from one person to the next checking gear.

Evans hurried to gear up as the Chinook took off, swooped down over the lake, and flew toward a target he couldn't see.

Less than three minutes later the helicopter slowed to a hover. The downward pressure from the rotors forced the waves to flatten. Evans' first look at the cannon was from the Chinook's rear ramp. The helo's belly lights were on, and the aircraft was so low, that every detail of the scene was visible. That included a gun barrel wrapped with what might have been cooling coils, the housing the weapon was attached to, and the hull below.

The cannon was mounted on a submarine! Why was the vessel still on the surface? There was a flash of light, followed by a deafening *BOOM*, as the cannon fired.

It was, Evans realized, a desperate attempt to destroy the Chinook. But the pulse missed the helo, raced up through the atmosphere, and disappeared.

"Follow me!" Hollis yelled, as he backed off the ramp and started to descend. The rest of the squad followed. Evans was last.

Fifteen or twenty cricks were firing up at the humans who couldn't respond effectively until they arrived on the deck below. Two Marines were hit. One fell, and the other continued to dangle, as the Chinook turned away.

Evans was off his rope, but was caught flat footed when a crick hopped into the air, and kicked him. He landed on his back. The officer struggled to recover as the alien lifted a gleaming short sword up over its head. Evans attempted to bring his rifle up to block the blade. But the process seemed to take forever. Then he heard a gunshot, and felt the resulting blood mist, as the bug collapsed. Hollis bent to offer a hand.

As Evans stood, he realized that the sub was sinking! Frigid water was starting to overtop his boots. "Don't worry," Hollis told him. "Rawlings is about to blow the hatch. Then we'll shut this hummer down."

That sounded good ... But would it work? The sub's controls weren't likely to include a glowing on-off switch.

Rawlings yelled, "Fire in the hole!" and Evans heard a *ka-thump* as the charge detonated. Someone shouted "We're in!" and shots were fired as the Marines entered the sub's control room. The water was higher by then, *much* higher, and Evans was about to summon the Chinook when the situation changed. "We've stopped sinking," Hollis remarked. "One of our lads found a way to shut it down."

Maybe. But there was a second possibility as well—chances were that the sub's computer wouldn't allow it to submerge while the hatch was open. Not that it mattered, so long as the gun platform continued to float.

"We've got to get this thing to a beach," Evans said, as he freed his radio. "Three-Two, this is Six. We have control of the platform, and we need a tow. Can do? Over."

"Roger that, Six," the pilot replied. "Hold on while we check to see if we have the right length of cable. Over."

The answer, when it came was "no." They didn't have the right length. But, by connecting two cables together the Chinook's crew managed to create a tether long enough to do the job.

The sun was rising by the time the sub was towed to a tiny beach where national guard troops were waiting. They hurried to cover the cannon with camouflage netting.

Colonel Lasky was there to greet Evans as he waded ashore. "Well done, Captain … It's going to be a bitch to hoist that thing up to the road. But hey, what are engineers for? What's this I hear about a spaceship?"

"It might be a spaceship," Evans replied cautiously. "Or it might not. But whatever it is got caught in the lava flow that Fenton told us about. What was that? Seven thousand years ago?"

"Give or take," Lasky replied. "So, it seems safe to assume that the cricks had an underground base way back then. All of this is top secret, Captain. Please make sure that your Marines understand that."

Evans nodded. "Sir, yes sir. Is my company going to remain here? Or, are we slated for something else?"

Lasky's expression darkened. "You and your leathernecks deserve a rest, but you aren't going to get one. Something like a hundred thousand Prax entered Mexico during the last forty-eight hours, and they're coming our way. The 2nd Battalion 1st Marines is one of the units that was sent to stop the bastards. Colonel Brock wants you back."

***

Washington D.C. The White House

President Vanessa Seton had been in the Situation Room for sixteen hours. After breaking out of Central America the Prax horde was surging north. And Seton was watching the carnage live. After overrunning the state of Chiapas, the aliens were approaching east-west Highway 185, recently dubbed the "Red Line."

That spot had been chosen because Mexico was only 124 miles wide at that point. And with the Gulf of Mexico on one side, and the Gulf of Tehuantepec on the other, it was a natural choke point. The Pentagon believed that the topology could make an important difference. It didn't. Seton could see thousands of aliens. No, hundreds of thousands!

The drone hovered above a company of Rangers and turned its camera south as a tidal wave of crick soldiers advanced on the American line.

The aliens didn't have any aircover, which left human and Mechan aircraft free to bomb and strafe them. Explosions obliterated hundreds of Prax. Cluster munitions killed thousands. And missiles streaked in to destroy their improvised vehicles. None of it mattered.

Like molecules of mercury the cricks oozed together to fill the holes in their ranks as *more* bugs hopped off trains, arrived on human trucks, or flew in from the south.

And there the company of Rangers stood, resolute in the face of the alien horde, which broke around them like the surf hitting a rock. "Watch out!" Seton said out loud. "They're going to flank you!" And the cricks *did* flank Americans, overran them, and hurried to feed. Seton began to cry.

A rumpled Secretary of Defense Morton Jones was seated at Seton's side. "We need to pull back, Madam President. And do so right away. If we don't, we'll suffer a defeat in detail."

Seton knew that Morton meant the Prax would be able to defeat the newly isolated units one by one. She wiped the tears away. "You're right Mort... We'll retreat to a point just short of Mexico City. Order our LAR Battalions and Stryker teams to fight a delaying action. Notify the Xyfor and what remains of the Mexican government."

Morton said, "Yes, ma'am," and turned to a two-star general. Orders began to flow.

Seton closed her eyes in hopes that the scenes of death and destruction would vanish. They didn't.

* * *

Aeropuerto Internacional, Mexico

So urgent was the need to get military personnel and equipment down to Mexico, that civilian aircraft had been pressed into service. That's why Charlie company was flying on an Alaska Airlines Boeing 737 MAX. The pilot spoke over the intercom. "We'll be landing at Aeropuerto Internacional in ten minutes. Please secure your seat belts and check to make sure that you have your belongings. You will deplane through the front door. May God bless and protect you."

Did the pilot think that the Marines were going to die? That's how it sounded. And, according to the scuttlebutt, that was a distinct possibility. The situation was, according to even the most optimistic news reports, bleak.

The company's orders were to join the 2nd of the 1st which was dug in on the historic Chapultepec Hill (Hill of the Grasshopper). A site which had been the scene of a last-ditch effort by 5,000 Mexican defenders to prevent U.S. forces under General Winfield Scott from capturing the castle that topped the hill.

According to Marine Corps lore the red stripe—that adorned the dress trousers of officers and noncoms—was commonly referred to as the "blood stripe." And was intended to commemorate the high number of officers and NCOs killed while storming the castle of Chapultepec in 1847. A hand-to-hand battle that led to a historic victory for the Americans. Could the Marines win again? Evans hoped so.

The plane thumped down. As it taxied to the terminal Evans saw all manner of aircraft waiting to load or unload. Airport tugs hurried this way and that, each towing trailers loaded with supplies, as columns of camo-clad soldiers snaked across the tarmac.

The Americans had to wait for fifteen minutes to exit the plane. This was followed by an hour-long delay before the Marines could collect their gear. How would they reach Chapultepec? That was anything but obvious.

Much to Evans' relief a second lieutenant appeared, came to attention, and delivered a smart salute. "Welcome to Mexico, Captain. My name is Christian Ramirez. Major Folsom sent me to secure your transportation and serve as a guide. It looks like you're ready to roll."

Evans returned the salute. "We're ready, thank you. What have you got for us?"

"Buses," Ramirez replied. "They were imprisoned in a parking lot surrounded by a fence. But, after negotiating with some security guards, my squad was able to liberate them." It was said with a grin.

"Well done, lieutenant. Please lead the way."

A line of bright red buses, all wearing the letters ADO, were waiting outside, each with a Marine driver. "Only one of my guys has driven a bus before," Ramirez confessed. "But we made it here."

Charlie company had been reduced to 226 Marines by then. But it was still going to require 5 buses and a flatbed truck to move the leathernecks and their gear. Loading began. "So, is this a combat zone?" Evan inquired.

"Mexico City is infested with cricks," Ramirez replied. "But they went to ground recently. Captain Chan figures they'll resurface when their army arrives." Chan was the battalion's intelligence officer.

"And when will that occur?" Evans wanted to know.

"It's hard to say exactly," Ramirez answered. "The crick Army doesn't carry MREs. So, they pause to eat when they find food."

Evans winced. It made sense. Kill humans, advance, eat and repeat. Did the bugs sleep? Probably. It was a very inefficient way to run an army. But, given tens of thousands of mindless soldiers, it would work.

Once the buses were loaded the convoy left the airport. The sun was high in the sky. And what Evans saw through a dusty window was far from pretty. Trash littered the streets. Ground level windows were shattered. Blackened store fronts signaled fires. Bullet-riddled cars squatted on flat tires. Gang graffiti covered the walls.

And, as the bus rounded a corner, Evans saw three crick skulls mounted on sticks. Grim reminders of a battle between a cartel and the aliens.

The whole thing was ugly, not to mention scary, since Charlie company was riding in defenseless buses. But Evans didn't spot any cricks, or humans, other than those who were peeking out of windows.

The highway took the convoy south, then west on the Viad, Rio de la Piedad, and slightly north to the Bosque de Chapultepec (Forest of Chapultepec), which was a 1,695-acre park with the famous hill at its center.

On the one hand, Evans liked looking at the surrounding trees. On the other hand, like any soldier, he would have preferred a well cleared free-fire zone. As it was the crickets could attack the hill from cover.

Marines waved the convoy down, Ramirez spoke to them, and the journey continued. It wasn't long before Evans caught glimpses of the castle.

It was tiered like a wedding cake, topped by a single tower, and surrounded by sheer walls. Evans approved of that. Even if they could be breached with plasma cannons, the walls would offer some protection.

As the convoy neared the end of its journey, Evans could see that a backhoe was being used to dig a partial trench around the castle, complete with mortar pits, grenade sumps, and ammo bunkers. It was a scene from a WWI movie. And that made sense.

Even though the Prax had Buck Rogers weapons, they fought like Doughboys.

A noncom was waiting for Evans as he got off the bus. He saluted. "Captain Evans? Sergeant Nichols, sir. Colonel Brock wants to see you right away."

Evans turned to Russo. "Get the download on quarters, latrines, food, guard rotations, and so on."

Russo nodded. "Yes, sir. Give me a holler once the meeting is over. I'll bring you up to speed."

Evans followed Nichols through a vast reception area, up one of two sweeping staircases, and past a beautiful mural. From there it was a short walk to a door and the stairway that wound its way up to a flat roof. The first thing Evans noticed was the number of light machine guns that had been set up, barrels pointed at the sky, ready to repel flying crickets.

There were sandbagged mortars too, a modest antenna farm, and a jury-rigged drone port. A Wasp recon UAV took to the air as Evans crossed the roof.

Brock and two staff officers were standing in front of a waist-high wall looking south through raised binoculars. Evans recognized Executive Officer Major Tracy Folsom and Captain Lester Chan. They turned as Evans arrived.

"There you are," Brock said, as if Evans had been missing. "It's good to have Charlie company back in the fold. You've been a busy boy. And Colonel Lasky likes you. That's no small thing."

"It's good to be back, sir," Evans replied. "Sort of."

The other officers laughed.

"The poop is definitely going to hit the fan," Brock admitted. "But we're the lucky ones."

"How's that, sir?"

"The Gulf of Mexico is about 180 miles thataway," Brock said, as he pointed east. "And the Pacific Ocean is 550 miles to the west. That's how long the new Red Line is. A whole lot of people have orders to hold areas that are flat. But we have a hill. And the hill consists of rock. Do you copy?"

Evans nodded. "I do, sir. The Prax will have to fight uphill. And it would be difficult for them to tunnel."

"But the hill won't stop the fliers," Chan observed. "We'll need air defenses. That's where Charlie comes in. The rest of the battalion will deal with the ground hoppers."

"Settle in and split the company in half. Twelve hours on and twelve off," Brock ordered. "Get the first watch up here ASAP. Do you have any questions?"

"No, sir."

"Welcome to Chapultepec Castle. Americans won here. They will again."

* * *

Washington D.C. The White House

After four hours of sleep, a hot shower, and a hurried breakfast, Seton returned to the Situation Room on crutches. Everyone stood and Seton waved them back into their seats. An Air Force colonel was in charge. His name was Beeson. "Good afternoon, Madam President."

Seton offered a crooked smile. "Is it good?"

Beeson made a face. "It could be worse. But no ma'am, it isn't good. And, if you look at the main screen, you'll see why."

Seton forced herself to remain standing even though her knee hurt. The image Beeson referred to was that of a train. Hundreds of humans were perched on top of boxcars which were snaking through a canyon.

Crickets were visible as well. Two on each car. "They call the train 'La Bestia,'" Beeson told her. "And they also call it 'El Tren de la Muerte.' The Train of Death.

"You might remember it from newscasts," Beeson continued. "Prior to the emergence. illegals rode the Beast north to Mexico City, where they could transfer to other trains. But the people on those boxcars aren't immigrants. They're prisoners, being used as human shields."

Seton frowned. "To protect the train?"

"Yes," Beeson responded. "To protect it from our planes. But more than that, to protect the crick soldiers packed into the boxcars. They're an important part of the Prax offensive. The bastards outnumber us ... And they know it."

"So, what's the plan?"

"The Pentagon is working on it. You'll have options by 1800."

* * *

Chapultepec Castle, Mexico City, Mexico

When the flying crickets arrived, they arrived with a vengeance. Evans was down in the castle's music room, a large space normally hung with paintings, all of which were now in storage. Sleeping bags lay side-by-side on the floor.

The only thing that made Evans' accommodation different from the others was the fact that he had a corner. And that's where he was, pulling his boots on, when a breathless runner arrived. "Prax fliers are coming, sir! Thousands of them."

Evans assumed that "thousands" meant hundreds. "Please inform Lieutenant Dawkins that I'll be there shortly."

The private hurried away. The off-duty Marines were staring at him. Evans stood. "Gun up, Marines, and follow me. The castle is under attack."

Evans secured his vest, grabbed his rifle, and waved the Marines toward the door. "What? You're going to let the 3rd shoot all the bugs? Remember, be sure to lead the fliers. Let's go."

Evans took off at a trot. The sounds of fighting could be heard as he neared the roof. What Evans saw when he arrived far outstripped his imagination. The private was correct. *Thousands* of cricks were flying toward the castle! So many that they nearly blocked the sun.

Those in the lead were firing their weapons, as were the Marines on the light machine guns. The combined clatter was deafening.

A Marine fell and Evans pointed to the unmanned machine gun. "Get on that LMG! Corpsman! We need a corpsman here."

The cumulative fire from the machine guns, the M27 assault weapons, and shotguns had a devastating effect on the alien formation—but weren't enough to stop it.

And, as some of the fliers circled above the castle, a new threat came into play. A crick took aim at a machine gun, dived and blew itself up!

Kamikaze cricks were something new as far as Evens knew, but there they were, and the tactic was working. As more fliers committed suicide, more Marines died. Often in groups of two or three. "Pop smoke!" Evans bellowed. "Aimed fire! Nail those bastards before they get close!"

Thanks to the infrared sights on their M27s the Marines could "see" through the roiling smoke and choose targets. That helped, but didn't solve the problem, since dead cricks exploded too. Evans yelled, "Take cover!" And crouched behind a wall.

That was when two Bell AH-1Z Vipers arrived. Rockets flared and three-barreled rotary cannons began to roar. The aliens were so close together that when one of the bomb carriers exploded, others did as well, creating a daisy chain effect. Hundreds of Prax died. Enough to stop the airborne assault. The roof was littered with bodies, both human and alien, all mixed together.

Marines called for help, grown men cried, and a corporal held his right foot up for his comrades to see. A tourniquet was cinched around his leg. "Look!" he said. "I'm the lucky one! I'm going home!"

Evans nodded numbly. "That's right, son ... You *are* the lucky one."

There were sporadic ground attacks during the next few hours. And, when darkness fell, snipers from both sides prowled the night.

After three hours of troubled sleep, Evans forced himself to get up off the floor, and go looking for coffee. There was some, thank God, plus boxes of pastries brought in by an air evac helo, along with boxes of MREs.

Evans eyed his watch, gobbled a doughnut, and washed it down with coffee. Then it was time to depart the fort for the morning burial service. A heavily guarded backhoe had been working during the night and the mass grave was ready.

Incoming planes were packed with troops and supplies. Outward bound planes were reserved for the wounded. Dead Americans had to wait and would be disinterred later.

"They won't mind," the battalion chaplain said, when questioned. "They're somewhere else."

The pit was ten feet deep in order to prevent the cricks from accessing and eating the dead Marines. The body bags were lined up in a tidy row, and as the sun rose above the horizon, the chaplain spoke. "We're gathered here to honor our brothers and sisters, heroes all, who fell while defending our country and are with us in spirit. May almighty God receive the Marines who gave their all, and protect those of us who remain. Amen."

A corporal, bugle in hand, took three steps forward and raised the instrument to her lips. As the plaintive sound of Taps floated across the still air, Evans remembered First Lieutenant Lester Russo, Second Lieutenant Maya Christou, and the others. Twelve in all.

And that's where he was, frozen in grief, as the process of lowering bodies into the ground began. "Excuse me, sir," a voice said. "The colonel sent me."

Evans turned to find a private standing next to him. The kid started to salute, remembered that saluting was forbidden in a combat zone, and dropped his arm.

Evans nodded. "What's the message?"

"The colonel wants you to take part in a meeting," the private explained. "It will be held at 0900 in the Viceroy's Office on the top floor of the castle."

A meeting? What about sleeping? But there was only one answer Evans could give. "Tell the colonel that I'll be there."

The Marine said, "Yes, sir," performed an about face, and jogged away. Evans watched him go. A newbie. More and more of them were arriving each day. The United States was bleeding out.

There were lots of things to do. That included elevating Andy Yamada to acting XO, putting Gunny Hollis in charge of the 2nd platoon, and shifting other Marines around to rebalance the company. So, the 0900 meeting came up quickly, and Evans was five minutes late. He entered the office to discover that a number of human officers were present, as were two Mechans.

The robots had identical features and wire mesh skin. "Aha!" Brock said. "Here he is... Form Leader Z, and Assistant Form Leader T, please allow me to introduce Captain Lester Evans. He has a great deal of combat experience, including time spent working with civilians."

Brock turned to look at Evans. "Charlie company is going to work with the Mechans to carry out an important mission."

Evans saw that Arabic serial numbers had been stenciled onto each Mechan's forehead. The identifiers consisted of a letter plus five digits. That was something new, and a lot better than the nicknames bestowed on Mechans during the silo mission.

Remember, Evans cautioned himself. *The Mechans are machines, not people. Don't shake hands with them.*

"Yes, sir … What's up?"

"Let's gather around Captain Chan's laptop. The boys and girls at the Pentagon sent us a video outlining the task and how to get it done."

Chan clicked his mouse and drone footage appeared. Evans could see a train track, a train coming straight at the camera, and humans crouched on boxcars.

"You're looking at *La Bestia,*" a female voice said. "Also referred to as *El Tren de la Muerte.* Which means the Death Train. Prior to the emergence, immigrants both legal and illegal rode on top of the cars as they tried to reach the U.S.

"The Prax captured it, and now the train is being used to transport thousands of cricket soldiers into the battle zone, which is one of the reasons why we're so badly outnumbered.

"In order to keep our aircraft from attacking *La Bestia,* human shields are positioned on the top of each car, with approximately one hundred cricks crammed into the space under them. That means eighty boxcars can deliver eight thousand Prax into southern Mexico in a matter of hours. That's the equivalent of two regiments."

The video dissolved and Evans found himself looking at President Vanessa Seton. "The following message is for Captain, now Major Evans.

"You helped to clear the SubTropolis. You defended the refugees at the Carlsbad Caverns. And you completed a classified mission in the Pacific Northwest.

"That's why this mission has *your* name on it. Free the hostages. The Air Force will destroy the train. Thank you for your service." The screen snapped to black.

CHAPTER SIXTEEN

Chapultepec Castle, Mexico City, Mexico

Evans was in shock. Colonel Brock laughed. "You should see the expression on your face! Sorry, but we couldn't resist."

Evans frowned. "How did the president know all that stuff?"

"I guess someone actually reads the reports that I send in," Brock replied modestly. "And congratulations on the bump to major. It's well deserved. But the celebratory bacchanal will have to wait. You have a mission to complete first."

"Let's talk about that," Evans said. "The president said we should rescue the hostages. She didn't say how."

"No," Brock agreed, "she didn't. But the brain trust in the Pentagon came up with a plan, and secured buy-in from the Xyfors, so we're ready to go. Captain Chan will fill you in."

Chan nodded. "You saw how the hostages were positioned on top of the boxcars with two cricks per car. And, I assume you're familiar with Mechan battle platforms."

Evans nodded. "Yes. They're used to transport Mechans and supplies."

"So," Chan said. "Imagine that our Mechan friends fly two platforms in next to the train. One on each side of it. Then, snipers kill the guards.

"At that point you, and your Spanish speaking Marines, invite the hostages to jump aboard. Once that's accomplished, the platforms will veer away, and the jet jockeys will destroy the train—including the eight thousand cricks riding inside the box-cars. Mission accomplished."

"And we can expect a bonus," Brock added. "The wreckage will block the tracks, making it impossible for the Prax to send other trains north."

The plan was slick. Evans had to admit that. And it should work. Then why did he have an empty feeling in his gut? Was it a case of the usual pre-mission heebie-jeebies? *Yes*, Evans decided. *That explains it.*

Evans knew that all eyes were on him, so he forced a smile. "I like the plan, sir. So, when do we head out?"

"This afternoon," Brock answered. "The train is being loaded, and if we can prevent thousands of cricks from joining the battle, then we will do so."

Evans nodded. "Yes, sir ... I'll get to work."

There was lots to do. Evans' first task was to follow the Mechan form leaders out to a parking lot where two battle plat-forms, or "bricks," were sitting on the ground. Both vehicles had energy cannons fore and aft.

Crews consisted of six robots each, including a pilot, two gun-ners, and three snipers. Each sharpshooter was assigned to a tripod-mounted, gyro-stabilized rifle, equipped with a high-tech scope. Their job was to kill the crick guards without harming the hostages.

Evans left the inspection feeling confident that the Mechans would do their part.

After returning to the castle, Evans turned his attention to the Marines chosen by Battalion Sergeant Major, John "Badass" Smith.

Second Lieutenant Christian Ramirez was going to serves as XO. The detachment consisted of six Spanish speaking "hos-tage wranglers," and two Navy corpsmen, one for each battle platform.

Acting from an abundance of caution, Evans suggested that a wide variety of weapons be made available to the Marines, along with plenty of ammo. "The energy cannons should be able to smoke any fliers that happen along," Evans told Ramirez. "But it's better to be safe rather than sorry."

Last, but not least was a virtual meeting with Air Force personnel, to make sure that everyone understood their role which, according to the lead pilot, was to "Kill the fucking train, and kill every fucking crick on it." And who could argue with that?

Evans had just enough time to gobble part of an MRE, and grab two bottles of water, before leaving the castle. And, thanks to Lieutenant Ramirez, everyone was ready—robots included.

Even though preparations had been hurried, Evans was glad that the mission was taking place that day, rather than the next. Get it over with. That beat the hell out of a long, sleepless night.

Evans and Ramirez were riding on different platforms to ensure that one of them would survive if a brick went down. The junior officer waved, and Evans waved back as his vehicle took off.

It was a bright sunny day. The air was pleasantly warm. And Evans felt an unexpected surge of exhilaration as he rode the alien assault craft into battle. He gloried in the press of air against his face, the adrenaline that was trickling into his bloodstream, and the sure knowledge that he was doing something important. The sense of well-being buoyed Evans up as he made the rounds, stopped to chat with each Marine, and Form Leader T as well. "This is an amazing machine."

Lifeless eyes met his. "Such platforms are useful," T allowed. "In spite of their design flaws."

The guileless response served to remind Evans of the fact that Mechans weren't political. And why would they be? The robots were rarely required to interact with sentients. That meant there were no constraints on what they could, or wouldn't say.

"What kind of flaws?" Evans inquired, as the brick sped south.

"Battle platforms are susceptible to ground fire," T replied. "The computer that designed them had to choose between weight and armor plating. It chose to limit weight in order to increase speed and maneuverability." The news was delivered in a monotone.

"I see," Evans replied. And he did. The tradeoffs between weight, speed, and armor affected tank design too. And the way Navy warships were constructed.

"Are the Xyfor aware of this?"

"Yes," T replied. "And they accept it."

"Do *you* accept it?"

"Of course," T answered. "Mechans are part of a complex system designed to kill Prax. If the system works, then we are part of the resulting equilibrium."

And that, Evans realized, was the essence of what machines were programmed to achieve. And democratic governments too … Or so it seemed to him.

The conversation was somewhat unsettling however, given where they were headed, and what they had to accomplish. Machinery thrummed, contrails crisscrossed the blue sky, and Marines ate MREs as the better part of two hours passed.

The silvery train track was clearly visible beneath the battle platform, as were the sparkling rivers, occasional bridges, villages, and sidings that slid past below.

Then an alert came in over the radio. The train was fifty miles ahead. And, given the speeds involved, the brick would pass over the locomotive in sixteen minutes.

Evans tried to look relaxed as he checked on the snipers, and joked with the Marines, prior to going forward. He was standing beside the bow cannon when *La Bestia* appeared, followed by a long column of multi-colored boxcars, all topped with human hostages.

Strangely, despite the fact that Evans was in command, he felt powerless. Could he tell the snipers when to fire? No. Their onboard computers would dictate those decisions.

Could he order the Marines to use their bullhorns? Yes. But that would be stupid. They knew what they were supposed to do, and had the freedom to act as they saw fit.

So, as the battle platforms separated and slowed, all Evans could do was watch. His brick was to the west of the track, with the other platform to the east.

The mission had been a leisurely affair up until then. Suddenly everything snapped into fast forward. The battle platforms dropped down so that they were level with the boxcars. Tree limbs snapped off if they got in the way. Shots were fired. And, thanks to the fact that the snipers were using AI to calculate all the variables, each shot delivered a kill.

As guards fell off the train, Marines began to yell in Spanish: *¡Ven a nosotros! ¡Saltar! ¡Hazlo ahora!* (Come to us! Jump across! Do it now!)

Thanks to the skill of the Mechan pilots the bricks were in close, only two feet away, and remained there for a full minute. Most of the hostages made the jump. A few fell through the gap, landed next to the track, and were killed. Others remained frozen in place as the flying barges moved on, unable to muster the courage to act, and dooming themselves in the process.

Evans saw a mother with two young children left behind and understood. She might carry one of them, and make the jump, but not two. He closed his eyes and opened them again. The family was gone.

Another boxcar was alongside. The new batch of hostages had witnessed what had taken place and were quick to react. Some chose the Ramirez barge, others chose the Evans barge, and he finally had something to do.

A woman jumped, nearly fell, and Evans pulled her in.

A crying baby sailed through the air and Evans managed to catch it. The child's father arrived seconds later.

A man with a bloody bandage wrapped around his head threw himself forward and Evans was there to break his fall.

Then the energy cannons began to burp balls of energy as the flying cricks appeared. Most of the Prax were destroyed in mid-flight. One managed to land on Evans' platform where a hospital corpsman blew its brains out.

Because *La Bestia* was traveling north, while the platforms flew south, the allies were nearing the end of the train. That was when they overflew a flatcar with two Yugoslavian M-55 A2 anti-aircraft guns sitting on it.

The triple barreled weapons were already *banging* away as the platforms passed overhead, and it was impossible for the Prax gunners to miss. Evans felt the brick shudder as rounds struck it. Black smoke poured out of the open wounds, and Evans was reminded of T's comment: "Battle platforms are susceptible to ground fire." Yeah, no shit. The brick slowed, but managed to stay aloft, as the force of a mighty explosion knocked Evans off his feet. The *boom* was like thunder.

A missile? No. Once the officer managed to stand, he realized that the other platform had been destroyed. His Marines, the Mechans, and the hostages. All of them were gone.

Evans was still trying to grasp that when T appeared next to him. "We lost an engine. One isn't enough. Not carrying this much weight. I suggest that you throw some of the hostages over the side."

The Marine could hardly believe his ears. But, like all machines, T was a pragmatist. Too much weight? Throw something overboard. Problem solved.

"*No*," Evans said emphatically. "We aren't throwing anyone off the platform. We'll land instead. What's up ahead?"

They had to push and shove to make their way through the crowd of terrified passengers. Smoke was pouring out of the hull, and the brick was losing altitude. Some people peppered the Marines with questions, others cried, and a lap dog barked incessantly as the odd couple arrived in the bow.

Evans scanned the area ahead, spotted a green clad hill, and pointed to it. "There! Order the pilot to land on top of that hill... A clean landing if possible."

"The top of the hill is higher than we are," T observed.

"Order the pilot to try. If we land below it, we won't stand a chance. This area is lousy with Prax." Evans heard the characteristic scream of jet engines, and turned in time to see the first of four F-16 jet fighters arrive. They'd been circling like vultures. Now they swooped in one after another. The planes were armed with AGM-65 Maverick missiles.

The first jet went for the engine, the next for the cars immediately behind it, and so forth—until the entire train had been targeted. Bright explosions marked hits, overlapping claps of thunder rolled across the land, and thousands of cricks were killed.

The first jet was circling back for a gun run as Evans heard a Marine yell, "*¡Prepararse!*" (Get ready!) through her bullhorn. And when Evans turned to look, he saw that the Mechan pilot had been able to gain some altitude and was about to crash land on the jungle clad hill.

All Evans could do was hang on to a railing and duck as the brick bashed its way through the treetops. Branches tried to sweep the deck clean, a tree toppled, and a flock of birds took to the sky.

When the pilot killed power, the barge dropped straight down, and crushed the secondary growth under its hull. Branches *snapped*, twigs *crackled*, and Evans felt a *thud* as the platform landed. Then, much to Evans' chagrin, an ex-hostage vaulted over the rail, followed by another and another as the braver souls chose to strike out on their own rather than remain with the gringos and robots.

Marines used their bullhorns to call out to the fugitives, and urge them to return, but to no avail. So, the translators turned their attention to calming the seventy-five percent of civilians who were still on board.

Evans told the radio operator to call for air support and a couple of Chinooks. The reply was pretty much what he had expected. Yes, regarding the air support, but it would be three or four hours before they could expect a dust-off.

No sooner had the message been received than a piercing *scream* was heard. Evans suddenly felt sick to his stomach. His worst fears were being realized. An unknown number of Prax had seen the platform land on the hill and they were hungry. Would the fleeing hostages be enough to sate them? No, of course not.

So, what to do? Call for jet fighters to attack the surrounding slopes? Knowing that humans would most likely be killed with the bugs? Or do nothing, and hope for the best?

It was another gut-wrenching decision, in a war marked by gut-wrenching decisions. Evans turned to the radio operator as *another* scream was heard. "What callsign is your guy using?"

"Eightball."

Evans took the mike. "Eightball, this is Charlie-Six actual. Have you got our twenty? Over."

"You're impossible to miss," Eightball replied. "No need for smoke. You're leaking it. Over."

Evans looked up, saw two jets circling, and wondered which pilot he was talking to. "Roger that. We have a pest control problem. There are bugs in the bushes all around our position. Over."

"Copy that," Eightball replied. "Keep your heads down. The exterminators are on the way. Over."

That was when the Prax attacked from the east, the brick's stern gunner opened fire on them, and the Marines began to yell, "*¡Abajo! ¡Abajo! ¡Abajo!*" (Down! Down! Down!).

The newly freed hostages hurried to obey as Marines and Mechans lined both sides of the platform and fired into the thick vegetation. Grenade launchers proved to be especially effective at clearing the perimeter, as were Mechan flechette guns, which shredded bushes, trees, and crickets. While that was taking place the fighters began to make pass after pass, firing rockets and guns, which turned the hill's slopes into an open-air abattoir.

The aerial attack came to an end shortly after the vegetation on the north side of the hill caught fire and ground combat ended. Evans took the mike. "Eightball, this is Charlie-Six actual. Thanks! Can you remain on station? Over."

"We'll be here for a while yet," Eightball replied. "A couple of 18s will take over when we run low on fuel. Over."

The waiting began. There were no further attempts to attack from the slopes of the hill. To guard against the possibility of a surprise attack, Evans put a staff sergeant named Alby in charge of establishing a defensive perimeter. It was thin, but heavily armed. And some of the hostages volunteered to help. By standing on a rock outcropping Evans could survey the plain below with his binoculars. There was movement, but no signs of an imminent attack.

Farther out, *La Bestia's* smoldering remains could be seen, and Evans felt a sense of satisfaction. Had eight thousand Prax been killed? He hoped so.

Try as he might, Evans couldn't spot the wreckage of the second battle platform, and that was consistent with the size of the explosion. It seemed safe to assume that bits and pieces of the brick were spread all over a wide area. *I'll write Ramirez up,* Evans decided. *And get him the highest decoration that Brock will approve.*

After what seemed like an eternity of waiting two Chinooks appeared in the distance. "Charlie-Six, this is Fly Girl," a female voice said. "We are two Chinooks in from the north. I see a tendril of black smoke. Is that *you*? Over."

"Roger that," Evans said. "So long as it's coming from the top of the hill in front of you. Over."

"It is," Fly Girl confirmed. "What, if anything, do you know about pinnacle landings? Over."

"Is that the kind where you back in, and hover? Over."

"Exactamundo," Fly Girl replied. "So, organize my passengers. When my crew chief waves them aboard I want them to hustle. Copy?"

"I copy," Evans assured her. "Over."

As the roar of helicopter engines grew louder Evans, Alby, and his interpreters went to work explaining what was going to happen, and dividing the civilians into two groups.

The propwash from the first Chinook's rotors whipped the surrounding vegetation into a frenzy, as the one-hundred-foot-long helicopter backed into position, and its ramp went down.

The Marines yelled, "*Andale! Andale! Andale!*" (Go! Go! Go!) as they herded the refugees up the ramp. Then, the moment the first group was aboard, the helicopter pulled away and the ramp went up. All the Marines and Mechans remained behind.

That was when the Chinook gunners began to fire down into the foliage below…And the Marines knew what that meant. Cricks were moving up slope!

"Put some 40 mike-mike on those bastards," Evans ordered. "And don't be shy about it."

Evans heard a *ka-thunk* sound each time a grenade went downhill, followed by a loud *bang*, and a geyser of smoke. It was impossible to assess how much actual damage was done, but Evans felt sure that the barrage would slow the attack down—if nothing else.

The second Chinook was backing in by then, machine guns firing, as the ramp went down. And, much as Evans wanted to rush aboard, he forced himself to wait until everyone else was on the aircraft. Then he made the jump.

T was standing on the Chinook's ramp. And, as the helo began to pull away, the robot produced what looked like a pistol. "It's a remote," T said emotionlessly. Then he pulled the trigger. A series of explosions rocked the battle platform and rendered it useless.

"I'm sorry you had to do that," Evans said.

"*Why?*" T inquired. "Machines can be replaced."

***

Carlsbad Caverns National Park, New Mexico
One of more than a dozen garden hoses that led from a faucet at the park's Visitor Center, down into the main cavern, was leaking. That's why FEMA Community Response Team Leader, Cassie Lang, was kneeling in the middle of the parking lot, using electrical tape to bind the wound. The *rattle* of a car engine caused Lang to stand. A constant trickle of refugees flowed into the camp, just as some decided to leave. But the camp attracted scumbags too. Hustlers for the most part, but thieves too, some of whom were violent.

So, Lang's right hand strayed to her .45 as a graffiti covered VW bus appeared—music blaring—and screeched to a halt. *On The Road Again* was silenced, the engine sputtered to a stop, and the passenger side door swung open.

That was when two mixed breed mutts jumped out, ran in circles, and came over to introduce themselves. Then the dogs took off again, as a sturdy looking middle-aged woman rounded the V-dub, and made her way over. "Hi! I'm Regina, but my friends call me Reggie. I'm looking for a woman named Cassie Lang."

"You found her," Lang said, as she offered her hand. As they shook, Lang noticed that Reggie's hand was callused, which suggested that the other woman was no stranger to physical work. And, judging from appearances, Reggie was willing to travel by herself.

"It's an honor to meet the legend," Reggie said.

Lang frowned. "'The legend?'"

Reggie looked surprised. "Yes, inside FEMA anyway. Is that the six gun that people talk about?"

"I suppose it is," Lang admitted. "So, you work for FEMA?"

"I do," Reggie replied. "And I'm you're replacement."

Lang was surprised. "You are? No one told me."

Reggie scowled. "Ain't that the way of it? Sorry about that."

Lang felt a combination of embarrassment and fear. "What did I do wrong?"

"It's more like what did you did right," Reggie replied. "The suits decided to promote you to Director of the Interagency Coordination Division. That's a big deal, and the pay's good, which matters since wartime Washington D.C. is very expensive."

Lang's head was spinning. A director? Washington D.C.? "No one asked me. I'm not sure I want it."

Reggie shrugged. "Okay, think it over. I'll get the paperwork out of the bus. Look it over, sleep on it, and let me know. Or, better yet, get on your phone and talk to your boss."

Lang had things to do. Finish the hose repair, meet with the latest security committee, and wait her turn for a hot shower. And all the while she was thinking about the opportunity and what it might portend.

Finally, with her hair still wet from the shower, she took her phone and ventured up to the surface. According to the voicemail greeting, Lang's latest supervisor, a guy named Nate Jennings, was busy but would call her back. And he did two hours later.

To Jennings' credit, he was very apologetic for failing to contact Lang, and didn't try to blame HR. "I'm sorry, Cassie. Please forgive me.

"But here's the situation... If you accept it, the job will be to work with FEMA partners across the country to allocate scarce resources and improvise when necessary.

"You're a legend in our universe. And, when you talk, people will listen. Plus, it's important to put individuals with field experience on the management team. Folks who aren't afraid to ruffle some feathers if necessary. So, how 'bout it, Cassie? Will you help us out?"

All sorts of thoughts swirled in Lang's mind, many of which were negative. But, when she spoke, the word "Yes" came out of her mouth.

What followed was a weeklong transition while Reggie took over, a scary drive to Holloman Air Force Base, and a flight to another world. One in which she slept better, apartments were almost impossible to find, and people called her "ma'am."

Fortunately, Lang was able to score a studio apartment, and with lots of help from a saleswoman, she purchased a new wardrobe. *Oh my God*, Lang thought, as she inspected herself in the dressing room mirror. *I turned into a suit!*

CHAPTER SEVENTEEN

Washington D.C.

Cassie Lang's office was located on the 4th floor of FEMA's nondescript office building in downtown D.C. The newly minted executive had spent the last two weeks familiarizing herself with the finer points of FEMA's bureaucracy, while trying to figure out which task to tackle first. Key West was the one she chose.

The resort town was located at the southernmost end of U.S Route 1, and was the only way to drive onto Key West, until some of the locals blew a hole in the Seven Mile Bridge. Why? To seal Key West off from the mainland, that's why. Because the bugs weren't designed for swimming and preferred to shuffle down the highway at night. There were fliers too of course, but the so-called "Conch Militia" had done a good job of keeping them at bay.

But even though Key West was reasonably secure, the locals felt that the federal government should do more, starting with FEMA—and extending to the Coast Guard and the Air Force. Both having repeatedly refused to provide the air taxi service that residents felt they were entitled to. To resolve the conflicts Lang was hosting a daylong meeting that included representatives from all three constituencies.

When the lunch recess arrived, Lang took the opportunity to retreat to her office, and chill out. That was when she saw the formal looking envelope on her desk. It was from the "Office of the President," and addressed to her. A rah-rah, let's work together message perhaps? Probably.

But, when Lang opened the envelope, something else awaited her: "The President requests that Ms. Cassie Lang, recipient of the Presidential Citizens Medal, join her on Tuesday..."

Lang stopped reading at that point, called her boss to see if the invitation was someone's idea of a joke, and learned that it wasn't.

Lang tried to put the award out of her mind as she returned to the meeting. There were four participants. Two military officers, and two citizen representatives, both of whom were in their sixties and sporting tropical shirts. "Okay," Lang said, "After listening to your input, I'd like to offer a compromise. FEMA will review the amount of support we offer Key West to ensure that islanders are receiving their fair share of MREs, medical supplies, and yes, toilet paper.

"As for an airborne shuttle service to the mainland, no, that isn't going to happen. Both the Coast Guard and the Air Force have their hands full dealing with the Prax.

"However, since the residents of Key West have boats, and the bugs are water aversive, it should be possible to establish a ferry service using the Conch Militia as security.

"Last, but not least, it's my hope that the Coast Guard will place a higher priority on med evacs for pregnant women, and those with life threatening injuries. Realizing that their primary mission, which is to defend coastal communities from the Prax, may cause significant delays. Okay, what do you think?"

It took the participants more than an hour to share what they thought. But eventually, all four of them came around, and a deal was done.

Once the visitors were gone Lang was free to address the most urgent matter: *What would she wear to the White House?*

A weekend came and went. Monday was spent working with her staff to draft the next budget. A gnarly process which involved so many rules, historical precedents, and "human factors" that it made Lang's head spin.

"Human factors" referred to politics both internal and external. So, it was a relief when Tuesday morning rolled around, and she could escape.

As Lang looked in the mirror, she thought the dark blue suit looked good on her. Then she didn't, and then she did. It took an act of will to leave her apartment, summon a taxi, and provide the address: "The White House, please." The driver wasn't impressed.

It was a short drive, and as Lang got out of the cab, she saw that two lines led to the gate. A uniformed officer approached Lang as she entered the area. "Good morning, ma'am. Are you here to receive an award?"

"Yes," Lang replied self-consciously, "I am."

"Civilian or military?"

"Civilian."

"Please join the line to the left. Have your ID and your invitation ready when you reach the checkpoint. Congratulations, and thank you for serving our country."

Lang got in line behind a well-dressed man and wondered who he was. Due to the need to empty pockets and phones, the queue advanced in a series of jerks. Then each person had to pass through a magnetometer and an EMP "burner" before proceeding.

When Lang drew even with the security kiosk, she proffered her federal ID card and invitation. The officer on the other side of the bullet proof glass scanned the bar code printed on the invitation, compared the results to the ID card, and returned both items.

A young man in a dark suit and wearing a government ID was available to provide instructions. "Please stay to the left of the cones. Thank you."

As Lang followed the other civilians, she saw that a line of men and women in uniform were entering the White House as well. One was in a wheelchair.

By that time Lang realized that the presentation ceremony would be nothing like those she'd seen on preemergence television. Everything had changed, including the way awards were given. The civilian briefing took place under a temporary awning to the left of the North Portico. A similar shelter for military personnel was visible on the other side of the portico.

"Welcome to the White House," a carefully coiffed woman said. "And congratulations! My name is Myra. We're going to make our way from here to the East Room.

"Please take the seat that has your last name on it. Once your name is called, please make your way to the podium. Let me know if you're going to need assistance.

"Once both civilian and military personnel are ready, the President will join us and deliver some remarks. The presentations will alternate between civilian and military award recipients.

"When your name is called, go forward, shake hands with President Seton and turn to the right. A light will flash as your picture is taken. Five copies will be sent to you. At that point, please follow the center aisle to the back of the room. After all of the presentations are made, refreshments will be served, and you'll be free to socialize. Please follow me."

Myra led the column into the White House, and over to the marble stairway that led up one level. The East Room was on the right.

The East Room looked the way Lang had expected: tall windows, floor length drapes, antique carpets, and a grand piano. Two sections of chairs were separated by a middle aisle.

Since arriving in the nation's capital Lang had noticed that most meetings started late, and wasn't surprised by President Seton's tardiness, for which the chief executive apologized.

Her speech was short and to the point.

"You're here for a reason. Some for bravery. Some for public service. And some for accomplishments in art, medicine and science. I'm here to celebrate you and what you accomplished. Thank you, one and all."

Seton's comments drew applause, a staffer gave her the first award, and the ceremony began. A civilian went first, followed by an Air Force staff sergeant.

Lang's mind started to drift after a while, and then, like a bolt of lightning out of a clear blue sky, she heard his name. "Would Marine Corps Major Lester Evans please approach the podium."

Lang craned her neck. Evans wasn't a major, and Evans was a common name, but still... Then she saw him! Evans was alive! Lang had been haunted by the possibility that Evans would be wounded or killed and no one would think to tell her. They weren't related after all.

But there he was, handsome as ever, receiving a medal for heroism! Lang felt her heart beat faster, thought how adolescent that was, and sat transfixed as the announcer read a short description. "Major Evans is receiving the Navy Cross with oak leaf cluster in recognition of his heroism in the battle for Kansas City, his actions in Refugee Camp 1106, and more recently—his role in killing an estimated 8,000 Prax in Mexico." The announcement drew enthusiastic applause.

Evans accepted the award, thanked Seton, and turned. A camera flashed and Evans followed the center aisle to the back of the room. Lang wanted to call out to him, but couldn't, and had to remain in her seat as the ceremony continued.

* * *

Even though Evans wasn't the type of officer who sought medals, or gave them much thought, he couldn't help but be buzzed. And, as he stood with the others at the back of room, Evans did his best to tamp his ego down, and focus his attention on those still going through the process.

Evans had never heard of them. Or that's what he thought until the MC called out a very familiar name. "Would FEMA's Director of the Interagency Coordination Division, Cassie Lang, please approach the podium."

Evans watched in shock as Lang rose from her chair and made her way to the podium. "In Director Lang's previous role," the MC said, "she managed Refugee Camp 1106 in New Mexico, and did so during a time of repeated attacks by outlaws and Prax soldiers. Ms. Lang even going so far as to shoot members of both groups with her now famous six gun."

The announcement drew applause and laughter as Lang accepted her award, and paused for the photograph, before walking to the back of the room.

Evans was waiting to greet her. "I missed you ... Thank God you're alright."

Lang looked up into his eyes. "And I missed you. Very much."

"Can I kiss you?"

"Please do."

They kissed. The embrace lasted a long time. Some people applauded and others whistled. Everyone turned to look, Seton included. "Do they know each other?"

"I assume they do," an aide replied dryly.

Seton felt envious. *What does it feel like?* she wondered. *To have someone. To hold them close.*

The aide was still there. "Madam President? Are you ready?"

"Of course, I am," Seton snapped. "Please proceed."

* * *

Evans awoke to find himself in a strange bed. The hotel? No, Lang's apartment. And there she was, sleeping next to him. The reunion began in a quiet bar, followed by dinner at a nice restaurant, and an irresistible invitation. "Stay with me tonight," Lang said. "While we have the chance." Evans knew what she meant. That could be their only night together.

So, they made love, and made love again, before finally falling asleep.

Evans eyed his watch. It was 0312. And he was supposed to attend a meeting at 0800. He slipped out of bed, put his uniform on, and wrote a note.

"Good morning! I have a meeting at the Pentagon. I'll meet you here at six. Here's my cell number. I love you."

Evans paused. Did he? Love her, that is? The answer was obvious. Evans drew a line under "I love you," and scribbled his name.

After a cab ride to his hotel, and a hot shower, Evans ordered breakfast from room service and ate in front of the TV. There was some good news for a change. Allied forces had been able to hold the second Red Line, and push the cricks back. Thank God.

That caused Evans to wonder what was next for him. A desk job at the Pentagon? That would be outstanding! Push paper all day, see Cassie every night, and put the nightmares behind him.

Did he have PTSD? Of course, he did. Now, after the emergence, most people did. And, even though Evans didn't think he could fully vanquish the memories, he believed he could live with them. Especially if he was with Cassie.

The trip from the hotel to the Pentagon was a time-consuming affair due to multiple security checks. "This is as far as I can take you," the cabbie said when he pulled over. "The Pentagon is two blocks *that* way."

Evans paid cash. The driver gave it back. "I served a hitch in the corps, so your money isn't any good. *Semper Fi.*"

Roaming MPs stopped Evans twice on his way to the Pentagon. Did he look like a crick? Of course not. But that was the military mindset.

After entering the building, Evans had to empty his pockets, and pass through a magnetometer followed by a "toaster." A corporal was waiting. "Major Evans? I'm Corporal Tegan. Colonel Lasky is waiting."

Lasky? Shit. So much for the desk job.

Evans nodded. "Please lead the way."

Tegan set a brisk pace. A ring corridor led to a hallway, which led to a fully loaded elevator. About 25,000 military and civilian personnel worked in the Pentagon, according to Tegan. So, at any given the time of day, many of them were arriving.

Tegan got off on the fourth floor and Evans followed. A short walk took them to a conference room. "This is it," Tegan proclaimed, "Here's my card. Please call me if you need assistance." Then he was gone.

A pair of plain clothes security officers bracketed the door. Evans had to show his ID and wai, while a guard checked a list. A tiny photo was visible beside his name.

Then, and only then, was Evans allowed to pass through a second EMP field and enter. Would his new Timex survive? Time would tell. Evans smiled.

Double doors opened onto a large room, with rows of tables and comfortable chairs. Most were taken. Evans didn't know any of those present except for Lasky, who was up front, chatting with a man and a woman. Video screens filled most of the far wall.

Evans saw an empty chair next to an Air Force officer, and made his way over. "Is this seat taken?"

"No, sir," the captain answered. "Welcome to whatever this is."

Evans sat down. "So, I'm not the only one. I'm Lester Evans."

"And I'm John Abbott," the other officer replied, as he offered his hand. They shook.

Evans eyed the other man's wings. "What do you fly?"

"C-17s," Abbott replied.

"So, we're going somewhere," Evans predicted. "I hope we like it."

Abbott laughed. "How likely is that?"

Evans didn't answer as the doors were closed, and Lasky took the podium. "Good morning. You're here, whether you know it or not, to participate in Operation Far Reach.

"This operation is classified and, to be blunt, even the Xyfor aren't aware of it. Let's keep it that way. It's our belief that they would approve of the mission's goal, but might have concerns about the technology transfer that's about to take place, and how it could affect them.

"Simply put, the mission is to access the heart of the Prax communications system, destroy it, and cut Prime off from crickets all around the world."

The announcement provoked a stir in the audience, expressions of delight, and scattered applause. Lasky nodded. "The research that made this opportunity possible was led by Doctor Anne Blake, who's a well-known entomologist, and Army officer.

"It was Doctor Blake who, along with a team of multi-disciplinary specialists, discovered the important role that cores play in the Prax communications network, and the fact that every core has the capacity to become a Prime. A theory that was confirmed when we capped the Prime living near Tiger, Georgia, and a new Prime came on line hours later.

"So why bother?" Lasky inquired rhetorically. "Because we were about to launch a nationwide attack at that time, and knew that taking the first Prime off line would disrupt the Prax chain of command—which it did. But the war continued.

"Now, thanks to additional Intel and analysis we have an opportunity to shut the Prax communication system down, and end the conflict. Here to explain is none other than Doctor Blake herself."

Such was Blake's fame that the audience rose to applaud her. She made the Army uniform look good. Her eyes scanned the room. "Thank you. Please be seated. I see some familiar faces out there, along with new ones, brought in to help us get the job done.

"Just to ensure everyone is on the same page let's review the basics. As the colonel said, there are more than a thousand cores, any of which can become the Prime. So killing one, two, or three of them is a waste of time."

A diagram appeared on the screen behind her. "Here's how the system works. The Prax use low frequency radio waves to communicate, because low frequency ground waves can be received up to 1,200 miles from the transmitting antenna.

"In order to reach farther than that, the Prax use what we think of as radio repeaters. Meaning a unit that can receive a signal and resend it. The Prax refer to such devices as 'nodes.'"

Blake turned to watch a flow chart appear on the center screen. Her laser pointer projected a red dot onto a circle labeled "Prime."

"It's important to realize that while we see the Prax as millions of individual cricks, each of which wants to eat us, they're actually part of a single organism. And that's Prime.

"Prime communicates with cores by sending messages to a central switching mechanism called the Nexus, which forwards them to the destination's node. After a core retrieves a message from a node, it translates Prime's directive into area specific activities, which soldiers carry out."

Blake turned to face her audience. "What that means is that the Nexus is a single point of failure. Without it, messages can't get through. We knew that, but didn't know where the Nexus was."

Blake paused as if to let the information sink in. "So, my team made use of the equipment in captured nests to send fake messages through the system, analyze the responses, and map the network. And, as it turns out, Nexus is located in Libya. Out in the Sahara Desert.

"Why there? We can't be certain. But it's worth noting that the sand varies from 69 to 141feet deep. Much deeper than other deserts around the world.

"As for power," Blake added, "we believe that the Nexus is powered by a geo tap that not only generates the electricity they need, but produces excess heat. And where better to vent excess heat than in the middle of a desert? A place where it wasn't noticed for thousands of years.

"Okay," Blake said with a smile. "Thanks for hanging in there. Here's the 'So what?' Based on recently acquired orbital imaging, we know where the Nexus is, and we know it's underground near the Birak Oasis.

"So," Blake continued, "if we can put a team inside the Nexus, and download a custom designed virus into the Prax communications system, we can destroy their network in a matter of minutes!

"And, since Prax soldiers lack the capacity to think for themselves, all of them are vulnerable. A period of chaos will ensue," Blake predicted. "But once that's over, Earth will be ours again. Thank you."

There was a moment of silence. Then everyone stood and applauded. Abbott turned to Evans. "I think I know where we're going."

Evans grinned. "Yeah, bring some sunscreen."

* * *

Aboard a C-17 over North Africa
Six thousand, two hundred and sixty miles—give or take. That was the distance from McCutcheon Field, North Carolina to the

Birak Oasis in Libya. And that was fine with Evans who, after a stressful prep process in a remote corner of Camp Lejeune, needed to recharge. Even if the recharging took place on a C-17.

Evans was in command of a company of Force Recon Marines, all of whom were the best of the best, and better at everything than he was. Evans had been forced to push himself to the max during the fourteen days of mission training led by a sadist named Captain Trevor Atkins. A tough bastard who could outshoot, outrun, and outthink every Marine under his command.

So, why was Evans in charge? The answer, according to Colonel Lasky, was that "You are extremely good at the weird shit. Nobody can teach that. You either are, or you aren't."

As Evans lay on his back, staring at the overhead, he hoped Lasky was right. The oasis was under constant surveillance from above. Evans had seen the imagery and knew the village was uninhabited. Was that because the residents and their animals had been slaughtered immediately after the emergence? Most likely.

The airstrip had been constructed by the Libyan Air Force back in the bad old days of Muammar Gaddafi. And though lightly drifted with sand, the strip had been declared fit for use by Captain Abbott's superiors. Were they correct? Evans hoped so.

A Marine loomed over him. "Major? Captain Atkins told me to wake you. We're thirty out."

Evans thanked the private, pushed the sleeping bag off, and went to the head. The face in the mirror needed a shave. Would the cricks complain? No, they wouldn't.

Evans emerged to find that Atkins was everywhere, coaching, complaining, and cajoling. "Seriously, Cantrell. You look like you're in the Army. Square that shit away.

"Good morning, Ling... Nice of you to get up off your ass.

"Hey corporal, get a haircut. You look like a hobo."

All of it was said good naturedly, and received that way as well. As a result, morale was good. And, should something happen to him, Evans knew Atkins would carry on. "Good morning, Trev...Or is it afternoon?"

Atkins grinned. "It's dark, sir."

Evans laughed. "Point taken. Why doesn't the chair force provide us with windows? I'll complain when we get back. Is everything ready to go?"

"Yes, sir. We'll land, set security, and check comms while we wait for plane two to arrive."

Half the company was on the C-17 with Evans, and the other half was on "the deuce." Supplies, gear and ammo had been divided equally in case one of the transports went down. That would trigger "Plan B," which called for the remaining Marines to complete the mission by themselves.

"Roger that," Evans replied. "The faster we unload, the faster the deuce will land." Atkins knew that of course, and Evans regretted saying it. *Don't be a pompous asshole*, Evans told himself. *Oops! Too late.*

"No prob," Atkins replied tactfully. "We're ready."

"We're five out," Captain Abbott advised over the intercom. "Please take your seats and strap in. The runway is roughly 3,600 feet long, and we need 3,500 feet of that, so you're going to feel it when the reverse thrusters come on. Welcome to Libya."

After a walk through, Company Sergeant Major Wanda Gilroy took her seat, and offered a thumbs up. Atkins nodded.

Gilroy was one of the small number of women Marines who had qualified for Recon. And, after watching her during the last couple of weeks, Evans was impressed. Though relatively small, Gilroy was incredibly tough, and well respected. The men called Gilroy "Marine Mama" behind her back, and stood ready to stomp anyone who dissed her.

The landing gear hit hard, and the Marines were thrown sideways, as the pilots stood on the brakes and the reverse thrusters came on. Evans tried to look nonchalant but didn't feel that way. After a series of bumps the big plane finally ground to a halt.

"Release your belts!" Gilroy shouted. "Remember the hymn! From the fucking halls of Montezuma, to the fucking shores of Tripoli, we kick ass! Hit it!"

A platoon of Marines thundered down the ramp, split into squads, and spread out—just as they were supposed to. And, in keeping with assumptions, there was no resistance. A sure sign that the tight security measures had paid off.

The air was surprisingly cold, the stars glittered above, and a slight breeze was blowing from the west. "Okay," Gilroy said. "Who wants to hump gear?"

It was her idea of a joke. The Marines on the plane shouted, "We do! Oorah!"

Evans laughed as unloading began. Supplies, gear and ammo. All of it had to come off. And Gilroy was timing the evolution with a stopwatch. Ten minutes. That was the target.

Evans and Atkins pitched in. It was part gesture, and part pragmatism, since the C-17 was not only vulnerable on the ground—but blocking the runway.

The record set in Lejeune was nine minutes and ten seconds. Gilroy clicked her watch as the last pallet of bottled water came off. "Nine minutes and six seconds!" she exclaimed. "It looks like Captain Atkins is buying the beer."

A cheer went up as Evans spoke into his throat mike. "Flyby, this Charlie-Six actual. We're clear … Thanks for the ride. See you soon. Over."

Abbott knew the Marines were clear because his crew chief said they were. "Roger that, Six. Make sure all of your people are off the runway. We're about to backup. Over."

C-17s were unique in that they could use their thrust reversers to back up on primitive airstrips, and weren't required to turn around.

Engines screamed and sand swirled as the 174-foot-long transport backed up, paused, and *roared* down the runway. Then, with only feet to spare, Abbott pulled back on the yoke and took to the air.

The second C-17 was ready. "Charlie-Six, this is Streamer. We're inbound from the north. Mark the strip with flares if you can … We're five out."

That was when Evans realized that Abbott had been able to put the first plane down *without* flares. No wonder he'd been chosen for the job.

The deuce landed without difficulty and, because all of the Marines were available to help, Gilroy didn't bother to time the offloading process. Then, like Abbott, Streamer backed down the runway, revved the engines and took off.

Evans could see that the sky was lighter in the east. The plan was to strike before the local Prax could bring reinforcements to bear. Assuming any were available.

If they existed, the crick reserves were well hidden, and had been able to escape notice as drones crisscrossed the area for two weeks. But it was never a good idea to assume, and the mission planners hadn't. Two teams of seven Marines, plus a corpsman, were slated to enter the Nexus via air vents Alpha and Bravo. Evans was slated to lead Team Alpha.

Meanwhile the rest of the company, under the leadership of Captain Atkins, was going to fortify the dilapidated terminal building and prepare to hold the strip against a theoretical air-ground assault by Prax soldiers.

If the cricks had the means to attack, they would be facing 134 well entrenched Marines, the combined armament of *two*

MQ-9 Reaper drones, and a pair of carrier-based fighter jets fly-ing top cover.

A lieutenant named Alan Finn was in charge of Team Bravo. Their heat vent was a quarter mile away from Alpha's entry point. Evans offered Finn a fist bump. "It's show time, Lieutenant. Stay in touch."

The entry teams were equipped with low-frequency Through-the-Earth (TTE) radios— identical to those employed by miners and cavers—in addition to conventional sets.

"I will, sir," Finn promised, and popped a salute.

Evans returned it, turned to his team, and waved them for-ward. "On me. Watch your intervals, keep those heads turning, and remember to look cool. We're Marines."

CHAPTER EIGHTEEN

The Candelaria Caves, in Guatemala

Because Prime was a bioelectronic computer it didn't feel fear. It could process a loss of equilibrium however ... And there were multiple reasons to do so. The first of which was the possibility that northern meats might push south to Guatemala.

And there was a second danger as well. After more than 12,000 years of continuous operation, Prime's nano drones had warned of a potential assault on Nexus, and that was especially significant without a backup system. Why was that?

Following a deep dive into its memory banks, where the actions of its predecessors were recorded for all time, Prime found only one mention of a backup plan. And that was an effort by Prime 3207 to gather the necessary resources and construct what it called N2.0.

But, because the college of cores knew the racial operating system was perfect, they concluded that 3207 was suffering from an undiagnosed malfunction, and voted to replace 07 with 08. N2.0 project was cancelled.

And that, the current Prime knew, was the correct decision. Why waste resources on unnecessary projects? Should the tower be breached, the resident tech forms would kill the intruders, and eat them. To reach any other conclusion was illogical.

Still, even though there weren't any soldiers stationed nearby, Prime thought it would be prudent to send reinforcements to Nexus. Equilibrium had been restored.

* * *

Above Nexus, in the Sahara Desert, Libya

The relentless sun was beating down on the Marines as they prepared to venture underground. Thanks to the heat mapping carried out during the past month, Evans had the GPS coordinates for all four vents, two of which were slated to serve as points of entry.

And the Alpha vent was well hidden. The grating was located at the base of a twenty-foot-high rock outcropping and impossible to see under a jumble of two-man rocks. All of which had to be shifted. A monitor lizard was standing guard and *hissed* as it scurried away.

The grating was identical to the one Evans had encountered at Crater Lake, and a good deal of effort was required to pry it free. A steady stream of hot air escaped and sand threatened to spill into the shaft as Evans brushed it back. "Send the drone down. Let's see what's waiting for us."

The Black Hornet drone produced a *buzzing* sound as it descended into the darkness. Evans figured that another grating was blocking the bottom of the shaft, ala Crater Lake. Would it be locked? Most likely. But the squad was prepared for that.

Walls blurred past as the drone descended, stopped, and hovered in place. Rather than the greenish glow Evans expected to see, there was a blueish glow instead, indicating that, while the vents were similar to Crater Lake, Nexus was different.

"Bring the drone up," Evans ordered. "And prepare to rappel. Carter will go first."

Though not a combat engineer, Lance Corporal Carter had been trained to blow obstacles, including the bottom grate. Assuming it was locked.

It didn't make sense to send anyone else down until the way was clear. Carter checked to make sure his rope was secured, offered a casual salute, and backed into the shaft.

"I'm standing on the grate," Carter whispered one minute later. "I'm going to shift my weight onto the apron around it. Hold on. Over."

The Marines on the surface formed a circle facing out. Should Prax soldiers attack, they were ready. Minutes dragged by. "Okay, it's locked," Carter announced, "I'm going to use a breacher strip to open it. Over."

The breaching tool had been prepared based on the situation Evans and his team faced at Crater Lake. All Carter had to do was unspool it, expose the adhesive strip, and press it around the grate. Carter then attached a wireless detonator and hoisted himself up out of harm's way. "Fire in the hole," Carter whispered.

Evans heard a muffled *bang*, knew Carter would open the grate, and drop into *what*? He was about to find out. The odor of ozone filled his nostrils as Evans descended in a series of long jumps. The air was cooler ... And that was a relief after the heat on the surface.

Evans heard the rat-a-tat-tat of an FN P90 personal defense weapon firing, and knew Carter was in the shit. The P90s were short, compact weapons, which made them ideal for the type of close quarters combat the team could expect inside Nexus.

Plus, the submachine guns used the same ammo as the five-seven pistols that the Marines were carrying. The problem was that the P90s ate a lot of ammo quickly. That's why Carter was firing short bursts as Evans landed next to him.

"I think they were waiting for us!" Carter exclaimed, as three white blobs dropped from somewhere up above, made use of tentacles to grab the rungs intended for that purpose, and fired streams of formic acid at the humans. Evans had encountered the blue cheese stink before, and knew the stuff could burn skin and even kill.

Fortunately, the cylindrical structure that the blobs were clinging to put them out of range. What the fuck were they anyway?

Evans had seen tech forms under the streets of Los Angeles months earlier. But unlike these blobs, they *looked* like Prax soldiers, even though they'd been hardwired to a core. So that's what Evans expected to see. And was Carter correct? Did the blobs, which was to say, did Prime, know the Marines were coming?

Evans freed himself from the rope as Carter popped number two of three, and was just about to smoke the third, when a tentacle shot out to wrap itself around the Marine's neck! A powerful jerk was enough to yank the Marine off the platform.

Carter screamed, and flailed his arms, as he fell into the twenty-foot gap that separated the inner cylinder from the outer casing. Darkness consumed the Marine as the rest of the squad arrived in quick succession. Blue light surged up through the semitransparent inner cylinder, and electricity *crackled*, as it made the jump to a large electrode.

The inner cylinder is Nexus, or contains Nexus, Evans concluded. *And we're near the top of it.* Staff Sergeant Tom Vernon was second in command. "Here they come! Three-round bursts only!"

"Watch their tentacles," Evans advised. "They can reach out and grab you!"

There was no railing around the platform, which meant the Marines would be that much more vulnerable as a swarm of techs rose from the depths. And it was reasonable to assume that other aliens were climbing up the far side of Nexus, where they'd been shielded from the Marines' gunfire. "Eyes right and left!!" Evans shouted. "More of them will circle around from the other side!"

The Marines opened fire and tech forms began to die. They looked like deflated balloons. But in spite of that, some of the blobs managed to climb Nexus to a point level with the platform, and fire pistols at the humans. Evans saw that one of the techs was armed with *three* weapons and killed it.

Then a tentacle shot across the twenty-foot gap to grab hold of Private Defoe's left leg. But rather than jerk the Marine off the platform, as was the case with Carter, the alien sent a power-ful electrical charge through its fully extended limb. Electricity *crackled*, Defoe jerked spastically, and attempted to scream. Then the alien broke contact. Evans watched in horror as the Marine's lifeless body dropped head first into the abyss.

There was no need to alert the rest of the squad. All the Marines had witnessed Defoe's death, and redoubled their efforts to fight the blobs off, as *more* aliens rounded Nexus and attacked. The squad had been reduced to six men at that point, the aliens were winning, and the Marines weren't even close to completing their mission.

We've got to move, Evans concluded. *And there's only one way to go: Downward.*

A curving ramp led down along the inside surface of the outer casing. Placed there for use by Prax soldiers perhaps? Evans assumed so. "Follow me!" Evans shouted, as he started down the ramp. And that, as it turned out, was a good decision.

Tentacles were handy for wielding tools, but feet were faster, and the Marines managed to outpace the blobs. That was good, but as more techs climbed upwards, the humans had to pause every thirty seconds or so and thin them out.

Corporal Miller was snatched off the ramp during one such interval, and continued to fire as he fell, killing two blobs on the way down.

Evans swore as the noncom hurtled past, and took a moment to shoot the tech responsible for Miller's death, even though it wouldn't bring the Marine back.

Then, as Evans turned his attention to what lay below, he saw the bridge. It was a skeletal affair that connected the ramp to the platform that circled Nexus.

And there, glowing like a beacon, was what appeared to be a control panel! That's what Evans hoped it was, because it stood to reason that a control panel would have an input port.

Evans felt a rising sense of excitement as he hurried down the ramp. Lieutenant Finn spoke over the radio. "Charlie-Six, this is Charlie-Three... You're above us. We'll meet you at the bridge. Over."

Evans felt a surge of joy. Having had no contact with Bravo Team, Evans had begun to fear the worst. "Copy that, Charlie-Three. Over."

There was no small talk as the teams came together. Evans was glad to see that Finn still had seven of his eight Marines. The fact that one had been killed pained him but, as with the other casualties, Evans had to put the loss aside.

The immediate priority was to upload the virus, haul ass, and rejoin the rest of the company. "Set security, Lieutenant. Staff Sergeant Vernon and I will cross the bridge and upload the virus."

Finn nodded. "Yes, sir."

Marines began to fire as blobs descended from above and rose from below. Vernon made it his business to protect Evans, as they crossed the vertigo inducing chasm.

Like every member of both squads, Evans was carrying the Prax equivalent of a human thumb drive, and was only dimly aware of the fighting as he removed the device from a pocket.

He stopped in front of the brightly lit panel, scanned the alien hieroglyphics, and spotted the pictograph he'd been taught to look for. And yes, there it was! The square aperture into which the alien storage device would fit.

The officer's hand was in motion, when a metal panel dropped from above, and blocked access to the control panel. Port included.

Evans swore. Did Nexus recognize him as a threat? Was something watching? A core? Prime? Anything was possible.

Evans returned the Prax drive to his pocket, placed both hands on the shield, and tried to push it up out of the way. The resulting shock caused the officer to step back, and he might have fallen into the abyss, had Vernon not been there to catch him. "Thanks," Evans said. "That was close."

"Charlie-Three, this is Charlie-Six. Send your boom-boom guy over. Maybe we can destroy the shield."

The "boom-boom guy" turned out to be a young woman named Lopez.

The Marine was all business as she planted chunks of C-4 on all four corners of the shield, wired them together, and connected a detonator. "We should cross the bridge before we detonate the charges off, sir. In case of secondaries."

Evans agreed. Who knew what sort of secondary explosions might occur?

So, they crossed the bridge, and retreated up the ramp. Lopez waited until everyone was clear, hollered "Fire in the hole!" and *clicked* her remote. The explosions overlapped each other and smoke billowed.

But, when the smoke cleared, the barrier remained. Bent at the corners, yes. Blackened, yes. But still intact. Evans felt a sense of gloom settle over him. To lose so many lives, and to fail, he couldn't imagine anything worse.

Finn cleared his throat. "Can I make a suggestion?"

"Go for it," Evans replied. "I'm all ears."

"The Bravo vent channeled my squad to the bottom of the complex," Finn explained. "And, once we fought our way out, we could see that tunnels branched off like spokes in a wheel. A cable led out of Nexus and into each tunnel."

Evans felt the first stirrings of hope. "And you think the cables lead to nodes?"

"Yes, sir," Finn replied. "That's what the brainiacs said. That cables extend out from Nexus like roots from a tree. And the nodes are attached to them."

"They *did* say that," Evans agreed. "And, if I'm understanding you correctly, you think the nodes are equipped with ports."

"Yes!" Finn said enthusiastically. "For testing and the like."

That made sense, or so it seemed to Evans. "I'm sold," Evans said. "Lead the way."

The lights went out as Finn led the team down the curving ramp. But, if the Prax thought that darkness would stop the humans, they were sadly mistaken. The Marines were wearing night vision goggles and could see quite well.

It seemed that the number of tech forms had been reduced, because rather than attack in masse, they arrived in twos and threes. And, it was at this point when a gigantic tentacle reached up out of the murk to grab a Marine and jerk him off the ramp. A single squeeze was sufficient to pop the private like a grape. "It's a giver!" Evans yelled. "Drop your grenades on it! All of them!"

The Marines were carrying four grenades each, and hurried to drop them on the monstrous creature below. The explosions overlapped each other, and Evans heard a bellow of what he assumed was pain, as shrapnel tore into the giver's flabby body.

A marine fired his P90, and Evans ordered him to stop. "That thing can absorb every bullet you have. Lopez! Drop some C-4 on the bastard!"

The team had to pause as Lopez cobbled the components together, dropped a block of C-4 into the gloom, and waited for it to land.

When Lopez triggered the charge, the explosion was so large that chunks of alien flesh were tossed high into the air. The blubber seemed to hang for a moment before raining down on the giver's remains. "Sorry," Lopez said. "I didn't mean to make such a mess."

Evans laughed. "Feel free to make a mess anytime, Marine. Well done. Let's finish this job."

The ramp led the team down to a gore-covered floor. Chunks of meat lay everywhere, and the humans had to step over cables, to access the nearest tunnel.

Evans turned to Finn. "Set security here. Vernon and I will go forward. I'll check in as often as I can. If the transmissions stop, try to complete the mission."

"We will," Finn promised. "Oorah!"

The rest of the team echoed the cry.

Evans led Vernon into the tunnel. The cable had been laid in a channel created for that purpose. It glowed as did the wiring attached to the ceiling, occasional junction boxes, and the snake that slithered away.

Evans was operating on the assumption that the nodes would be attached to the tunnel, but when two opposing side openings appeared, he realized that wasn't the case. Evans paused which forced Vernon to do likewise. The entrance to the side tunnel was small, but it would be easy for a blob to ooze into the corrugated tube, and use its tentacles for locomotion.

As for a human, not so much. And, since Vernon was bigger than Evans, the choice was obvious. Evans began to strip. "Charlie-Three, this is Charlie-Six. There are side tunnels which, if our theory is correct, lead to nodes.

"It's going to be a tight fit. I'm going in with nothing more than my night vision, radio, and the Prax drive. Charlie Two-Seven will stay in touch. Over."

Evans was about to enter the opening when Vernon intervened. "Hold on. I'm going to tie my rappel rope to your ankles."

That was a good idea. Evans didn't like tight spaces to begin with. And the possibility of getting stuck, and being unable to back out, was his worst nightmare.

Once the rope was fastened Evans tried to enter the tube, quickly discovered that fastening the radio to his chest had been a mistake, and ripped it off. He winced as some of his chest hair came with it. "I can't lie on this thing," Evans complained. "Tape it to my back."

Vernon fastened the unit to the officer's back with all-purpose electrical tape. "There you go, sir. Give me a count."

"One, two, three, four, five."

"I copy. You're good to go."

"Good," wasn't the right word. Not in Evans' opinion. But he stuck his head into the pipe anyway. If he could kill the Prax comm system, it would be worth whatever price he had to pay.

There was barely enough room for the radio. The inside of the pipe was corrugated rather than smooth and the bottom grooves were half full of sand.

With his arms fully outstretched, Evans managed to move forward, using his fingers to pull, and his toes to push. How far would he have to go? The thumb-thick cable stretched on with no end in sight.

Then something stung him! A scorpion? No, not a scorpion, because it was happening over and over. And the bites ran the length of his body. Evans jerked uncontrollably, tried to touch his wounds, and couldn't.

Then he realized that the stings were caused by electric shocks rather than insects. From the cable? No, Evans didn't think so. He felt a rising sense of panic, a need to escape, and to do so quickly. Every fiber of his being wanted to call Vernon.

Then Evans noticed the teeny-tiny dots circling in the air ahead of him. The only reason he could see them was because they were radiating heat, and he was wearing night vision goggles.

Then the truth occurred to him. Nano drones! Fucking nano drones. Were they acting on their own? Hell no. Prime, a core, or Nexus had ordered the tiny machines to attack. A sure sign that Evans was getting close. That realization was enough to keep the Marine's fingers scrabbling for purchase, to push with his toes, and to will himself forward.

There...Evans could see something ahead. Something warm! A node? Yes, he thought so...Could the bugs turn it off? Could they turn *all* nodes off? The possibility was enough to stimulate more adrenaline and a series of frantic movements.

Evans was no longer conscious of the electric shocks, just the urgent need to reach his objective, and stop the Prax forever. Finally, he was there, only a foot away. And sure enough, there was a square port! The storage device was taped to the officer's left wrist. Sore fingertips tugged at the black plastic but to no avail.

Evans brought his left wrist up to his mouth in order to use his teeth. It worked. The device came free. The port was waiting and Evans took aim. But his right hand was shaking, causing Evans to fumble, before finally shoving the memory stick in.

A blue light appeared on the drive, flashed three times, and turned steady.

That was it! That was fucking it! The thing he'd been trained to look for...Doctor Blake's Angel Virus was racing through the comm system, doing what it was supposed to do, or was it? Evans felt a moment of despair. What if the indicator light was wrong? What if he'd failed? What if...

"Charlie-Six," Finn said over the radio. "This is Charlie-Three. The blobs were attacking. Then they collapsed and fell to the floor. It looks like they're dead. Or inactive. Maybe fifty of them. Did you cause that?"

Evans felt a surge of relief as he began to back out of the pipe. "Yes, Charlie-Three, I think so. But I didn't do it. *We* did it. Over."

"Sorry to interrupt," Captain Atkins said. "But be advised that a Mechan battle platform carrying Prax soldiers is circling the terminal and firing at us. We expect it to land. Over."

Evans had been vaguely aware of radio traffic between Finn and Atkins throughout the long crawl, but had tuned it out. Now, as Vernon dragged him out of the pipe, Evans was reminded that more than a hundred Marines were in harm's way.

Did the crickets on the battle platform know that the war was essentially over? No, of course they didn't. They'd been sent to protect Nexus, and that's what they intended to do. But a Mechan battle platform? What the hell? *They must have captured it*, Evans decided.

"Get ready," Vernon warned. "I can see your feet."

Evans emerged moments later. The floor felt cold. The first few moments were spent touching some of the nano "bites." Vernon stared at the red marks. "What the hell happened?"

"I forgot my drone repellent," Evans replied, as he pulled his pants on.

It took ten minutes to finish dressing, gear up, and hurry back to Nexus. Finn was waiting. "It's good to see you, sir."

"You too," Evans replied. "Did you take any additional casualties?"

"We lost Doc Henry," Finn replied.

Evans made a face. "Damn it."

"Yeah."

"What about ammo?"

"We went looking for bodies, took their tags, and their ammo. That gave us a bump."

Evans eyed the grimy faces assembled around him. There had been sixteen Marines to begin with. A quarter of them had been killed.

"Good job Marines … Our work here is done. We're going to climb the ramp and exfil through the Alpha vent. Then, once up top, we'll save the rest of the company from the bugs. They will be extremely grateful." That produced guffaws, grins. and loud oorahs.

Evans waved them forward. The ramp was steeper than Evans remembered it. And it wasn't long before he was breathing heavily. Were the Recon Marines aware of that? Probably.

The ramp led to the platform under the Alpha vent, and *another* climb, but not up a rope thank God. Evans allowed Finn to lead the way this time, and used the time to rest, as the others followed the rungs upwards. Then with teeth gritted, Evans made his way up, and was happy to accept Vernon's hand when he surfaced. He could hear firing to the south, interspersed with explosions. "Put the Black Hornet up," Evans ordered. "Let's see where we can make a difference."

Finn led the way, as the Marines hurried toward the sound of fighting, and paused behind a dune. The drone was in position and the situation was clear.

With no other cover to hide behind, the Prax were crouched in and around the battle platform, which sat atop a dune. A position that allowed the bow gunner to send a steady stream of plasma bolts at Atkins and his Marines. And, thanks to the protective energy field surrounding the bug, it could fire with impunity.

"We'll approach them from the north," Evans announced, "get close, and seize control of the barge. Once we kill the gunner the rest will be easy."

After informing Atkins of what to expect, and the danger of a friendly fire incident, Evans led the team forward.

Then it was time to move closer, drop down, and low crawl. The sand was hot. But it was also soft. That helped as did the fact that the cricks were focused on the terminal. And there was no sign of a rear guard.

That's the way it seemed until a half-buried crick popped up no more than ten feet in front of Finn! Fortunately, the officer had a suppressed pistol in his hand. Evans heard a soft *clacking* sound as Finn shot the alien in the head.

And, thanks to the din generated by the ongoing battle, the aliens gathered around the battle platform didn't hear the shots. Evans stood, waved the squad forward, and began to run.

His boots sank into the sand, which made the sprint more difficult, but it also muffled his footsteps. Evans opened fire from fifteen feet away. Working from left to right the officer killed three cricks with as many short bursts.

Then, as other team members engaged the bugs, Evans took the opportunity to jump up, and get a grip on the rail that ran along both sides of the barge. A pull-up, followed by a heave, allowed Evans to tumble in among the Prax.

The aliens turned, ready to blast the meat, only to receive fire from Finn and the surviving corpsman. That gave Evans an opportunity to roll over and shoot the crick that loomed over him. The alien staggered, released its sword, and fell over backward.

The bow gunner was still firing, when Lance Corporal Lopez spotted the power cable that led from a deck housing to the cannon, and wondered if she could unplug the weapon.

Lopez attempted to pull the plug—it refused to budge. But then, after a half twist, it came free! The protective force field collapsed with a *pop*, a sniper kneeling on top of the terminal building shot the gunner through the head, and the crick slumped sideways.

The battle continued for ten minutes or so, but the remaining aliens were no match for a company of Marines, and were annihilated.

But the job, so far as Evans was concerned, wasn't over. His orders were clear: Protect the site, especially Nexus, and wait for the science team to arrive.

A platoon of Marines was dispatched to retrieve their dead comrades, secure the installation, and standby in case it suddenly came back to life. It didn't.

The night passed without incident, and a gaggle of scientists led by Doctor Blake arrived the next morning, along with her own security team.

Once relieved, Evans and the first contingent of Marines boarded Abbott's C-17, discovered that three trunks of ice-cold beer were waiting for them, along with Colonel Lasky. He popped a can. "To the Marine Corps!"

"*Oorah!*"

"To Recon!"

"*Oorah!*"

"To Major Evans!"

"*Oorah!*"

"Prepare your can!"

"*Yes, sir!*"

"Deploy your can!"

"*Yes, sir!*"

"Consume your beer!"

"*Yes, sir!*"

The war was over.

CHAPTER NINETEEN

Luke Air Force Base, Arizona

Vanessa Seton wasn't the first president to use an Air Force base as a backdrop for a press conference, and she wouldn't be the last. Airforce One was parked behind her, and mountains were visible in the distance, as the governor delivered his introduction.

More than a month had passed since Major Evans had squirmed his way through a pipe deep below the Sahara to upload the virus that ended the war. But it was going to take a long time, and trillions of dollars, to restore America to its former glory.

In the meantime, it was Seton's job to convince the public that it could be done, to direct scarce resources to those who needed them most, and to defend those decisions. It was a difficult, energy sapping task, but absolutely necessary in the face of unending criticism by ambitious politicians of all stripes. "And so," Governor Larson said, "it's my pleasure to introduce Vanessa Seton, President of the United States!"

A large contingent of supporters were present to applaud. Seton approached the mike and launched into the usual speech. She was thrilled to be there. She wanted to thank Air Force personnel, as well as the other branches, for "Their selfless bravery and self-sacrifice during the war with the Prax." Law enforcement officers, civil servants, and volunteer groups came in for praise as well.

Then, after previewing major plans to rebuild the country's infrastructure on the way to what Seton called "America 2.0," she announced her willingness "To take a few questions."

Consistent with her press secretary's advice, Seton called on a local reporter first. "Yes, Sandra … What's on your mind?"

Seton had what some people claimed was a supernatural capacity to learn and remember names. The sort of implied compliment that worked on politicians, foreign officials, and reporters. Sandra smiled. "Thank you, Madam President, … Even though the Prax can no longer communicate with each other, and thousands have been killed, so-called 'loners' continue to attack citizens in the Denver area. What's being done to stop them?"

By then everyone knew that "loners" were hungry crickets which, after losing contact with a nest, were responsible for attacks on animals and vulnerable people.

"Thank you for that," Seton replied. "Local law enforcement has the primary responsibility for loner attacks.

"That said, individual citizens can play a defensive role too, although the careless use of firearms can result in needless injury and death for innocent bystanders. I join Governor Larson in urging people to attend the new 'One for All' defense courses being offered all around the state. Larger numbers of cricks are the province of the Arizona National Guard, and when necessary, other branches of the military.

"Brody, I like the new haircut. What's up?"

Brody Nelson was a reporter for the *Washington Post*. "Madam President, it's no secret that government teams have been gathering alien tech for the purpose of learning from it, and some people claim that the U.S. is building a spaceship. Are those rumors true?"

"No," Seton replied emphatically. And that was true. It was way too early for that. But would the U.S. construct a ship in the near future? Of course, it would.

"What *is* taking place," Seton told them, "is a concerted effort to identify alien tech that may be of immediate value to American companies and consumers. Take the Xyfor battle platforms for example. What keeps them aloft? Could auto companies use it? Inquiring minds want to know."

"A follow up please," Nelson put in. "How would tech of that sort be allocated?"

"That's a good question," Seton replied. "I'm about to send a request to Congress asking it to craft appropriate processes and laws."

"What about the Xyfor?" a reporter shouted. "When are they going to leave?"

"They are scheduled to depart in twelve days," Seton answered, knowing that the departure would dominate the news. "And let's remember what they did for us. Thanks to their intervention, we were able to hold the line long enough to develop the Angel Virus.

"Okay, one more question … Yes, Cindy … Go."

"How about foreign policy, Madam President? Are you reaching out to other countries?"

"Yes," Seton said. "We're in touch with NATO countries, members of the EU and active members of the UN. That said, as many as twenty-five percent of the world's governments have gone dark, and descended into chaos.

"We will, where possible, send experts to advise local officials on how to restore and maintain order. But that effort has just begun, and I don't have any hard data for you at this time."

Seton's Press Secretary was a man named Milton Hughes. He knew when to step in and did so. "That's it for today. Thank you for keeping citizens informed. Please contact me electronically with any follow ups you may have."

And with that Seton's Secret Service agents closed in around her as she walked toward Air Force One. One of them was Nick

Omata. "So, Madam President, was that better or worse than your time spent in Russia?"

Seton laughed. "Things are getting better, Nick... Our best days are up ahead."

***

Key West, Florida

Mallory Square was busy, and would become even more so later on when tourists arrived to watch the sunset. But for the moment Cassie Lang had a bench all to herself. It was located just yards from the shimmering blue water.

Lang eyed her watch. It was 5:46. And at 6:00 Lester Evans was going to meet her there. It was a moment she'd been looking forward to ever since the date had been set using email.

Something like eight weeks had passed since the awards ceremony in D.C., the dinner, and the lovemaking at her apartment. And they hadn't seen each other since then. Attempts had been made. But something always got in the way.

More often than not it was Evans who had to beg off, and for good reason. He was a hero in the wake of the Libyan mission, and as such, a PR asset that the Marine Corps was eager to employ as part of their post-Prax recruitment drive. Yes, the aliens had been defeated, but there were lots of trouble spots around the world. And a strong military would be required to prop up shaky democracies and confront a new crop of dictators.

And if FEMA had been busy during the conflict, it was doubly so as communities all across the country struggled to feed and house displaced citizens. A reality that forced Lang to travel, live on the road, and battle dozens of bureaucracies, including the one she represented.

But not this weekend, Lang thought. *The next three days will be all about us.*

Lang checked the time. It was 6:06. She stood to look around. There were men, but not the one she was looking for, so she sat down again.

Time seemed to drag. Lang checked email. There were none. And no text messages either. Surely Lester would contact her, if only to say that he was running late, or had been forced to cancel. By the time 7:00 rolled around Lang was in a funk. *He dumped me*, Lang concluded. *Just like Ken dumped me. With no warning and no explanation.*

Then hands covered her eyes, and she heard a familiar voice. "Guess who?"

Lang stood, and turned. "A Marine?"

Evans smiled. "Yes, a paper pushing, Pentagon Marine. Sorry I'm late."

She held his hands. "The Pentagon? That's wonderful!"

There was applause as the sun dropped toward the horizon. The kiss lasted for a long time. So, when Lang opened her eyes, the sun was gone. But a beautiful red-pink sky remained. And her world had changed.

AUTHOR'S NOTES

Those who follow my fiction know that the CRICKETS novels are a departure from the near future, alternative history, *Winds of War* novels I've been writing during the last few years. And, I have no plans to write additional **CRICKETS** books.

There are eight *Winds of War* books starting with **RED ICE**. But, while all of the novels are set in a futuristic WWIII, each has its own separate plot, characters and setting. That means they can be read in any order. **RED DOG** is the most recent addition to the series, and for those who like Winds of War, I want to assure you that there will be more books in the future.

All of the *Winds of War* books are available in e-book format on amazon, as well as trade paperback, and in most cases audio as well.

At the moment I'm working on volume one of a two-book **Legion of the Damned** ™ sequel. This will be my first Legion novel since **Andromeda's War** in 2014.

Many thanks for reading my fiction! Take care, and watch your six.

ABOUT WILLIAM C. DIETZ

To contact William C. Dietz, or to learn more about his fiction, please visit williamcdietz.com.

You can find Bill on Facebook at: www.facebook.com/williamcdietz.